Growing Season

Growing Season

ALDEN R. CARTER

COWARD-McCANN, INC.
NEW YORK

Library of Congress Cataloging in Publication Data
Carter, Alden R.
Growing season.
Summary: Dismayed by his parents' decision to move to
a farm in the middle of his senior year, seventeen-year-
old Rick accompanies his family out of loyalty but finds
that life in the country has something very special to
offer him.
[1. Farm life—Fiction. 2. Family life—Fiction]
I. Title.
PZ7.C2426Gr 1984 [Fic]   83-15322
ISBN 0-698-20599-5

CA

ACKNOWLEDGMENTS

Many thanks to all those who helped me in writing this novel, especially my mother Hilda Carter Fletcher, my agent Ray Puechner, my editor Refna Wilkin, my friends Anne Lee, Dean Markwardt, and Don Beyer, and, most of all, my wife Carol.

I owe special thanks to the Maynard and Barbara Nelson family whose example of dedication, love, and courage originally inspired GROWING SEASON. However, the personalities and incidents in this novel are entirely fictional and GROWING SEASON should in no way be interpreted as their history. This book is admiringly dedicated to the Nelsons.

Growing Season

1

THE BALL HUNG awkwardly on the hoop and then tilted out slowly and fell, rebounding on the cracked asphalt court with a hard rubber ring. I caught it chest high and dribbled back outside the free throw circle before turning fast to shoot again. The ball spun wide and dropped outside the court, rolling and bouncing across the stubby brown grass until it stopped in the muddy hole scraped by countless dragging feet below the tilted seat of a swing.

My heart wasn't in the game anymore and I scuffed slowly across the grass and sat on the swing, spinning the ball idly in my hands. It isn't much, I told myself, a worn-out, blue-collar suburban playground—a couple of basketball courts, some rusty swings and a ball diamond too small to play hardball on. Nothing to get upset about losing. I've outgrown it anyway. In the fall there's college and a new life. Only six months away and I'll be back in the city. Hell, I'd want to get away for the summer anyhow, so what's the big deal about a few months on a farm?

The rationalization didn't help much, so I tried thinking about college instead. For years I'd dreamed about becoming an architect. It would take me six years, five if I could get in some summer school. Once the family got started on the farm, I could come back to Milwaukee and pursue my own future without worrying about theirs. My folks' lifelong dream coming true, I owed them the summer anyway.

My watch said 4:30. Bill was late as usual. If he didn't show in another fifteen minutes, I'd go, walk around the neighborhood one more time, and get home by 5:30 to help finish the packing.

Suddenly a deep voice startled me. "Ah, wool gathering again, Mr. Saunders, er . . . Simons? Time flies; waste not, want not; let's get the show on the road." It was Bill's nearly perfect imitation of the assistant principal and it left me convulsed with laughter. "Ah, sport, it's not really that funny, you know." Bill's voice was concerned under an assumed English accent and I realized I was laughing too hard.

He plucked the ball out of my hands and jogged toward the court. I followed and we played one-on-one for twenty minutes. Bill is four inches shorter than I am and normally I can beat him easily, grabbing rebounds and shooting over his stubby outstretched hands with little effort. But I was listless this afternoon and he won 20–12, sinking the last two points on a lay-up I didn't even try to stop.

Afterward we sat on the swings letting the sweat cool. Bill smoked a cigarette slowly.

"You know your wind would be better if you quit those things."

"Ya, I know. This summer I'm going to give 'em up, ride my ten-speed, and really get in shape."

"I'll bet."

"No, really. I'm going to get this body all set for those college girls. Come the fall, watch out."

I left it without comment and we sat not talking much for five minutes or so before Bill crushed his second cigarette and stood. "How about a beer?"

He was recovered, full of energy again and dancing to be off.

"Your old man will give you hell again."

"Naw, he'll understand. Your last night in town and all."

"What are you going to do tonight?"

"Got a date with Jennifer. Ho boy, been chasing that little girl since Christmas. Going to get hot tonight." He did a few quick dance steps and swung his invisible partner into a bent-backed Hollywood embrace. "Want to come along? I'll get you a date if you don't have one."

"No, I promised Mom I'd baby-sit. I thought you might want to come over and watch the tube for a while. The Bucks are on tonight."

"Well, hell, if you'd said something earlier . . ." He shrugged. "Come on, let's get that beer."

We walked down the street toward his home past the rows of brick houses that varied in sequences of four so that the first was a copy of the fifth, the second a copy of the sixth, and so on block after block. Still, the houses had a certain attractiveness with their cleanly kept yards faintly green in the mid-March evening and neat little gardens waiting for spring planting. I've never imagined tending anything bigger than one of these backyard plots, but now the family owned 240 acres of dairy farm and for the next few months I'd be a part of that.

I stopped below the steps leading up to Bill's porch. He trotted up and paused at the top. "Aren't you coming in?"

"No, I promised Mom I'd be home soon."

"A beer will only take a minute."

"No, I'd really better not."

"Well, I could drop Jennifer off early and come by for a few minutes around twelve. You be up?"

"I guess not. Mom wants to leave by seven, so I'll have to be up around five."

"Wow, they're not giving you much slack working into the old farming routine, are they?"

"I guess not."

We stood awkwardly for a moment before Bill came down the steps and extended a hand. We shook. "Well, I guess we'll be seeing you. Try to come down for a few days. I'd come up, but you know a milk bottle is the closest I ever want to get to one of them bossies."

"Sure, I'll be down in August for registration. We still going to get that apartment together?"

"Jeez, I don't know, Rick. The old man wants me to stay home another year. He says as long as he's footing part of the bill, I might as well save on some rent."

"I thought you weren't going to take anything from him."

"Might have to. College ain't cheap, you know, and the financial-aids people don't think I'm going to get much."

"Ya, well, we'll talk in August."

"Sure, sure, you take it light now."

"You too."

I walked home with my shoulders hunched against the cold breeze coming off the lake as the sun fell behind the houses.

Mom was standing with her back to the door when I came in. A few packing boxes still stood against the walls of the kitchen. The movers had taken most of the stuff in the morning, leaving only the items Mom insisted on moving herself. I'd spent most of the day loading all but the last few boxes into the U-Haul trailer hitched behind the waiting car. I thought it was a little silly moving so much ourselves since the movers seemed professional enough, but Mom had said days before, "If someone's going to break my china, I am, not someone I don't know."

She turned, hands still on her wide hips. Her face was tired and I was glad I hadn't stayed for the beer. This is hard on her too, I reminded myself.

"Hi, Mom. Sorry I wasn't home sooner."

"That's all right, dear. You weren't gone that long." She seemed about to say more, but instead she sighed and walked into the next room, giving me a pat on the shoulder as she passed. I could hear her walking slowly through the other rooms as I checked what was warming on the stove—hamburger—and what was in the refrigerator—nothing but milk, eggs, bacon, and three cans of pop. I took out the milk, poured a glass, and turned up the heat under the pan.

Mom came back in with her coat on. "Well, that's it, I guess. I'll send Pam and Jim over as soon as I get to the Andersons'. Tommy will stay there with me. Judy and Connie are over at the Bauers'. Don't let Jim and Pam stay up too late and don't get the stove dirty; it's all cleaned up for the new owners."

"Don't worry, Mom, we'll survive."

"I know, I know. I'm just worried about everything today."

"It'll be okay."

"I know." She stood at the door, unwilling to leave yet. Finally she stepped over and gave me a quick hug. She backed away, still holding me by the arms. "You've gotten so big, it's hard to hug you anymore." She paused, biting her upper lip thoughtfully. "You're a good son, Rick. I know this is harder for you than the others. They're still children. You're not anymore. We won't stop you from doing what you want to do. If we can just get started . . ."

"It's okay, Mom. I don't mind."

"Sure." For a second I thought she was going to cry and I felt panic, but instead she smiled, gave me another hug, and left quickly. I watched her hurrying down the street without a glance back at the house where she'd lived and raised a family for nearly twenty years.

I was finishing the dishes when the door slammed and Jim and Pam rushed in. "Is there any pop?" Jim shouted. This was going to be an adventure for them. Mom was staying at the Andersons' for the night, and it was obviously time to get the party started here.

"There's one can for each of us. Why don't you save it for later?"

"Gee, just one can apiece?"

"One can each and that's enough."

"You sound like Mom."

"Ya, and I'm going to keep sounding like her. We've got to get to bed early."

"Ah, hell, you sure take the fun out of everything."

"Don't swear. You can watch the ball game as long as it's over by nine-thirty."

"Can we split a can now?"

"Okay."

They took the can and ran upstairs to play the new game they'd discovered in the last few days. Without the rugs on the floor they could now run and slide half the length of the hall in their stocking feet. I called up the stairs, telling them to be careful and not to spill the pop or break any bones, then went back to cleaning up the kitchen. But five minutes later there was a shriek and a boom. I hurried up and found Jim flat on his back with the wind knocked out of him. Pam was giggling and I glared at her as I knelt by Jim to see if any moving parts were out of place, but he needed more healing for his ego than medical assistance. As soon as he could breathe again, he started muttering excuses and I knew he was all right. I called a halt to further sliding and took them downstairs where we played cards on the bare floor until the Bucks came on.

It was a lousy game. Phoenix jumped off to a big lead early and the Bucks seemed to give up by halftime. The kids got bored and I let them switch to another station to watch a comedy. After the first ten minutes, I lost interest and wandered into the empty living room.

Beside a framed family picture in a box of odds and ends, I found a science fiction book I'd been saving for the right time. I sat down cross-legged on the floor and started to read, but the book didn't hold my attention either and I found myself gazing at the picture. We're a big family, but there's not much family resemblance since only Pam and I are natural children and the other four are adopted.

The next oldest are Connie and Judy, the twins. They lost their parents in a car accident a few years ago and got moved around quite a bit until my folks adopted them. They're two years younger than I am and a pain in the butt a lot of the time, but I don't mind their teasing too much, I guess. They have sex and dating on the mind all the time, even though Mom and Dad don't let them go out much. That's just as well, since they don't get asked much either. They're in the pimply, baby-fat stage, but that doesn't stop them from doing each other's hair for hours at a time and drooling over every young male TV star. One of their favorite pastimes is asking about my social life and constantly suggesting new girls I could ask out. They have rotten taste that way, so I ignore them. But they're proud of me for some reason and think I'm handsome (I'm not particularly), and that's nice for the ego, I'll admit.

Jim is twelve and came from a bad home. I don't know all the details of the story, but I guess both his parents were alcoholics and Jim never got much care. When his old man walked out a few years ago, his mother started seeing lots of other men and sometimes didn't come home for days. Finally, social services took Jim away from her and put him in a foster home. The social worker told Mom later that neither of Jim's parents even bothered to show up at the custody hearing. He was pretty screwed up when he came to us a few months later. Considering what he'd been through, it's a miracle he wasn't worse.

Still, after more than three years with us, he's still got a lot of problems. He's very sensitive and broods even about little things. When the pressure builds up too high, he blows. His hysterical tantrums last for hours and it sometimes takes him days to recover. They're terrible experiences for the whole family. Still, I think he's growing out of them and most of the time he's a pretty good kid. Dad works awfully hard with him and so do I when I can find the patience. It doesn't take much to set Jim off when he's feeling lousy—losing at a game or getting corrected will do it. And, of course, it hurts most when big brother is responsible. So I try to control myself and make allowances for him, but it's hard to remember all the time, especially when he insists on tagging along with Bill and me.

Tommy, the youngest, is a skinny little kid of five with huge thick glasses. He's going blind and the doctors can't seem to do much about it. Pam and he are inseparable. She's small for nine and I guess Tommy makes her feel big and grown-up when he depends on her. Mom and Dad still get some money from the state to help with Tommy's medical bills, but it's never enough.

Pam is my favorite. She's always cheerful and kind to everyone and everything, birds that fall from nests, stray cats, and the like. Dad jokes that she'll grow out of it and be just like every other teenager, but I don't think so. She's real quiet, but she almost always has a smile, and I think she'll always be kind, never bitchy like so many of the junior high girls you see.

Obviously, I wasn't in a mood to read, so I put the book back in the box and went to the kitchen for my can of pop. The kids were engrossed in the program and didn't even glance up as I passed. Back in the bare living room, I again sat looking at the picture of the family. How would the move from city to country change our lives? Mom and Dad came from the country, but that was a long time ago and all of us kids were city born and raised. I, at least, didn't want to change. I was happy in the city. Sure, a weekend in the country was nice now and then, but farming? No thanks, not this boy. Still, it didn't seem like I had much choice—not for a few months anyway. My eyes focused on my father in the center of the picture. He stood smiling uncomfortably, his arm around Mom's fat waist.

Dad is a small, good-natured man, thin and wiry and remarkably strong for his size. He's forty-two and, until he quit in December, he'd worked the last eighteen years for a dairy here in Milwaukee. Every day he drove a truck around delivering cartons of milk, cream, and eggs. It wasn't what anyone would call a stimulating job, but it always put food on the table. Once a week he went bowling with his friends and sometimes he'd come home a little too jovial and get a sharp word from Mom, but mostly he stayed home at nights watching the TV or puttering. Dad's got to have his hands moving all the time, so even when he watched the tube, he'd be polishing or fixing something. He's always been good about playing with the younger kids or talking with me. We all miss him since he's been up on the farm.

Mom has stayed home raising us kids all these years. She picks up a little extra cash doing some sewing now and then, or helping to cook for parties and weddings. She's wonderful and always busy, but she weighs too much and goes to Weight Watchers once a week. It bothers her a lot to be fat, but as hard as she tries, she doesn't seem able to stick with the program. It's a vicious circle really. Whenever she gets nervous or depressed, she has a habit of snacking. And then, of course, she feels guilty and more depressed. She's embarrassed by her habit too, because she knows she isn't fooling anybody. So, Mom keeps the snacks small, one or two cookies, or a little cake. "Just a little something to go with my coffee," she'll say. The trouble is that half an hour later, she'll have just a little something more. And when her nerves act up, she can't sleep very well, and that gives her still more time to raid the refrigerator or the cookie jar.

But I don't want to make Mom sound like she's always nervous or depressed, or that things are really grim around here. We've had a nice home—a little cramped, but nothing wrong with it. Maybe we've never had a lot of money, but we haven't been poor either. All in all we've been a pretty happy family, even if we aren't made up like most other families.

Mom had a lot of trouble having children—I guess when she had me there was some damage. She lost the next three, and after Pam, the doctors gave Mom a hysterectomy. When I was still very young and Mom and Dad were still trying to have children of their own, they started taking in foster kids. The extra income never amounted to much, because Mom always spent generously on the kids. But money wasn't the reason she took them in anyway. Mom just loves kids. Hell, she probably would have paid social services for the chance to care for foster kids, problems and all.

I can hardly remember a time in my childhood when there weren't foster kids around. Some stayed a few weeks, others months, and three or four were with us a couple of years. Most of them were nice, but a few really had troubles. Still, Mom would never give up hope on any of them—even on the couple of occasions when kids stole money from her purse and ran away. When they returned days later with their tails between their legs, she welcomed them back. Every Christmas we get cards from some of those kids. Several are grown now and married, but they don't forget Mom and Dad.

Bill once asked me how I'd felt about sharing my childhood with so many strangers. I had to think for a while. "I guess I never really minded much. You know, they didn't stay strangers very long. I think I would have been lonely without them."

"But, hell, you must have felt left out sometimes. I mean, not getting your fair share of attention and all."

"Well, maybe now and then, but a lot of those kids became my friends. You remember playing with some of them, don't you? Like Bud and Fred and Jenny?"

"Sure. But it must have been a real zoo around your house sometimes."

I laughed. "It hasn't changed much."

Mom and Dad eventually stopped taking in foster kids, because it was always too hard on Mom when one of them got adopted or went to a relative or something. What they wanted was a permanent family. So they started adopting children. Connie and Judy came first about five years ago, Jim a year and a half later, and Tommy two years ago. They were all considered difficult kids to place in homes because of their ages and problems, but Mom didn't care. They were kids who needed love and attention and that's all that mattered to her.

I liked the change too. The foster kids had been okay, but it was better this way. Even if my new brothers and sisters had their problems, at least they were permanent parts of the family. We no longer had to adjust to new people every couple of months. We still had our fair share of turmoil, more maybe, but generally life settled down a little. I really didn't expect things to change too much in the rest of the time I lived at home. But then this farming deal came along.

As long as I can remember, my parents have been talking about getting a farm. They both grew up on farms and came to the city to work. They met in a factory and I guess their first conversation was about farming. It was pretty much fantasy for them for a long time, but a couple of years ago they started getting serious. I didn't notice at first, but farm equipment catalogs and agriculture magazines started coming in the mail and Mom and Dad began to sit up late talking about money and the price of land. Usually they'd be grumpy in the morning and the catalogs, magazines, and calculations would go untouched for a week or so. But they'd always go back at them, once again trying to figure out how they could find enough money to buy a farm.

The turning point came last fall. I got home late from school to find the table set with the Sunday china and all the kids buzzing about a "big surprise."

"What's going on?" I asked Connie.

"They won't tell, but it's something to do with a letter from Uncle Fritz. They said they had to wait to talk to you."

I had a sudden sinking feeling. Uncle Fritz is Mom's older brother. He's worked all his life as a hired hand on farms and I guessed immediately that the surprise must concern farming.

Mom came to the kitchen door. "Good, you're home, dear. Come into the living room; your father has something to tell you. You others stay here."

Not quite willing, I followed her. Dad got up as we came in and made a great show of opening a bottle of wine and pouring us each a glass. Whatever had happened, it was something big. We almost never had any kind of liquor in the house and, except for a can or two of beer on a hot day of fishing, Dad had never offered me a drink.

"What's the occasion?" I asked.

Dad coughed, spent ten seconds clearing his throat, glanced at Mom, coughed again, and finally began. "We got a letter from your Uncle Fritz today. He's found a good farm at a very good price." He studied my face for a moment, looking for a reaction, but I tried to remain deadpan. Dad went on. "He also said he can raise about a third of the down payment. So . . . well, I think I'll go up and take a look at it. If it's as good as Fritz says it is, I guess we'll buy it." He paused again.

I looked down at my hands. They were shaking a little and I hastily took a sip of the wine to cover my agitation. Mom was talking now. "You know we've been thinking about it for a long time. But since you're the oldest, we thought we should tell you first."

My voice, like my hands, was a little unsteady. "When would all this happen?"

"If we buy it," Dad said, "about the first of the year. I'd go up and help Fritz get things in shape and the rest of the family could move up in the spring after school lets out. The thing is, son, you'd have to take most of the responsibility for keeping things going around here this winter. We can't expect you to do that if you don't agree abut buying the farm."

This was the kind of blackmail parents get so good at: You're a big boy now, sonny, so make a big boy's decision. And if we don't agree with it, that'll just show you're not really a big boy after all. Then, of course, your opinion won't be worth a damn and we'll do what we want anyway. So, agree with us and everybody will be happy. I shrugged. "I guess if it's what you want to do, I'll manage."

"Good boy." Dad's tone showed his relief. "I knew we could count on you. Ellie, why don't you call the rest of the kids?"

They must have practiced how they were going to tell them because they made the farm sound like heaven. They talked about having dogs and horses and lots of sunlight and room to have fun. At first there were some pretty confused looks, but Connie and Judy are always talking about horses and about a hundred magazine pictures of horses share the walls of their room with the portraits of TV stars. Mention of having a real horse turned the tide and before long all the kids were asking questions a mile a minute. I felt kind of left out and thought of going for a walk, but that wouldn't have looked good. So, I helped myself to a little more wine and sat trying to look enthusiastic.

I didn't think then that I was going to the farm at all. I just imagined helping Mom through the winter while Dad was up on the farm. After the family moved, I figured I'd get an apartment in Milwaukee and work until school started in the fall.

That all changed about six weeks after Dad went up. I knew they were trying to save money on phone calls, so when he called one Wednesday night I guessed it must be something important and ran upstairs to get on the extension. As I got the receiver to my ear Dad was talking: ". . . it seems like every piece of machinery needs work. There's a lot to do on the outbuildings too. Monday, half the cows will be delivered and then we'll have to worry about milking. We just don't have time to make decent meals and keep the house clean." He took a deep breath and sighed. "Anyway, I think we ought to move the family up here as soon as possible."

It was like somebody had thrown a pail of ice cold water on me when I least expected it. Mom and Dad started talking about selling the house, getting the kids into the new school, and so on, but I hardly listened. Move halfway through my senior year? It just wasn't fair. I had plans! A whole lot of plans! This was the climax of all my years of school! I'd miss the prom, the senior banquet, all the spring parties, and graduation—just because a stupid bunch of cows had to be milked!

I slammed down the receiver and stalked to my room. Hell, there was track too. I had run varsity half of last season and I was sure to be on for the full season this spring. I stood at the window glaring into the night. Damn it, I wouldn't go. To hell with them. I'd stay at Bill's or somewhere.

Mom knocked lightly on the open door. "Were you listening, Rick?" I nodded, but didn't turn. She sat down on the bed and sighed. "I see you're upset. I can understand that. You've worked hard and it doesn't seem right for you to miss part of your senior year." She paused. "It's just that this is our big chance to do what we've always wanted to do. Your father and uncle are working very hard, but they need help. We don't expect you to stay, Rick, but if you could just help for a few months . . ."

I glared at her, angry words on my tongue, but the sight of the tears in her eyes stopped me from speaking. We stared at each other for a long minute. Then I nodded dumbly, afraid that if I tried to talk I might start crying too. She got up, patted me on the shoulder, and left, quietly closing the door behind her.

For the next couple of days I fought with myself about it. Was there still a way out? I knew Mom had interpreted my nod as agreement, but maybe I could convince her that it was better if I stayed behind.

I spent all Saturday morning at my desk carefully writing out and rehearsing my arguments. In a way I knew I should go, but damn it, I wouldn't be there for long anyway! I knew nothing of cows or farm machinery, so how could I really be that much help? I'd just about gotten everything down on paper and was working up my courage to confront Mom when Pam rushed up the stairs.

"Ricky, Dad sent you a letter." I could hear Tommy clumping awkwardly up the steps behind her.

"Thanks." I took it from her.

They stood watching expectantly as I tore open the envelope and unfolded the sheets covered with Dad's scrawl. "What's it say?" Pam asked.

"Just a second." I read it to myself.

Thursday, P.M.

Dear Rick,

   Things aren't easy down on the farm, I can tell
you. It rained and snowed and sleeted and God
knows what else all day long. Fritz and I came in
soaked and shivering like a pair of drenched cats.
He's already gone to bed, but I thought I'd drop you
a note first. Lord, every bone in my body aches.
Enough complaining.

   I'm sure your mother has explained why we've
decided to move the family early. I'm also sure it's a
disappointment to you and I'm sorry, but there's just
no other way we can pull this deal off. We need
more hands up here and we need them right away.

   Son, I'm very proud to know I can trust you to
get the family packed and safely up here. Believe
me, it's a load off my mind now the decision is
finally made and soon we can all be settled and
making this place go.

   It will be a big help to have a third man around
too . . .

   The letter went on about the problems they were having
with the machinery, but Pam and Tommy were tired of waiting and kept asking what Dad had said, so I turned back to the
first page and read it to them, skipping a line here and there.
When I was halfway through the part on the equipment, Pam
asked, "Is there any more exciting stuff?"

   I glanced ahead. "It doesn't look like it." They left.

   The letter ended, "So anyway you can see how much work
there is to be done. You'll be a big help, son. It's good to know
I can count on you. Love, Dad."

   I sat for a few minutes looking out my window at the familiar street. Then I reread the beginning and end of the letter,
folded it, and put it in my drawer. Carefully I tore the sheets

with all my reasons for not going into small pieces and dropped them in my wastebasket. None of them stood up very well anymore—not after Dad's letter.

But even then I didn't realize I'd committed myself for the whole summer. Somehow everyone assumed that. Mom started talking about what a big help I'd be and Dad wrote me another long letter about how many acres would be planted in this and that and how we'd go about doing it. Despite my disappointment, I felt complimented that my parents had so much confidence in me, so I didn't complain. By summer perhaps things would change and I could come back to Milwaukee to work until school started. At least I wouldn't have to spend the rest of the winter in high school seven hours a day. I've always been a pretty good student and I already had enough credits to graduate, so I took half credits in a couple of my classes and arranged with my other teachers to finish by mail.

Still, as I sat brooding on this last night in the vacant living room of the only home I'd ever known, I couldn't help feeling a deep resentment again. And there was fear too—fear of a new world where all my city-bred skills would be scorned and useless.

I'd lost track of the time and was surprised when I glanced at my watch. Nearly 10:00 and the kids were still up. They'd be cranky in the morning. They were half asleep on the air mattresses in front of the portable TV, so I got them into their pajamas and settled in the sleeping bags. I thought of stepping out for a last stroll around the neighborhood, but I was tired too and only stood on the stoop in the sharp March night for a few minutes.

A car pulled up and parked in the shadows across the street. The couple in the front seat started making out immediately. Peggy Mathews, I thought. I wonder who she's got with her this time. I grimaced thinking of the couple of times I'd been out with her. I'd been pretty clumsy. She was definitely out of my league. But God knows it had been instructive. A lot of

guys had found an evening with Peggy a real "learning experience."

The door of the car popped open and Peggy hopped out and
ran to the house. What the hell? I thought. It's only a little
after ten. Is she going in now? A wild thought struck me.
Maybe I could wander over. She'd probably think that was
funny—getting dropped off by one guy and have another show
up a few minutes later. If her parents weren't home . . .

But the car didn't move. A light came on upstairs. Hell, she
probably just forgot something. In a couple of minutes she was
back in the car and, after another quick round of making out,
they rolled off. So much for a last night adventure for me.

I slipped back into the house, careful not to wake the kids.
Lying in my sleeping bag, I thought, This is the last night in
my home. Tomorrow this will all be part of the past. Until I
fell asleep, I watched the shadows of the bare branches of the
oak in our yard gently tossing in the pool of light the street
lamp splashed on the ceiling.

2

I SLAMMED THE stubborn door on the trailer again and this time the latch caught. I checked to see if I still had the key to the padlock in my pocket, then slid the hasp through the ring and snapped the lock shut.

"Do you have the key?" Jim asked.

"Ya, I've got the key," I said irritably.

"Gee, I was just asking."

"Well, don't you think it would have been better to ask me before I locked it?"

"Hey, don't pick on me. I was just trying to help!"

Oh, hell, I thought. On this of all mornings I don't want to set him off. "I know, I know. Forget it. Why don't you check the oil and I'll try to round everybody up?"

"Okay." He ran off to find a rag, happy to have a grown-up job. I'd already checked the oil myself, but it would keep him occupied.

"Rick, where are the twins?" Mom called from the porch.

"I don't know." For God's sake, was I supposed to keep track of them too? "I'll find them."

They were sitting on the steps leading up to the backdoor.

Beyond, our postage-stamp backyard, with its few scraggly, leafless shrubs, looked forlorn in the gray morning light. Judy had her legs drawn up and her head buried in her arms. Connie was talking to her softly, one hand lying gently on her shoulder. I paused irresolutely for a second, then came closer. Careful, I thought.

"Hey, you guys, we're about ready to go." Judy sniffed wetly. Connie had been crying too, but her eyes were dry now. "Judy, we're all kind of sad," I said, "but we don't want to get the little kids going. Mom has enough trouble already."

Judy raised her head, blinking back the tears, and nodded. Connie handed her a fresh tissue. We could hear Mom calling our names from the front of the house. Connie gave Judy a hug. "Come on, let's go."

I hurried back to the front. Mom was standing on the porch, her coat on and her purse over her shoulder. She looked tired and irritable already. Pam and Tommy were already in the front seat and Jim was officiously closing the hood of the Plymouth. "It's okay, Mom," I said. "They're around back saying good-bye to the place. They'll be here in a minute."

Mom let out a sigh of exasperation, but I could tell it was put on because her eyes were a little red too. "The oil's okay, Rick," Jim called.

"Good. Thanks, Jim." The twins came around the porch and headed for the car. "I think it's time to go, Mom. If we stand around, somebody's going to start crying. Probably me."

She smiled, blinking her eyes rapidly. "You're right, dear. Farming, here we come." She gave the door to the house a final tug and descended the steps quickly. "Okay, kids. Everybody got his seat belt on? Here, you sit on Momma's lap, Tommy. Now everybody watch your fingers when you close the doors."

I got in on my side, fastened my seat belt, and started the engine. My total experience with driving a car with a trailer behind had been the eight or ten blocks between the rental

agency and our house. And then the trailer had been empty. I
let out the clutch slowly and the car jerked forward and stalled.

The twins giggled and Jim yelled, "Give it more gas, Rick."
I swore under my breath.

"You kids be quiet," Mom snapped.

I got the engine started again and this time, none too
smoothly and with more giggles from the back seat, we pulled
out onto the street leading away from our house.

The suburbs of Milwaukee fell away slowly. In the rearview
mirror I could see the twins sitting with their heads turned to
the windows. They had known changes before, bigger changes
than I ever had. Judy wiped away a tear, and Connie reached
over to pat her shoulder, but no one else seemed to notice
their distress.

Jim was having a great time evaluating my driving and
offering an occasional helpful comment. Pam had Tommy
involved in making a cat's cradle out of a piece of string. Mom
just rode quietly, her eyes straight ahead, her thoughts hidden
from all of us.

With the traffic and the strain of trying to master the drag of
the trailer, I didn't have much time to think about other
things. But soon the traffic thinned and before long I'd gotten
used to the trailer. One by one the kids dozed off. I even
thought Mom had fallen asleep, but when I glanced over, her
eyes were still open. She shifted Tommy's weight on her lap
and smiled down at Pam asleep against her left arm. Her lips
moved, said "Thank you" inaudibly, and I knew that she had
just said a prayer: thanked the God she believed in so strongly
for the burdens she bore. He'd better be up there, I thought.
Mom's going to have a whole lot more burdens soon.

For the first couple of hours after we cleared Milwaukee the
kids were pretty quiet, but by midmorning they were awake
and antsy. Mom tried leading some singing (she's the only one
who can sing worth a hoot) and then we played some word

games. Of course, we had to stop at rest areas a couple of times
to let people empty their bladders, but otherwise we kept rolling steadily northwest.

Lunch by the road helped to dissipate some of the kids'
pent-up energy and I hoped they would be quiet in the afternoon. No such luck. Mom tried the singing again and also the
word games, but everyone was pretty bored with howling the
few songs we knew in common and playing twenty questions.

We were a little more than an hour away from the farm
when I heard a strangled voice from the back seat. "Stop the
car!" Oh, no! I thought. I put on the brakes as hard as I dared
with the trailer behind and pulled over on the shoulder. Too
late. "*Buuuuraaaackkkk!*" . . . "Oh, God, gross!" . . . "Ich,
let me out of here!" Jim vomited noisily again. The twins were
already clambering out the back doors. The smell hit us in the
front seat and Tommy, squirming on Mom's lap, immediately
heaved on her legs. Chaos. I jumped out my door and jerked
Pam out as if the car was on fire. Two vomiting kids were
enough and I didn't want her to sit there with the smell upset-
ting her stomach too.

Mom set Tommy on the ground and slowly got out. Jim was
over in some weeds either getting sick again or contemplating
suicide. Mom looked around at all of us. "Well, we can't
abandon the car. It'll take us all night to walk and I hear there
are wolves and hostile Indians in the woods around here."

There were a few giggles. Tommy looked up at Mom. "Indians? Where are the Indians?"

"Rick," Mom went on, "unlock the trailer. There's some
detergent and a plastic pail in that last box I packed. Pam, get a
sweater on Tommy. And one on yourself too. Connie, Judy,
when Rick gets the pail, you go to the house we just passed and
ask for some water. Be polite, mind. Now hop to it. I've got to
see to Jim."

"Where are the Indians?" Tommy asked Pam.

"That was just a joke, silly."

"Oh." Tommy looked disappointed.

Mom didn't have to tell me—I was to be in charge of cleaning up. I pulled out the soiled floor mats and, when the twins got back with the water, we scrubbed them. Mom cleaned up her clothes as well as she could and a half hour later we were back on the road.

It seemed to take forever to cover the last fifty miles. Ahead the road buried itself in brown hills under gray clouds. Everything was muddy and dreary. Dirty snowdrifts lay crumpled in the ditches and the recently thawed streams flowed fast and dark through the culverts crossing under the road. The car smelled horrible. Despite all the scrubbing and open windows, the odor of vomit stayed with us.

In the back seat, Jim sat morosely, muttering every now and then, "It must have been something I ate." No one paid much attention as we rode cramped and peevish.

Finally, Mom pointed ahead to a white frame church standing at the top of another brown hill. "There, that's the turn off. A mile more and we're home. Thank God."

I don't believe much in God, but I also thanked whoever or whatever is up there too. I took it slow down the bumpy gravel road, turned left on another country road, and swung in a half mile farther down the road at the farm I recognized from the pictures Dad had sent. The large white frame house was badly in need of paint around the windows and on the porch. To the left of the house stood a red barn with three silos of various heights clustered around it. A garage and several sheds fronted on the circular driveway that ran past all the buildings.

As we pulled in Dad came hurrying out of the barn wiping his hands on a rag and smoothing back his thinning hair. I barely had the car stopped when the kids were out and running toward him with Tommy a little behind peering through his thick glasses at this new and wondrous world. Connie and Judy hung on Dad's arms asking nonstop questions about the horse. Pam had him around the waist and Jim, trying to act the man, stood a step back inquiring formally about Dad's health and the next second asking excitedly about the dog.

"Hold on, hold on, just a second, be patient." Dad freed his arms, squeezing and hugging each of them, and squatted down. "There's Tommy." He opened his arms and took the little boy into a long hug.

"Hi, Daddy, I got sick in the car. Jimmy threw up and that made me sick."

"It was something I ate, something in the lunch," Jim protested.

"It's okay. Don't worry about it now." Dad stood with Tommy in the crook of his elbow and dropped an arm over Jim's shoulders. Jim tried to squirm away, but Dad held him, ruffling his hair. "It's okay now. You're here and we don't have to worry about who got sick for what reason."

"There's Uncle Fritz," Connie yelled, and they all dashed toward the barn where a little bowlegged man stood smiling with crooked, gaping teeth. Tommy pushed on Dad's shoulder, and he let him down to follow the others and turned to us.

"Hello, Ellie."

"Hello, dear." They embraced and I turned away to start unpacking the car. I was embarrassed. I'd forgotten how little Mom makes Dad seem when they're close. He's a small man, standing only about to my chin. Mom's shorter yet, but her weight makes her seem much bigger. I hurt for her because she can't help being fat and homely. But Dad never complains and always jollies her up. Maybe on the farm she'll be able to stop eating so much, I thought.

"Hello, Rick." Dad came over with his hand out and I took it, very glad to see him. I noticed for the first time he was growing a mustache. I glanced at Mom and she rubbed her upper lip, grinning.

"You're growing a mustache."

"Ya, how do you like it?" He took a quick look at Mom.

"I don't have to kiss you," I said.

"No, I guess you don't. What do you think, Ellie?"

"It's fine, dear, it makes you look even more handsome."

He laughed self-consciously and spent a long minute getting his pipe going. "Ya, well, long trip, huh?"

"Not so bad," I said. "We beat the traffic out of the city."

"Well, traffic isn't something we have to worry about around here, unless it's getting run over by the cows when they're coming in for milking. You all set to get your hand back at milking, Ellie?"

"Oh, no you don't. I'll leave that to the men, at least until I get the house in shape and the garden in."

"You don't milk by hand, do you?" I felt a twinge of panic. This might be worse than I'd imagined.

"No, no. Not in this generation. You've got a lot to learn." He slapped me on the shoulder, laughing. I wasn't very sure I wanted to learn at all. He surveyed the trailer. "Guess we'd better unpack this beast before dark." He turned and I followed his look out into the field where the kids formed a little knot around Uncle Fritz, who was coaxing a nervous gray horse to join the group. A heavyset black mongrel with long fur stood by the driveway, whining and shaking, too shy to do more than wag her tail fiercely as she watched the kids. "Oh, well, let them explore a little more first," Dad said. "We've got the yard light to work by. Come on, Rick, let's back 'er around."

It was a long evening. Mom stood in the middle of the dining room directing the flow of boxes. Pam took care of ·Tommy while the rest of us worked. We could hear them roaming the house, laughing and occasionally yelling questions from some distant room. Dad had taken us all on a quick tour earlier, but Pam and Tommy had forgotten much of what he'd said.

The house was quite a bit bigger than our home in Milwaukee and, although it needed a lot of fixing up, everyone seemed happy with it. Dad had assigned the twins a bedroom, Pam and Tommy another, and, much to my relief, Jim a room of his own. So, for the first time, I would have a room to myself. I'd shared with Jim in Milwaukee and, before he came, with a succession of foster kids. For years I hadn't thought much about it—it was just the way things were in our family—but as I'd gotten older, it had become a pain in the ass. Jim's last major tantrum in February had forced me to move downstairs for two days. At least I'd have a little privacy now. The room was hardly large, but there was enough space for a decent-size desk and some shelves in addition to my bed. Not bad.

Dad, Uncle Fritz, and I carried in the boxes from the trailer. The twins and Jim unpacked them and put away the contents under Mom's direction. Jim could hardly wait to see the milking and, when it was time, Dad and Uncle Fritz took him to the barn, leaving me to finish unloading the trailer.

About 7:30 they came back in and we all stood around the kitchen eating sandwiches and canned soup. Mom looked distastefully at the stained table and three broken-down chairs left behind by the previous owner. A few other pieces of decrepit furniture were scattered about the house. "Those go out first thing in the morning. And so does most of the other junk they left here. If I'd known you men were living like this, I would have moved everybody else up here sooner. I'll bet you two spent half the day doing the last month's dishes."

Dad and Uncle Fritz grinned sheepishly. "Well, Ellie," Uncle Fritz said, "that's not exactly true. We only had a couple of plates and you've got to wash them every week or so. The old food kinda gets caked up around the edges after five or six days."

Jim and Pam giggled and Tommy joined in, not really sure what was funny. The twins gave cries of "Oh, gross!" and "Ich." Mom shook her head. "You're probably telling the truth for once." I grinned at Dad, who was sucking at his pipe and studying his stocking feet earnestly.

We went back to the unpacking soon after and were pretty well finished in an hour. Mom shooed the kids off to bed. "Bright and early, kids," she called after them as they lugged the sleeping bags up the stairs. "We have to get this place cleaned up before the mover comes."

I started gathering up the boxes and wrapping paper to take to the burn barrel out back. Dad and Uncle Fritz had gone back down to the barn, but I had no desire to join them—I was going to put off my first barn visit as long as I could. Mom came back into the kitchen. Even after the long day her face was lit with happiness. She put her hands on her hips and I remembered how, the night before, she'd looked so old and tired in a similar pose.

"This house is going to be just fine. Lots of closets, lots of room. I can't wait to get some wallpaper and paint on these walls." She glanced at me. "We'll even have a guest room for visiting big-shot architects." She laughed and kicked her way to the stove through the pile of wrapping paper I'd just gathered. "Thank the Lord, I feel like I have a real home again." Without thinking, she took a cookie from a plate on the table and munched it as she poured a cup of coffee. "Want some coffee?"

"No, thanks."

"Well, I'm going to take a cup down to your father and Fritz. Been here six hours and haven't even seen the barn."

I watched her swinging her fat figure down through the frosty evening to the barn, the steam from the coffee pot arching behind her. I shook my head. I'm the odd one out here, I thought. Everyone else has fallen in love with the country. Well, that's good, I guess. Maybe they won't make such a big fuss when I go.

I got my coat on and carried some of the boxes out to the burn barrel. I got the fire going, made three more trips for the rest of the boxes and paper, then stood back watching the sparks fly up into the chill air. The fire shone through the rust holes in the barrel, throwing strange shadows on the brown lawn. Every now and then I stirred the fire with a long steel rod, the rustling of the burning cardboard sending a new cloud of sparks whirling up into the dark. Despite the cold I was comfortable near the fire and I needed the solitude to think.

Maybe the move really was for the best. The city had gotten pretty bad in the last few years. Not that it bothered me. I liked it in spite of the dirt and the crime. Still, twice in the last couple of years, Dad had been mugged on his milk route and I knew Mom worried about him more and more. And there was the busing thing too. My parents aren't racists or anything, but the prospect of the kids taking long bus rides into the inner city concerned them deeply. Now no one would have to worry about any of that. Still, there were new problems. The farm had cost a lot of money and things would be damned tight for the first few years. I shuddered to think of what would happen if there was a sudden illness or an accident. My parents and Uncle Fritz had bet their life savings and everything they could borrow on the farm—a little bad luck could wipe them out.

Yet, I had to admit what bothered me most was the fact that I no longer had a home in the city. After this, my family would be hundreds of miles away. I'd go to school in the city, then hopefully land a job with a good firm. Eventually, if everything worked out, I would become a partner or found my own company. But whatever happened, I'd never again have my family close by to provide aid and comfort. After the next few months they would become voices on the other end of the long distance line: people I saw in person only rarely and for short periods. All my life I'd thought of home as a constant thing in my future. Sure, I would move away, get married, and eventually have a family of my own, but for many years my parents would be only a short car ride away. No longer. Once I left the farm (a departure I planned to make at the earliest opportunity) my family would never again be readily available to protect me when things went badly.

After a while the dog came up, accepted a pat, then lay with her head on her paws watching me. I've always liked dogs and it was good to have one around again. Our last dog in the city had been killed in the street in front of our house by a passing car and I hadn't wanted another since then. But it was all right here and, despite my worries, I found myself almost happy burning the boxes with the dog for company.

It was nearly 10:00 when they came out of the barn. Mom and Dad went into the house, laughing and talking, and Uncle Fritz came over to me. I realized then that we really hadn't had time to say more than hello. Uncle Fritz is quite a bit older than my parents, maybe fifteen years, and he's worked all his life on farms around here. Since I was a small child, he's always come for Christmas and a few times he's come with Dad and me on fishing weekends in the summer. At Christmas he always brings nice presents and my parents always bawl him out for spending his money on us, but he only laughs and says, "No man ever wrote out a check in a casket. I'll just drink it up if I don't spend it on you folks." Still, over the years, he's saved some money and now that he's getting older he wants more security, I guess. He's never had a wife or children, so he doesn't want to own the farm. He said in his letter in the fall, "I just want a steady place to work and not to have to worry when I'm too old to put in long days. Besides, Ellie's food is worth all my money."

I was happy to see him coming over to talk, limping on his gimpy leg and smiling with his bad teeth. We shook hands. "Hi, Uncle Fritz, how you been behavin'?"

"When you get to my age, boy, you ain't got much choice." I laughed and he squatted down to pet the dog. After a moment, he pushed her muzzle aside and got his short black pipe going. I tossed a couple more boxes in the barrel and prodded the fire. He laughed low. "Boy, your parents sure are happy. I swear Ellie's mouth is going like a hummingbird's ass in huckleberry season." He shook his head and blew smoke out through the gaps in his teeth in two thin streams. "Yep, they've got their dream farm. It's a good one. Good soil and solid buildings. Needs a tad of fixing up, but it's the best buy I've seen in a long time." He stroked the dog's head and she whined, rolling over to get her belly rubbed by his strong, gnarled hands.

"Well, I hope it makes them happy. Looks like an awful lot of work to me."

"Yep, it's all of that. Farming is always a lot of work, kinda like juggling five bowling balls while running backwards through an obstacle course. But a man's his own boss and you're out in the open. Ain't no two days alike and you never get bored."

"I guess you're right. I just hope they know what they're getting into."

"Oh, they know all right. They've farmed before. A lot of things have changed, but I've seen it all happen and I'll be around for a lot of years yet to help them." He paused for a long minute and I stirred the fire. "Your pa tells me you're going to college in the fall."

"Ya, I want to study architecture."

"Architecture, huh? Well, I don't know much about that except for building a barn or a milkhouse." He smoked his pipe thoughtfully for a minute. "Why architecture?"

That was a hard one to answer in words. I'd thought about architecture both on the ride north and while burning the boxes and wrapping papers, but now that he asked, I was hard put to explain. How could I tell him that to me buildings were like living things: some warm and welcoming like old friends; some like tall, graceful, but distant beauty queens; some heavy and powerful like football linemen; and so on and so on— lines, angles, and curves, almost as alive as my parents, brothers, and sisters. It would sound crazy if I tried to say it that way, so I shrugged. "I don't know, I just like buildings, I guess."

"Hmm . . . how they look or what they do?"

"Well, it's kind of the same thing, isn't it?" I searched for words. "Someone once said that form follows function, but that doesn't mean that the form has to be commonplace just because the function is common." I paused and met his quizzical stare. "I mean even a milkhouse doesn't have to be ugly just because it's a milkhouse," I finished lamely.

He tapped out his pipe against his worn half-Wellington

boots. "No, I guess not, although I don't quite see why it has to be much more than four walls, a roof, and a floor, if that's all you need. A cow is a complicated thing, but she doesn't have to win a beauty prize to be a good milker."

"But, Uncle Fritz, a milk cow is a milk cow! You don't design a cow, nature has done that already. You do design a building and just because the building has a function doesn't mean the form always has to be the same! Why, look at office buildings or homes or almost any building you can think of. The functions may not change, but we can find an almost infinite number of forms to serve them."

He grinned. "Ever hear of the guy who built a round barn, then went crazy trying to find a corner to piss in?" He chuckled, pulling his tobacco pouch from an inside pocket.

I stared at him, my arms hanging lax in confusion and frustration. Couldn't I explain it to him? Uncle Fritz was not a stupid man. "Well, that's not exactly what I meant . . ."

He relit his pipe and even in the weak light of the match I could see his eyes twinkling. "I guess it's too complicated for an old sodbuster like me. Tell you what, next summer when you and me are up reshingling the house, you can explain it all to me again."

I nodded, a little numb. It wasn't that Uncle Fritz had bested me in an argument, it was just that he, like almost all the adults I had ever known, had a way of squelching you when you were doing your best to make a point. They'd make some dumb joke or just snicker and shake their heads. Or, if you were really getting the best of them, they'd say, "Well, when you are as old as I am . . ." or "Now in the real world . . ." And that was that. They didn't allow you any comeback. The argument was over and you, sonny boy, could just take your ideas back to the playpen.

I turned away abruptly and gave the fire a vicious poke with the steel rod. Uncle Fritz hummed softly for a couple of minutes, then spoke seriously. "I didn't mean to cut you off, Rick. You know your old uncle can't never pass up a chance for a joke. Go ahead, I'm listening."

I felt chastened. I shouldn't have gotten angry with him. "I'm sorry, Uncle Fritz, it's been a long day."

"I can imagine. Maybe you can explain all that form and function stuff to me another day."

"Sure." I tried to smile at him.

He smiled back, then studied his pipe for a moment before tapping it out and dropping it in his shirt pocket. "Well, morning comes early on a farm and it's past my bedtime." He stood and shook himself. "Whew, still pretty nippy. Well, I'm glad you're here, Rick. Don't worry about your folks none. We'll have a good summer. You an' me will even sneak off sometime and do a little fishing."

"Sounds good. That's the kind of work I enjoy."

"You and me both. Good night. Sleep well."

He called the dog and went off toward the garage. In a couple of minutes I saw the light come on in his room upstairs. I burned the last few boxes and waited for the fire to die down. By the time I went to bed Uncle Fritz's light was off and the farmhouse was dark.

3

THE GRASS CRACKLED with frost under my shoes as I trudged out to the barn, its windows already glowing with light in the faint dawn. I'd been up about twenty minutes and, although I'd forced myself to hurry, I was still the last to the barn. Dad, Uncle Fritz, and Jim were already at work among the cows. This morning, like the three mornings before, I'd been jarred awake by a hard rap on the door and Dad's cheery, "Up and at 'em, Rick, daylight in the swamp." I'd heard the same shout on the dawn of many fishing trips in the past, but it was infinitely harder for me to wrench myself from the warm covers to go down to the barn for the milking than it had ever been to rise for an early morning on a mist-covered lake where we shivered both from the cold and the anticipation of the first bite.

Jim didn't mind at all. He'd jump up like a startled bird at Dad's first knock on his bedroom door. He'd almost fly down the stairs, pausing only long enough to grab a slice of toast before dashing across the yard to the barn, one sleeve of his coat trailing in the wind. For me it was agony. I'd linger as long as I dared over coffee and a second piece of toast, then make my way down to the barn slowly.

Even on my fourth morning I dreaded the overpowering smell of the barn that would hit me on first coming in from the sharp outside air. I'd tried breathing through my mouth on the first day, but it was impossible to get away from the stench of the creatures that stood tossing their heads in the clanking metal stanchions around their necks and rasping their tremendous hooves on the concrete floor of the stalls as they waited to have the milking machines attached.

I was stunned by their size. I'd seen cows grazing by the road ten thousand times in my life, but up close in the barn these seemingly gentle beasts took on awesome proportions. Dad said a good-size holstein weighed nearly fifteen hundred pounds and, for effect, told some gruesome stories of the damage a hoof could do to the unwary farmer's foot. To me, their huge brown eyes were equally menacing. Instead of the gentle brown of storybooks, their eyes seemed at once both frightened and resentful. I tried to appear nonchalant around them, yet I moved hesitantly as I helped Dad attach the milking machines or apply the iodine solution that prevents infection to the udders after the machine is detached and the last milk stripped by hand.

But Jim loved it all and I felt humiliated by my little brother's ease around the cows. He'd always hated school and would have happily spent the entire day helping Dad and Uncle Fritz. I would just as happily have gone to school for him, even if it meant being a somewhat overage seventh-grader.

The milking was not complicated, yet seemed to take forever. There were twenty-six cows in the barn, only a small herd, but one that Dad hoped to expand once the resettling bills got paid. We worked two milking machines on either side of the barn with the milk pumping into closed stainless steel pails through long hoses. As each pail was filled, another was attached and the full pails carried into the adjoining milkhouse to be emptied into the bulk tank for pickup later by the driver from the cheese factory. I should have thought of it before, but I was surprised by the hot frothy character of the milk as it poured from the cans into the steamy reaches of the deep, semicircular tank. For me even the thought of warm milk had always been disgusting. Milk was supposed to be ice cold in a glass with water condensing on the sides in cool driblets. But that was a fake. This was real, genuine milk and this was a real, genuine farm. And I hated it.

Still, I'd kept that pretty well hidden until the evening of the third day when I'd walked past a cow at the worst possible moment. Suddenly a gush of green slime as thick as my forearm hit me like a firehose. I looked down to see my clothes from shoulder to waist plastered with cow diarrhea. I almost vomited when I raised a slimy, putrid hand to try to wipe the thin strands from my cheek and hair. Then I heard the howls of laughter from Dad and Uncle Fritz and the higher pitched giggling of Jim.

I take pride in almost never losing my temper; you can't in a family as big and diverse as ours. But I did then. I dropped the milk pail I was carrying in my other hand, peeled a big handful of the slime off my pants, and hurled it at the cow. It missed, splattering on the wall and sending one of the barn cats leaping for cover. Dad, Uncle Fritz, and Jim were almost collapsing with laughter. I tried to give them a withering look, but it must have been all the more absurd with the green slime hanging from my hair and clothes. I felt like cursing them, the cow, the whole damn farm, but no words came and all I could do was stalk out of the barn.

I undressed to my underwear in the yard, ignoring the cold and not caring who saw. I threw my manure-soaked clothes in a heap on the porch and stomped into the house. Mom and the twins were in the kitchen.

"What on earth . . .?" Mom exclaimed.

"What happened, Rick?" Connie yelled.

I ignored them both and just kept going through the kitchen and up to the bathroom. I passed Pam and Tommy on the stairs. Pam let out a little cry of surprise and Tommy squinted at me. I ignored them too. Behind me Tommy asked, "Why don't Ricky have no clothes on?"

"I don't know, but he looked real mad."

"I thought he looked funny."

I scrubbed myself in the shower until my skin was raw. I would have happily jumped into a vat of acid to rid myself of the stench of cow diarrhea, of the barn, of farming itself.

I didn't go down to dinner, but sat on my bed burning with humiliation, too mad even to read.

What the hell was I doing here anyway? I wasn't a farm boy! I should be back in the city where I belonged. While I was working my ass off on the farm, Bill and my other friends were enjoying their senior year in high school. After all the years of study and going through crap, our class had finally made it to that last year when we knew all the ropes and could enjoy ourselves for once. Yet right in the middle of that, I'd been dragged away to . . . get shit on by a cow!

Maybe I should go. Tell my parents, "Sorry, but I'm just not cut out for this. I'm going back to the city. Good luck. You can write to me at Bill's." But hell, that would never work. It would just be a big scene and my father's arguments and my mother's tears would win in the end. Don't kid yourself, boy, you are stuck here until the fall!

I got up and looked out the window. Thin icy snow and patches of brown grass lay in the circle of the yard light. Milking was over and the barn was dark. I could hear the voices of the men below in the kitchen. Some laughter drifted up to me. Probably at my expense, I thought. I flopped back down on the bed and tried to think.

A lot of what really bothered me was simply envy. All my brothers and sisters were already adjusting to life in the country. Adjusting! Hell, they loved it! They all loved their new school, our big, roomy house, and the multitude of wonders on the farm. Pam and Tommy seemed to feel that they'd been suddenly dropped into a Noah's Ark of animal playmates. Signa, the big black mongrel, escorted them everywhere. To their delight, Dad had put them in charge of caring for the numerous barn cats. The cats had been doing fine without little kids around, but they seemed to guess instinctively that the small humans meant lots of petting and milk. Fat times ahead.

I'd never seen Jim so happy. Every morning Dad had to order him out of the barn in time to wash, change, and get a real breakfast before the school bus came. If we worked in the evenings after milking and supper, he'd work with us until Dad chased him back to the house to do his homework or get ready for bed. Farming seemed to be in every corpuscle of Jim's blood.

I thought Judy and Connie were getting off pretty easy. Except for feeding and watering the horse, they didn't have to help with the farm work. Mom had said to Dad, "Let them get used to the place first, Paul. There's lots to be done around the house and you men can manage down in the barn." I wished maliciously for a moment that it had been one of them who had been in the way of that blast of diarrhea. They wouldn't be so quick to laugh at me after that.

I slapped my hand angrily against my leg. What was I doing being envious of my brothers and sisters? They were still children. My parents expected me to be an adult. I expected myself to be an adult! So act like one then, I told myself. But I was still too goddamn angry. Getting shit on by a cow . . . what would my friends say if they knew about that?

It was well after I heard the final clink of dishwashing and the giggles and whispers of the kids going up to bed when Dad knocked lightly on the door and came in. He sat, half smiling, on the end of the bed sucking meditatively on his pipe. I stared down at the book I'd grabbed off the bedstand at his knock. After a minute he put a hand lightly on my leg. "I'm sorry if you're embarrassed, son. It's just . . ." He paused trying to hold his laughter, finally making a show of coughing into his fist. He tried again, but had to chuckle. "It's just you looked so damned funny. I swear the look on your face must have curdled half the milk in that barn." He shook his head at the memory. I could have throttled him. He drew a deep breath and tried to be as serious as he'd intended to be at the start. "Hey look, a lot worse has happened to me, to Fritz, to your mother, to anyone who's worked around animals, or anywhere else for that matter. None of us likes being laughed at, but, hell, we all come in for our share of bad luck. That's only natural and it's natural to laugh too. It'll happen to Jim too one of these days and you'll laugh just as hard at him as he did at you. Forget it. Clothes wash easy. Just don't let your feelings get so hurt you can't wash them out with a little laughter." He paused, then squeezed my leg. "Come on, what do you say?"

"I think you're turning into some kind of country philosopher."

"You bet. In this business you have to. Come on down and get a bite to eat."

I followed him down the stairs trying to take what he'd said to heart. It was all true, I knew that. I'd known I was acting like a child ten feet outside the barn door, but the disgust I felt had been stronger than my good sense. Less than six months left in this stinking hole, I reminded myself for the thousandth time.

In the kitchen Mom and Uncle Fritz stopped talking when we came in and made a show of drinking coffee to hide their grins. "It's okay," I said, "you can laugh if you want to."

Mom got up to get my plate out of the oven and Uncle Fritz leaned back smiling wistfully. "You know, boy, in my day that was called a baptism. Nothing like it to wake you up on a cold morning unless it's a slap in the face with a cow's tail. Wait until a critter catches you with one of them flyswatters. Gets your attention, that's for sure."

Mom put my plate in front of me and tousled my hair, something I've always hated. "Don't worry, Rick, worse has happened to us."

"Ya, Dad told me."

"Careful, he's still a bit sensitive," Dad said and they all laughed. I just ate my food.

After a pause Uncle Fritz slapped his thigh and said, "Hey,

Ellie, you remember that cousin of ours who stayed with us that one winter when we were kids?"

"You mean Francie?"

"Yep, that was it. Why, I'll never forget the time she was reading one of them romance magazines out there in the outhouse in the middle of January. Ma wouldn't never allow them things in the house so the girls had to read 'em out there." Mom started laughing then and Uncle Fritz got laughing too and it was a couple of minutes before he could go on, Mom still giggling so hard her face turned red. "Anyway, one day Francie got so involved in a story she froze right to the seat. Ma had to go up with a kettle of hot water and thaw her off. That girl had a red ring around her ass all the rest of that winter." They exploded with laughter and I joined in until my sides hurt. When I looked over at Dad he was watching me, smiling around the stem of his pipe. "You heard that one before?" I asked.

"About a hundred times. It's still funny, though." He knocked the ash out of his pipe and winked at me. "Time for bed; those cows are already making milk for the morning."

Now in the early morning light I braced myself at the barn door for another volley of jokes about my "baptism." Instead I found Dad and Uncle Fritz squatting beside a cow lying on the cement floor, Jim looking curiously over their shoulders. I recognized her as the same cow that had been stubborn about getting up the night before and a few minutes later had given me my "baptism."

Uncle Fritz leaned over and put his ear to her side. "That paunch is pretty quiet. No sound in that stomach, no milk. I guess we've still got hardware problems then. Better call the vet. We don't want something working through the stomach wall into her heart. She's a stubborn old cuss, but she's a good milker."

Dad grunted and stood. Passing me, he smiled wryly. "Another bill. Better get started with the milking, Rick. Milk is money and we ain't got much of the green kind these days."

When Dad came back in, I asked, "What's all the talk about hardware?"

"Fritz thinks she's swallowed a lot of metal and it's screwing up her system."

"Well, I think it would!"

Dad chuckled, but I could tell he was pretty worried. "All these cows have metal in their stomachs—screws, nuts, bolts, barbed wire, all sorts of crap. Cows aren't careful eaters. That's why we put magnets in them sometimes."

"You're kidding!"

"Not a bit. The day before you guys came, we put a magnet and a half dozen laxative pills in her."

"Thanks for telling me now!"

He glanced over. "Oh, ya. Forgot about that. Well, even a healthy cow will do that sometimes. Cough at one end and blow out the other. Happens pretty often." He dug in a coat pocket and handed me a cylindrical piece of metal about three inches long and a half inch in diameter. "That's one of the magnets. The pills are almost the same size."

"Wow," I said hefting it, "how do you get it down her? Or, do you put it up her?"

"Down. I'd hate like hell to try to get it in from the other end." He laughed at the thought. "We use what's called a balling gun. I'm sure you've seen ours around. It's that metal contraption about eighteen inches long. Looks like a big syringe. We load the magnet in the gun, stick it over her tongue and into her throat, and push the plunger. They take it pretty good most of the time. Usually the magnet picks up all the metal and the whole mess lies at the bottom of the stomach where it can't do any damage. But this time it didn't work. I'm not sure why, but probably a nail or something is stuck in the stomach wall. So, the vet will have to cut her open and see what he can find."

It was close to 4:00 when the vet drove his truck into the yard and parked. I'd been helping Uncle Fritz fix a cracked manifold on one of the tractors since lunchtime. I liked this

48

work better. I've always been handy with machines. That's not to say I'm any expert, but I know the right end of a screwdriver and I don't mind getting my hands dirty.

When we heard the door on the vet's truck slam, Uncle Fritz looked out from under the tractor, then slid the creeper out and stood. He wobbled for a second and leaned against the tractor.

"You okay?"

"Ya, ya, I'm okay."

He was breathing a little fast and I noticed his face was pale. "Are you sure?"

"Oh, ya." He laughed. "Just getting old. Get a little dizzy when I stand up too fast, that's all."

The vet, a balding, chunky man with horn-rimmed glasses, was talking with Dad when we came in. The vet shook hands with Uncle Fritz warmly. "Hey, Fritz, ain't seen you around in a while. Thought maybe the boys from the fox farm had come and hauled you away."

Uncle Fritz laughed. "Ain't no one going to make mink food out of me for a while yet, Doc. How's the hack and slash business?"

"Oh, I keep my hand in. What do you think we've got here?"

"Hardware most likely. Put a magnet in her a few days ago, but no luck. She gets up when she feels like it, so I know she still can. Stays down mostly 'cause she's lazy."

"Well, let's get her up and have a look."

Uncle Fritz deftly snatched a passing barn cat from a hay-bale, grinned at me, and held the enraged cat against the cow's hindquarter. The cat spit and scratched and the cow came up with a surprised bellow. "Best damn cattle prod there is." Uncle Fritz laughed. He tossed the cat toward a corner where it landed expertly and turned to give us all a malevolent glare.

The vet looked in the cow's mouth and eyes, listened to her side, then inserted a large thermometer in her rectum. "She been constipated?"

"No, diarrhea, actually," Dad said. I winced and Uncle Fritz nudged me.

"That's funny," the vet said. "Usually they're all stuck up. Been pumping a lot of laxatives into her?"

"We gave her some with the magnet," Dad said.

"Well, maybe that explains it." He stood considering for a moment, then glanced at his watch and removed the thermometer. As if commenting on the indignity of her treatment, the cow let out a long blast of gas. "Whew, that should solve the gas shortage." The vet waved his cap and Dad and Uncle Fritz laughed. It was apparently an old joke, but one always enjoyed.

The vet read the thermometer. "I think you're right about the hardware. She's not too sick yet, but she'll get a whole lot worse unless we find out what's bothering her. . . . Well, let's get to work. Young fellow, get me some hot water and soap, please."

The water heater in the milkhouse was on the blink again, so I had to go to the house for hot water. I was balancing the basin of water carefully as I walked back across the yard when the school bus stopped at the end of the drive. Jim was the first out and came running down to me. "What's happening? When did the vet get here?"

"About a half hour ago."

"Hope I ain't missed anything." He ran on to the barn.

I stepped over his books just inside the barn door. Dad looked over from talking to the vet and shouted at Jim, who was peering with great interest into the vet's bag. "Get inside and change or your mother will skin you alive for wearing your school clothes in the barn!"

"I don't want to miss anything."

"Then hurry! It'll be a few minutes yet."

Jim nearly upset both me and the water as he charged out the door. I set the basin on a hay bale and watched. Uncle Fritz was standing by the cow's head, stroking her nose. A long I.V. line ran from a plastic bottle hanging on a beam to a vein in her neck. The vet was clipping a two-foot square on her left side. He touched up a spot or two with a straight razor and gave her an injection. "That'll freeze her if the sight of Fritz don't." He laughed.

"Watch it, Doc," Uncle Fritz said. "There's lots of things I could tell that examining board about you."

Laughing, the vet came over to the basin. I watched in amazement as he stripped off his jacket, wool shirt, and undershirt and started scrubbing himself down. It had never been above forty degrees all day and now with the light dying, the breath of the men and animals was hazy in the cold barn. His skin quickly turned pink and steaming. He shuddered and laughed. "God, I love my work!" He pulled a bottle of dark liquid from his bag. As he doused his hands and arms, I recognized the pungent smell of iodine.

While he was washing the shaved patch on the cow's side with more iodine, Jim rushed back in. "Has he started yet?"

"Hush," Dad said, "just watch."

The vet drew a scalpel down the cow's side just behind the last rib. For a second I didn't think he'd pressed hard enough, but then the skin gaped open a couple of inches, revealing a ten-inch slash of red muscle tissue. I felt the bile rush to my throat, but I swallowed hard. After playing the child the night before, I was determined to act like a man tonight.

Despite my discomfort, I soon found myself fascinated with the deftness of the vet's hands as he separated the tissue. The cow took it all with remarkable calm, gazing placidly at Uncle Fritz. I turned to say something about it to Jim, but he was gone. In the dim light outside, I could see him leaning against the tool shed getting sick.

The vet had reached a grayish membrane below the muscles and there was a sucking sound from inside the cow as he cut through. He spread the incision wide, revealing the greenish white insides of a cow. I swallowed hard again. The vet stuck his arm forward as far as he could, grunting and grimacing with the effort. He felt around, then withdrew his arm and sat on his haunches resting. "I don't feel any adhesions at the head of the stomach, so that's good news. Nothing's penetrated the stomach wall yet." He took a deep breath. "Well, let's get the rumen out. Paul, you can handle one suture." He turned to me. "Think you can handle the other?" I nodded. "Okay, here we go."

He reached inside the cow, grabbed hold, and pulled a big, steaming glob of gray stomach through the incision. I think my eyes were about a yard wide. The vet fastened a long suture to the bottom of the basketball-size section of stomach. He was just starting to put another at the top when the cow coughed. A huge blob of stomach, three or four times what he'd already pulled out, slithered out of the cow. "Hold on, bossie!" he yelled. "We don't need that much!" He good-naturedly stuffed the excess back into her while Dad and Uncle Fritz laughed and I fought back the desire to gag.

He got the second suture in place and beckoned to me. "Hold the end down below where I'm going to work. I should give you the other so you'd get the full benefit of the experience, but I'll let your pop have the fun." Uncle Fritz laughed. Grinning, the vet handed the other suture over the cow's back to Dad. Dad made a face.

The vet picked up a scalpel. "Ready?" He slit the stomach, and a cloud of white steam rushed out, rising to nearly envelop Dad. The smell was horrible, and from the look on Dad's face I wasn't the only one in the barn who was tempted to be sick. The vet raked out great handfuls of partially digested hay from the stomach and threw them in the gutter.

"Caught your breath yet, Paul?" Uncle Fritz asked. Dad replied with an obscene remark I'd never heard him use before and the vet and Uncle Fritz laughed.

The vet felt around carefully, reaching far forward inside the cow. "Here it is. Feels like barbed wire and the magnet is stuck right to it." He grimaced, pulled, and brought out the magnet with a six-inch piece of barbed wire, a few screws, and a big nail hanging from it. Everything was covered with metal

filings. "Cow must think she's a goat," Uncle Fritz said. The
vet chuckled.

He pulled the rest of the contents of the stomach out, wiped
the magnet clean, and ran it around inside her stomach again.
"You know, I've taken the damnedest things out of cows. Last
year I took a pitchfork tine out of one. Another time a knitting
needle. The critters will eat anything." He laughed. "About
five years ago a farmer called me and said one of his cows had
swallowed the damn balling gun while he was trying to get a
magnet in her. I think she was trying to get back at him. I took
not only the balling gun out of that cow, but nine damn
magnets. No wonder she felt like hell. That farmer thought
any problem could be solved with a magnet. His elevator
never did go to the top anyway. . . . There, that should do it."
He pulled out the magnet. It was covered with another glob of
miscellaneous hardware. "Want to leave the magnet in,
Paul?"

"Sure. Doesn't look like she'll change her habits any."

"Probably not." The vet cleaned the magnet, stuck it back
in, and started sewing up the incision. Things went fast after
that. Soon he cut loose the sutures Dad and I were holding
and wrestled the stomach back into the cow. "Lucky they go
back together almost as easy as they come apart." He started
stitching again. In fifteen minutes he was done. He washed
the cow's side with iodine again, gave her another shot, and
grinned at us. "No damage that won't heal. Keep her on
penicillin for three days and she should be fine."

He washed quickly then and I handed him a towel. As he
pulled his clothes back on, I noticed he was shivering. He'd
been rock steady all through the operation, too absorbed in his
work to notice the cold.

"Coffee, Doc?" Dad asked. "Or a little whiskey, maybe?"

"No thanks, Paul. I've got another call to make over on the
Andersen place before I go home and you've got a lot of cows
to milk. Next time we'll gab awhile."

"Well, thanks. You know where to send the bill."

"Sure. If it's okay, I'll just set you up on a monthly account."

"That's fine. Don't work too hard."

"I'll try not to. Good night. See ya, Fritz. Take it easy, son."

We called good night after him and set about the milking. Supper would have to wait; the operation had taken quite a while. Dad looked over at me as we worked one of the milking machines into place. "How'd you weather your first barnyard operation?"

"I'm okay, Jim didn't feel so good."

"Ya, I noticed. He took off like a ruptured duck. Let's get the milking started and then I'll go look for him. Probably embarrassed."

"He shouldn't be. I didn't feel so good myself a few times."

"I probably didn't the first time I saw one either. Takes getting used to. I like animals or I wouldn't be in this business, but you can't be sentimental or squeamish about them either."

"I'm starting to see that."

He went out to find Jim while Uncle Fritz and I went on milking the cows. In a few minutes they came back and Dad worked with Jim, talking and joking with him in low tones. For a while I almost enjoyed the quiet bustle of the barn. Uncle Fritz was quick and efficient, whistling softly, occasionally giving me advice or showing me how to save a few seconds or steps. Everything was going pretty well and I was looking forward to dinner when the last cow in our line planted a big hoof squarely on my big toe. I let out a yelp and a curse. Dad called over, "What's the matter, Rick?"

"Damned cow just stepped on my foot!" There was laughter again, but I gritted my teeth and ignored it. My foot throbbed and I was limping when we went in to dinner. That night when I took off the sock, the nail was already turning a deep purple. By morning it'd be black and I knew it would take half the summer to grow back.

4

"AND MR. WEBER, he's our algebra teacher, is really cute, especially when he blushes. Half the girls have a crush on him. But man, does he grade hard! I got a C on a quiz and I only made two little mistakes."

Judy was reporting on the day at school. Every evening the twins dominated the supper table conversation with news of their day.

Jim fought to get in his stories too. "Connie, do you know Jerry Tidwell? He's a big football player."

Judy cut him off. "He's a jerk. Always strutting around with Debbie Rank like he owned the place."

"Ya, she makes me sick," Connie put in. "She's a dork."

"Now, Connie, . . ." Mom said.

"Well, she is, Mom."

"We've all got our faults. Remember Christian charity."

Connie lapsed into a pout, muttering, "Well, I still think she's a dork."

Jim leaped into the pause. "Well, I think Jerry is a nice guy. After school he threw the football around with a couple of us." He looked around for expressions of interest, but found none.

Judy leaned over to Connie. "You know what I heard about Debbie Rank?" She whispered fast and I couldn't make it out, but they both started giggling so hard they couldn't eat. Dad and Uncle Fritz looked up from their own conversation about milk prices.

"Connie! Judy!" There was a warning in Mom's voice and they bit their lips and tried to stop, but a few more giggles escaped.

For a couple of minutes there was only the rattle of dishes, knives, and forks. Dad decided to get some of his parenting duties out of the way. "Well, Jim, been playing any ball after school?"

Jim glared at him. "If anyone had been listening, they'd have heard about me playing catch with probably the biggest star in the school."

"I'm sorry, son, I didn't hear you. Who was that?" Jim told his story in detail and Dad listened politely, then turned to look where Tommy sat between Mom and Pam. "And how was Tommy today? Were you a good boy?"

"Yes, Daddy. Mommy took me to the store." He babbled about the wonders of the supermarket while Dad nodded patiently.

When the story had apparently reached its conclusion, Dad, his obligations as head of the household again successfully discharged, murmured, "That's good. I'm glad you had fun," and turned back to his interrupted conversation with Uncle Fritz. The twins began talking and Jim again tried to join in.

Pam stood up. "Mom, can I be excused? I'm not very hungry."

"Don't you feel good?"

"I feel okay. I'm just not very hungry. Can I go, please?" Mom nodded and went back to helping Tommy with his meat.

Having had little to say about milk prices, football, grocery stores, or who was or was not a dork, I finished five minutes later, excused myself, and went in to the living room to watch the news. After supper there would be more chores to do in the barn and I hoped the others would eat slowly. I was sitting on the low stool in front of the TV, fiddling with the antenna control, when I heard something fall in the basement. What the hell? I thought. Rats?

I descended the stairs softly in the dark and at the bottom flipped on the lights, hoping to spot the little buggers. Pam jumped up from an old couch in the corner. It was covered with a jumble of boxes and miscellaneous junk left, like the abandoned couch, by the previous owner. Trying to find a place to sit, Pam had tipped over a shoebox of ancient, mildewed playing cards which now lay scattered by the score across the cement floor.

"What are you doing down here?" I blurted.

"Nothing. Just thinking."

"In the dark?" She had her head bowed and I couldn't see her face well.

"I like to think in the dark." Her voice had a catch in it and I went closer.

"What's the matter, Pammy?" She collapsed on the couch and started sobbing into her hands. After standing irresolutely for a moment, I pushed some boxes aside, sat down and put my arm around her. She was rigid and I had to tug at her gently before she leaned her head against my chest. We sat like that for several minutes before her crying eased. "Do you come down here often?" I asked. She nodded. "Why?" She didn't answer. "Why, Pammy? You can tell me."

"Because I feel like old dead dog bones," she choked out.

"Like dead dog bones?" I was incredulous; it was almost funny. She nodded fiercely. "Why do you feel like that?"

Another half a minute passed before she curled her legs up under her and lay more heavily on my chest. I patted her shoulder. Finally, she said very softly, "Because nobody ever pays any attention to me. It's like they don't even notice me. Dad asks about Jimmy and Tommy, but not about me. Mom is always bawling out Connie or Judy or helping Tommy. And no one pays any attention to me!" She started crying again.

"Tommy pays attention to you."

"He's only a little boy!"

"Well, how about Jim? You two have always been buddies."

"Not since we've been up here. He's always with you guys and he never has time to play with me anymore."

I was getting desperate. "Well, I pay attention to you and so does Uncle Fritz."

"No, you don't!" I was about to argue with her, but I stopped. It was true; we really didn't. Nobody in the family did. We took her for granted: smiling, shy, good-hearted Pam. She didn't complain or throw tantrums or act bitchy. She was the perfect little kid, so no one paid any attention to her. "I'm sorry," I said softly. "I guess you're right. I'll try to do better."

"I'd like to help in the kitchen more, but Mom and the twins rush around and I don't get a chance. If I try and then do anything just a little bit wrong, Connie or Judy yells at me and tells me to get out of the way. . . ." She sniffed. "It's just not fair."

"Well, maybe we can do something about that."

She burrowed a little closer. "Even at school I'm ignored. I'm the littlest in the class and the kids don't play with me and the teachers don't call on me."

"Oh, that's not true all the time, is it?"

"Most of it. . . . I wish I was adopted. Then I could have lots of problems and people would notice me."

"Pam, you really don't mean that! We're the lucky ones. We've had a family all our lives."

She sniffed and didn't reply. Finally she said, "I miss Linda."

Linda! My God, I'd completely forgotten about Linda. Linda was Pam's best friend in Milwaukee. A tiny, red-haired girl with a million freckles, she was forever proposing games and adventures Pam would never have tried on her own. The only times I could remember Mom really yelling at Pam was when one of Linda's projects got them in trouble—especially the time both girls and Tommy got covered with green paint trying to paint the front porch swing. But Linda had been good for Pam even then. "Well, maybe she could come up for a visit this summer. I'm sure you two would get in enough trouble to be noticed then."

She giggled and I tickled her. "No! Stop! Don't!" She was laughing now and I kept tickling her until she tried to wriggle away. She caught her breath, then said seriously, "But I don't want to wait until then to be noticed. Even a little bit."

I nodded. "Well, I guess you'll have to force yourself to speak up. Maybe even argue a bit. Tell you what, tomorrow at suppertime I'll ask you what you did at school. And we'll make everybody listen. That'll be a start. Okay?"

"You won't forget?"

"I promise."

She bit her lip. "Okay."

I thought about Pam during chores and, after she'd gone to bed, I asked the twins if they wanted to go into town for a Coke. I figured they'd be easier to talk to than Mom or Dad, who'd think they were being accused of incompetent parenting and get real hostile real quick.

The twins, of course, jumped at the chance, but not before getting in a few barbs. "Wow, he must really be lonely tonight," Connie said mockingly.

"Must be. I bet he wants us to introduce him to some girls," Judy said.

"We could take him by Debbie Rank's. I'm sure Jerry Tidwell is already home getting his beauty sleep."

"Sure, I bet she'd be raring to go." They both started giggling.

"Come on," I snapped. "Do you want to go or not? I'm leaving in two minutes flat, whether you're there or not." That shut them up and they dashed for their coats.

Outside a damp, raw wind chilled us as we hurried to the pickup. Although it was thawing during the day now, at night the temperature still fell below freezing. I backed the truck around and we bounced off along the frozen mud ruts of the drive to the gravel road and, after a mile, turned onto the highway leading to town. The fields stretching away on either side were almost bare of snow, but in the occasional groves of hardwoods and under the pine windbreaks an icy layer of rotting snow still lay.

I was trying to find the right words to begin when Connie spoke. "There are a couple of senior girls very interested in you, Rick."

I was immediately suspicious. "Oh ya? What did you do, show them a picture of some TV star and tell them it was me?"

"Why, we didn't do anything," Connie replied in a hurt voice. "Nothing except tell them who you were."

"How do they know me?" I was interested despite my mistrust of my sisters.

Judy answered. "They saw you at the feed mill around noon on Tuesday. We all waved when you drove out, but you just sailed by with your nose in the air."

"They thought you were cute," Connie added.

"Who are these girls of doubtful taste, Six-Pack Sally and Ton-of-Love Sue?"

Connie did her Miss Prim. "I'll have you know they're two of the prettiest girls in the school. They were both on homecoming court."

"Then they must have boyfriends."

"Not steady ones," Judy said, "and I'd bet they'd go for someone with your exotic range of experiences."

"Give me a break. Are you telling the truth?"

"Scout's honor," Judy replied.

"Give me a Bible!" Connie screeched, making me wince. "I want to swear on a Bible!"

"Okay. Okay. How do I meet one of them?"

"They said they'd meet you at the drugstore for a Coke tomorrow noon," Judy said.

"Hell, I can't get away then."

"You can if you want to meet them. Besides, they're farm girls, they won't mind if you're not all slicked up."

This was beginning to sound very interesting. I'll admit to being no great hit with the girls, but maybe I'd gotten lucky this time. "Well, maybe I could."

We rode in silence for a couple of minutes. It sure would be nice to have a little social life for a change, I thought. In Milwaukee I'd had a lot of friends of both sexes, but since moving to the farm I'd seen almost nothing of people my own age. A few dates would make life a lot more tolerable. Not that I should expect too much. I knew from past experience that my sisters' idea of what made an attractive girl differed considerably from mine. Still, why not take a chance? Connie, nearest the door, giggled and Judy said, "Shut up, Connie."

I gave them a hard look. They were trying to look innocent, but I could tell something was fishy. What was it that kept bothering me? Something about . . . I exploded. "Two girls, my aching butt. April fool, huh? That's it, isn't it?" They dissolved into screams of laughter. April first tomorrow. I should have known. "Why you two little brats. You are going to walk home!"

Judy was the first to recover enough to talk. "We were going to leave a note with the soda fountain man saying 'April Fool.'" That touched off another explosion of mirth.

"I would have murdered you both," I said sourly.

They had more or less gotten possession of themselves by the time I swung in at the all-night truck stop. I was still pretty burned up. It showed too, because after we'd found a booth and ordered Cokes and fries, Connie said, "Oh, you know we wouldn't have done it, really. We would have told you in the morning."

"I'll bet," I said sarcastically. Still, I decided to let it go. Their time would come.

After our orders arrived, I started in on what I'd meant to talk about. "I talked with Pam tonight. She was pretty upset because she doesn't think anyone pays any attention to her."

I waited as they exchanged looks. Connie spoke first. "So, what does that have to do with us? We're not to blame."

"I'm not saying anyone is to blame. I just think we ought to do something about it."

"Like what?" Connie snapped. "I think she gets plenty of attention. Little Miss Perfect, always pretending she's so good."

"Ya, Mom never yells at her, just at Connie and me. I think she's got it pretty easy."

Wow, had I walked into a buzz saw! "Hold on, will you? She doesn't see it that way. You've got each other and she's just lost her best friend. Jim's loud enough to get some attention and Tommy's little yet. Pam just feels left out."

"Then why is she always playing so goody-goody? We get a lot of crap and she gets away with everything." Connie was very angry.

Judy joined in. "So, I suppose we have to be nicey-nice and let her come everywhere we go."

I slammed my botttle down, making the plates rattle and getting a dirty look from the waitress at the counter. "Now I didn't say that! What the hell are you guys so mad about, anyway?" They looked uncomfortable. "Hey, what's going on here? This isn't like you two."

Connie toyed with her fork a moment, then said, "Last Friday we rode around with some guys for a couple of hours after school, then caught the late bus home. We told Mom we'd been in the Home Ec room, but she got really mad and said we were lying. Pam must have told her."

"Did you tell her not to?"

"No, but she should have known. You know how strict Mom and Dad are."

"Well, maybe she shouldn't have, but that doesn't mean she did it to get you in trouble. Mom probably just asked her where you were and Pam told her. Besides, Jim could have told her."

"No, we asked him," Judy said.

"Well, I still don't think it's Pam's fault. You should have called from school or told the truth." They both looked back at me stubbornly. I was getting nowhere—making things worse, actually. "Hey listen, I didn't mean to tell you this . . ." I told them all about Pam crying in the dark and what she'd told me, including the bit about dead dog bones.

When I was done, they sat quiet for a minute, then Connie said grudgingly, "Well, what should we do about it?"

"Just let her talk at the supper table now and then. Maybe we could ask her to come along more often. I mean, I know she's only a little girl, but that isn't easy either. You guys know that."

"I guess," Connie said. Judy nodded. They were still resentful, not quite convinced.

"Look, I'm not asking you to do anything big. Just pay a little attention to her now and then. Let her help in the kitchen a little more, even if she isn't as fast as you guys. . . . Okay?" They nodded. I went on, "And I don't think you should expect her, or anybody else, to lie for you. I've found the best way to deal with Mom and Dad is just to be completely honest."

"Wow. Now look who's playing the perfect one!" Judy snapped.

"Ya. I'll bet you told them all about the party you and your friends had over at Bill's in January. I heard things got pretty wild," Connie said.

"At breakfast you sure looked like you'd had a rough night. We saw you sneak back to bed when Mom went to the grocery store. I'm sure you told her *all* about it," Judy said.

Connie smirked. "And how about that first time you went out with Peggy Mathews? You sure were attached to your turtleneck sweater that next week. You didn't have something on your neck you were trying to hide, did you?"

I blushed. "Okay. Okay. Maybe I didn't mean completely honest. I've been no saint, I'll admit, but I think you could have told the truth about riding around with your friends. If you'd called first, I don't think there would have been any problem. They're not that strict."

"You ought to try being a girl," Judy said bitterly.

"Ya. Mom seems to think we're going to jump into bed with any boy we see. You should have heard the big lecture we got on the birds and the bees and preserving our virginity before we got to go to the Christmas dance at school. I'll bet they never gave you such a rough time," Connie said.

"Well, I've gotten some of that stuff, maybe not as much, but . . . Look, I don't know what to tell you guys, you're just going to have to work it out with them. It'll probably take some time, but you're only fifteen, after all."

"Almost sixteen," Judy said.

"Okay, almost sixteen. You'll just have to show you can be trusted. I think Mom still thinks about that foster girl who came to us pregnant after she'd tried to slash her wrists. She was only fourteen. You've heard about her, haven't you?"

"Oh, ya. We've heard all about *poor* Cindy. Mom brings her up every time she gets a chance," Connie said.

"Well, you know she means well and she's probably right a lot of the time. You've just got to be patient and talk to her about things. That's all I can suggest." There was a pause. No one seemed to have anything else to say. "I guess we'd better get home."

We finished our Cokes and the last cold fries and I went to the register to pay. I got my coat and joined the twins, who were talking to some high school guys at a table near the door. On our way out one of the guys called, "See you, Connie. Take 'er easy, Boots." There was some laughter.

When we were in the car, I asked Judy, "What did he mean calling you Boots?"

"Oh, nothing. It's just something a few of the kids called me. It doesn't mean anything."

I didn't pursue the matter. Instead I asked them more about school, and soon they were jabbering away about this teacher and that clique, and I tuned out. It was strange how so little of that interested me anymore. Only three weeks before I'd been in high school too, but it already seemed distant. I reminded myself guiltily that I still had those courses to finish. Somehow I'd thought I would have more time on the farm. Even if I didn't need them for graduation, they would look good on my high school transcript when I applied for college. I'd have to find some time.

The next evening we had supper before the evening milking, since Mom was going for the first time to her new Weight Watchers club. (All week she'd been trying to cut down on her snacking so she could go with a clean conscience.) As usual, the twins started the conversation with the day's school news roundup, but when I cleared my throat and gave them a significant look, they shut up and I was able to ask Pam what she'd done at school. She'd been waiting, her topic already chosen. She told about learning a few words in Spanish. Her voice wasn't very loud and when she counted to ten it sounded like one long word. Still, she got an impressed reaction from both Mom and Dad and the attention of the rest, so I counted it a success. That isn't to say that it was any big deal, but I knew it made her feel a little better.

I was still feeling pretty good about it when we finished the milking. Dad applied iodine to the udders of the last cow and stood up, putting a hand against the small of his back as he straightened his spine. "Oh, boy, getting old. Stiffer every night." I grinned. It was an old complaint. He looked at me. "Well, son, it's Friday night. Going to go out and whoop it up?"

"No. I'm kind of tired and there's a movie on the tube I want to watch. Also Pam wants me to help her write a letter to Linda. I'll save my whooping for tomorrow night."

"Just as long as you can get up Sunday morning. Your

mother is putting her foot down and all us godless heathens have to go to church."

I'd been expecting this. Mom is a firm churchwoman and now that we'd been here three weeks, it was time to get the family back among the saved. But I'd decided I didn't want to be included anymore. "Dad, I think I'll skip church for a while."

He looked hard at me. "Why? You always went before."

"I know, but I haven't believed in it for a long time. Now I guess I'm going to stop being a hypocrite."

He got his pipe going and leaned back against the wall. "What is it you object to?"

"Lots of things—all that crap about Adam and Eve, Jonah and the whale, and Noah's Ark. I mean, who can believe that stuff?"

He chuckled. "I know what you mean. I don't believe a lot of that myself. But I don't think that's the most important part, anyway. The New Testament has the really important things."

"Ya, but how about the loaves and the fishes, Dad? That's just as wild as Moses parting the Red Sea."

He looked bemused for a moment. "Well, I'm not going to argue theology with you, Rick. If you've got those questions, maybe you ought to talk to the minister or someone else at church, but I don't think you're going to find the answers by not going. Besides, your mother expects you to go." End of the discussion. He turned for the door.

I could hear Uncle Fritz in the milkhouse adjoining the barn whistling as he cleaned up. Jim was trying to imitate him. "Dad, I'm sorry, but I'm not going."

He turned, his blue eyes cold. "You're expected to go and that's it! I'm not going to let you upset your mother over a few little quibbles about whales and arks and the Red Sea."

"They're not quibbles, Dad! They're serious questions and I'm not going to sit in church pretending to believe when I don't. I'm almost eighteen and I think I have a right to decide these things for myself!"

66

"As long as you're living in my house, you'll do what your mother and I say!"

"I don't want to live in your damn house! Who do you think I came up here for? It sure as hell wasn't for me. If I'd had my way, I'd never have left Milwaukee." We stood glaring at each other.

"Hey, Paul, Rick, what's keeping you?" Uncle Fritz yelled from the milkhouse.

I wasn't sure if he'd overheard or if his interruption was just chance, but it came at the right time. Dad half turned. "Be there in a minute." He looked at me. "You think about it. Just consider how it's going to make your mother feel. We'll talk tomorrow." He left the barn.

Late the following afternoon I was trying to make some kind of order out of the chaos in the workshop when I saw Dad come out of the barn and walk toward the shop. Here it comes, I thought. I was sorry we'd fought but I was still angry about him laying the parental authority trip on me.

He came in. "How's it going?" he asked.

"Okay."

He sat down on a box. "We got into it a little last night, didn't we?"

"Ya, I'm sorry I said a couple of those things."

He took off his hat and ran his fingers through his hair. He always does that when he's about to say something important. "I guess I was wrong too. You are almost eighteen and pretty soon you'll be on your own. It's just, well, you know how your mother is about church. I don't really care if you go or not, but she sure does."

I threw a couple of lag bolts into a box, hung up a hammer, and turned to him. "I'm sorry if it hurts her, Dad, but what am I supposed to do? If I go against my own conscience, aren't I hurting myself?"

"Are you saying you don't believe in God?"

"No, I'm not saying that. I believe there is divine order in the universe, but I sure as hell don't believe Jonah was swallowed by a whale or that a couple of loaves and fishes fed hundreds."

"So, just because you don't believe a couple of stories, you think that the church is no good?"

"Don't twist my words, Dad!" I paused and took a deep breath. I wanted to keep this cool. "Dad, if other people want to believe, that's okay with me. Maybe it is good for them. But I don't believe and it's not good for me. Not right now. And I'm sorry if it's going to hurt Mom, but that's the way it is."

He rubbed the stubble on his chin, then got out his pipe and spent a minute getting it going. "Well, I guess I see your point, but the problem is that a little inconvenience for you, a little hypocrisy if you want to put it that way, will spare your mother a lot of pain. Things are in pretty precarious balance right now, and I'd hate to see a lot of trouble over something minor. Now hold on, I know it's not minor to you, but there are some other things more important right now."

"I don't think I follow you."

He twisted uncomfortably on his seat, then studied his pipe before lighting another match and holding it to the bowl. "It's just that your mother has gone through quite a bit in the last few months. Right now she seems to be handling it pretty well, but I just don't want to load too much more on her. This would be the wrong time for a big dustup over going to church. It might really throw her for a loop."

"I don't understand. I don't think I've ever seen her happier."

"Well, things aren't always quite what they appear. Oh, she's happy about moving to the farm, but there's a lot of strain too. She worries about the kids adjusting to school, about fixing up the place, about her weight, about money, about everything. Tommy's probably going to have to have another operation soon. We have to make a profit this year or maybe lose the whole works. And so on and so forth. She's got a lot to worry about."

"Including my soul."

He grinned. "If you want to put it that way." He was serious again. "Look, Rick, I guess it shouldn't come as any news to me that you aren't very happy here. But with everything else, I haven't given it much thought. By fall things will be better. Until then, we need you. I need you. And I know it's asking a lot. If you really think that you can't go to church without being a hypocrite, well, I guess your mother and I will have to deal with that. Still, I want you to think if it's worth adding another care to her load."

I stared at the toes of my boots. He sure knew how to make me feel guilty. "Ya, I'll think about it."

"Good." He got up. At the door he turned. "And, Rick, I appreciate what you're doing." He left.

Parents! You couldn't make them happy no matter what you did! I returned to the cleaning with angry energy. To hell with them. In a few more months I'd be out of here and then they could take the farm, the church, and all the guilt and expectations and stick them where the sun didn't shine!

After milking and dinner that night, I took the truck and drove down to Mason, twenty miles south. It is the nearest big town, about twenty thousand, and I hoped, using Dad's phrase, to whoop it up. But there wasn't much to do and I finally ended up going to a movie by myself. God, I missed my friends. Saturday nights had never been as lonely or boring in Milwaukee.

During milking on Sunday morning Uncle Fritz had a great time contemplating the prospect of going to church. "Yes siree, that minister's really gonna figure something's wrong when he sees me arrive. Fritz Gebhardt ain't darkened the door of a church in a coon's age. 'Cept for weddings and funerals, that is. Why that preacher will probably think the end of the world really is at hand. Probably have to change the subject of his sermon." He finished getting a milking machine in place and went on. "But, you know, that minister ain't a bad fellow, really. I've seen him in Irma's a couple of times having a beer and laughing at the boys' dirty jokes—kind of sampling the sin so he knows what to talk about on Sunday." He laughed. "Yes sir, going to get me some religion today. Expect it'll do me any good, Rick?"

I grinned. "I don't know, Uncle Fritz. You're already in trouble pretty deep, I hear."

He laughed. "You must have been talking to some of the real old-timers. I did most of my big sinning before you was even a pup. I'm too old for it now. Don't you think there's one of them statutes of limitations on some of them sins?"

"You're asking the wrong guy, Uncle Fritz, but I think it's worth checking out."

Chuckling he went off to empty milk into the bulk tank. I went back to thinking about church. I really couldn't see how I would be hurting anyone by not going. Mom couldn't be that sensitive. Besides, it would be wonderful to lounge around the house with everyone else gone.

As the four of us walked back to the house, I'd just about made up my mind not to go, but my resolution faltered when we came into the kitchen. Mom looked up from braiding Pam's long hair. "Hurry now, you men. We don't want to be late on our first Sunday. The kids are all cleaned up, so you can use the shower upstairs and the tub downstairs. *Mach schnell!*"

"*Andale!*" Pam said, showing off her Spanish.

Dad looked at me. I gulped and said, "You and Uncle Fritz can go upstairs. Jim and I'll stay down here." He winked at me and grinned.

So I went. What the hell, it wouldn't last forever—not church or life on the farm.

5

MIDWAY THROUGH THE morning milking Dad glanced at his watch. "We're running a little late. Can you finish alone?"

"Sure, no problem."

"Good, I've got to shower, change, and get a decent breakfast. Have to make a good impression on the loan officer. Can't smell bad or sit there with my stomach growling." He smiled wryly—there was little humor in asking for another loan.

"Good luck," I called after him as he headed for the door.

"Ya, thanks."

He was just getting into the car when I came out of the barn. It was a nice day, cool but cloudless, with a bright spring sun. By noon we might be able to work with our coats off. The motor turned over, caught, and stalled. I didn't like the way it sounded. Dad ground the starter again, but this time the motor wouldn't catch.

"Hold on a second, Dad." I went over, lifted the hood and took off the top of the air cleaner. The filter was black. I stuck a finger into the carburetor. No, it didn't seem to be flooded.

"Try her again. I'll handle the throttle." Dad turned the key and I pulled the long rod of the carburetor linkage all the way toward me. The choke flap popped open obligingly. The engine coughed twice, then went back to turning over without effect. I worked the throttle a couple of times, but still nothing happened.

Dad turned off the ignition and got out. "Flooded?"

"I don't think so, Dad. I'm not sure what's wrong."

"Let me see." He started to reach into the engine compartment.

"You'd better not, you'll get your clothes dirty."

He pulled his hands back. "I guess you're right. I forgot." I smiled. He looked odd and awkward in suit and tie. "Well, I've got to go. You'll have to make do without the pickup this morning. See what you can do with the car. I bought parts for tuning it up a couple of weeks ago, but never got around to it. They're still in the trunk. You might as well change the oil too."

"Okay. I'll start after I help Uncle Fritz with the cleaning up."

"Just so it's done by this afternoon. I think your mother is planning on going to town." He hurried off.

Cleaning the barn was not one of the great pleasures in my life, but it went fast this morning and we were done by 9:30. I tackled the car while Uncle Fritz drove out in the field to spread the manure.

Whoever designed the slant six engine must have had a mean streak. It's a reliable engine, but it sure is a bitch to work on. The spark plugs are impossible to reach without putting a joint and two extensions on the socket wrench and you almost have to climb in to get at the distributor.

I begrudged the time I was spending on the car, since a thousand other things waited to be done. Almost every day now, between the morning and evening milkings, we were working on the equipment. I'd never realized before how much machinery is necessary to run a farm. At first I'd barely understood what much of it was for but, as I said, I've always liked machinery and my best hours were spent figuring out how each piece worked. Besides the three tractors, there were three hay wagons, three chopper wagons, a grain drill, a silo unloader, a corn planter, a cultivator, an elevator, a grain auger, three plows, a couple of disks, a hay baler, a haybine, a corn picker, a corn and hay chopper, a manure spreader, an ancient combine, and dozens of smaller pieces of equipment. Most of them were in poor repair, since the previous owner had been sick a lot in his last few years and unable to keep up with the maintenance. So all those undone tasks now stretched in front of us like stalks in a row of corn running to the horizon. No sooner was one machine fixed when we found yet another that needed mending. Everything not necessary for the spring planting had to wait, but the car was an exception.

Thinking about the other things that had to be done, I wasn't paying close attention to what I was doing. When I took a turn on the last spark plug in the line, the one farthest toward the back and the hardest one to reach, I didn't have the socket seated right, and snapped the head off the plug. Damn! That made things twice as hard. To hell with it. I'd change the oil and come back to it in a few minutes.

Dad drove in while I was putting in the new oil. He waved, parked the pickup, and went in to change. He came back out a few minutes later looking more at ease in his overalls and patched jacket. "How's it going?"

"Okay. Everything's done except the spark plugs."

"You put in the new points and rotor?"

"Ya, I did that first, but I snapped the head off one of the plugs and I can't get it out."

"Let me try." He took the socket wrench. "Quite an arrangement, here." He found a different socket, replaced a long extension with a shorter one and leaned in under the raised hood. The socket must have been worn, because when he applied pressure to the wrench, it slipped on the plug and his knuckles smacked painfully against the air cleaner housing. He cursed, jerked his hand back, and studied the gouged skin. He swore again, glared at me for a long second, then turned on his heel and stalked away toward the house. He almost took the porch door off the hinges when he went in. What was he so mad about? Hell, it hadn't been my fault. If he'd left the longer extension on, it never would have happened.

I took the socket wrench and replaced the extension. This time I got the plug out without too much trouble. I gapped the new plugs and started putting them in.

I was on the fourth one when Dad came out of the house and walked over. "Get it out?"

"Ya. How's the hand?"

"All right. Nothing that won't heal." He watched as I got the last two plugs in and reconnected the wires. "Shall I start her up?"

"Sure, go ahead."

The engine sounded good. I checked the timing, adjusted the idle a little, and shut the hood. Dad turned off the engine and got out. "I'm sorry, Rick. I didn't mean to seem so angry. Things haven't been going my way today."

"No luck at the bank, huh?"

"Oh, some. It's just that they make you crawl, then give you half what you need. It's humiliating. They can't really cut us off, because we owe them so much already. If we go bankrupt they'll lose a pile, but you'd think from their attitude that I was some junkie stumbling in off the street to get a loan for dope." He grimaced. "I just hate to ask them for more money." He got his pipe going and stared off toward the horizon. He was talking as much to himself as to me. "I bought a farm so I could be my own boss, but now I owe five times what I ever did before. I'm less my own boss now than when I was working for the dairy." He shook his head.

"Is there really a danger that we're going to go broke?"

He looked at me in surprise. He really had forgotten I was there. "Well, yes. Yes, there is a chance. Right now we're actually losing money. What I borrowed today should give us enough to survive until midsummer. By then production should be up enough to meet the payments and expenses with a little left over. I hope to get a half dozen more cows next week at auction and that'll help. But if there are too many unexpected bills, we'll be sunk."

I nodded. So it was that bad. "We really need a good year."

"You bet. Everything is going to have to be pretty near perfect—weather, prices, crops, cattle, and people. We don't have much margin for bad luck. . . . Well, this isn't getting anything done. Where's Fritz?"

"He went up to his room as soon as he got in from spreading manure. He said he was feeling a little poorly and wanted to lie down for a few minutes."

"Hmmm. Well, let him rest. We'll call him at noon. Let's see if we can fix that damn blower."

"Okay." I gathered up the tools and followed.

With spring planting coming soon, Dad and Uncle Fritz often worked until nearly midnight on the equipment. They'd come in tired, Dad grouchy and Uncle Fritz pale and quiet, to eat a sandwich and go to bed for the few hours before the morning milking. Most nights I'd help too, but as we got well into April I had to start begging off a few nights a week to do my schoolwork. I'd done little in the first few weeks and now I had to hurry to get everything sent down to Milwaukee before the end of May. I didn't dare wait any longer since the plowing and planting would take all three of us sixteen hours a day once the weather warmed.

Even though Dad couldn't spare me much during the day, he sometimes sent me inside to help Mom sand or paint or repair small items like a cracked floorboard in the stairs. I didn't mind too much because it was warm and dry inside and often a cold wind was blowing a fine spring rain outside.

Still, I'd often feel like I was missing something as Dad and Uncle Fritz at last found a broken part or finally got a stubborn machine to work well again. The small triumphs could make many hours of work seem worthwhile, but as often as not, we'd come in with little to show for a day's labor except blackened fingernails and bruised knuckles. Uncle Fritz was good at trying to cheer us up then. He had an endless store of colorful expressions to fit any possible situation. The problem was that the color was often more off-color than anything else. In the open spaces of the country the kids were kicking up their heels and sending the inhibitions of city life flying. Uncle Fritz's language seemed tailor-made to fit their new sense of freedom and they adopted it, much to his amusement, off-color humor and all. It's not that he swore much, he just had an earthy perspective on life.

I remember one evening when we came in particularly tired after an unsuccessful battle with a stubborn tractor engine. The last snow of the season had fallen in the late afternoon, big soggy flakes that melted almost as soon as they reached the ground, but left the air cold and wet and the drive ankle-deep in mud.

It was after 10:30 when we sat down, still muddy, around the kitchen table to eat sandwiches and drink coffee. After a couple of swallows of steaming coffee and a bite or two of bologna sandwich, Uncle Fritz surveyed our dour faces and grinned. "Hell, you guys worry too much. In a year or two we'll be enough ahead to buy some new iron. This old stuff will last until then. Buck up, by fall we'll have this place running like cowshit through a greased funnel."

"Now, Fritz, watch your language," Mom said in a mildly warning tone.

"All I said was cowshit. Hell, Ellie, I'm just an old farmer talking his natural way."

"Well, just remember there are lots of big ears around here waiting to take your quaint little sayings off to school with them and I don't want any teachers calling me up about my kids swearing."

"Well, I'll try, Ellie, but you know trying to change an old farmer like me is a little like trying to get ten pounds of cowshit into a five-pound bag." She screeched and threw a dishrag at him and he roared.

It was always something like that. But often Dad would only smile and go back to puffing moodily on his pipe. Sometimes he'd mutter, more to himself than anyone else, "Gotta make do. Just gotta make do with what we've got for a while."

Dad was quieter these days and often I'd hear Mom and him talking late in the kitchen. The subject was always the same—money. How could we cut expenses or raise a little more to make ends meet.

I didn't ask for any money myself, although I'd hoped at the beginning to earn something over the summer toward college. But that seemed distant now and I'd accepted that my responsibility to the family had to come first. Every now and then Dad would give me a few bucks and tell me to go into town and have some fun, but there really wasn't much to do since I wasn't eighteen yet and couldn't go into the bars to shoot pool or down to the discotheque ten miles away to dance. So I usually ended up spending the money on a movie or some machine part we needed.

There was a youth center in town, but most of the kids there were a lot younger than I was and I couldn't see spending all my money on Cokes and electronic games anyway. The twins were getting involved in the church youth group and they dragged me in once, but the kids there were young too. And, besides, I still felt like a hypocrite when we all bowed our heads to pray at the beginning of the meeting. On Sunday evenings after that, I'd just drop them off and spend the next couple of hours in the library or at the movies until it was time to pick them up.

From what I could tell, all the kids had settled down pretty well at their new school. Judy grumbled now and then about how the old school in Milwaukee had been more fun, and, of course, Jim was still of the opinion that all school was a waste of time. Still, that all seemed like pretty normal bitching. Pam complained to me again a couple of times about being the littlest in her class, but I assured her that would probably change.

Spring vacation came in the middle of April. It was good to have the extra help at home. Pam could take care of Tommy and do some of the smaller chores, giving Mom more time to work on the house. The twins, after some complaining, pitched in to help with the remodeling. Jim was the happiest to be away from school for a few days. Uncle Fritz would watch him running for tools or helping with some chore and grin. "Boy's a natural-born farmer. Takes to it like flies to fresh cowshit on a hot July day."

About the fourth time he said that, I asked irritably, "Don't you ever get sick of cowshit sayings?"

"No siree, boy. Cowshit is the foundation of farming. Hell, cowshit is the foundation of life. It fertilizes the fields, the fields feed the cattle, the cattle feed us, and fertilize the fields all over again. Cowshit is beautiful."

"Ya, and smells like hell too."

"Smell! Boy, that is perfume you are smelling now. And, son, you ain't had a fulfilled childhood until you've been in a cowpie-throwing fight or had a contest to see who can chuck one the farthest. Hell, I bet the guy who invented them frisbees grew up on a farm throwing cowpies. This summer I'll show you the knack and next year you can impress all your big uppity city friends. It's a great and glorious art, I tell you."

"And I imagine the guy who invented the discus took the idea from a cowpie too?"

"A discus? You mean one of them things they throw at the Olympics? Why, sure. They ought to change it back, too. Lot more skill in throwing a cowpie than one of them metal things." He laughed happily at the picture of an Olympic manure-chucking competition and I shook my head.

Somehow Uncle Fritz could always make things a little

78

cheerier. I even thought I'd take him up on the cowpie throwing. Just to see it done.

A major interest for Jim and all the kids this vacation was the anticipated birth of the first calf of the season. Four of the cows were "close-up," as Uncle Fritz called it, but it looked like a small two-year-old heifer would calve the earliest. This would be her first and, just like an inexperienced human mother, she seemed nervous and restless. Dad and Uncle Fritz had been talking about possible problems. She weighed only about seven hundred pounds and her hips were narrow. Since a vet isn't usually called to attend a cow except in exceptional cases, we'd have to deal with any problem until he could get there.

When we sat down to lunch on the Wednesday before Easter, Dad said to Mom, "Fritz thinks it will be sometime late this afternoon or early in the evening. She's been up and down most of the morning and it looks like the labor is beginning."

"Oh boy," Jim yelled, "I'm going to go watch."

"You sit down and eat your lunch first," Mom said firmly.

"But I don't want to miss anything!"

"It'll be a long time yet," Dad said.

Jim spent the rest of the afternoon watching the cow in fascination as her discomfort built. Uncle Fritz or Dad would occasionally check on her, but otherwise she was left in Jim's care.

Late in the afternoon, Dad took a few minutes to play with Pam and Tommy. For weeks he'd been chiding himself for not spending enough time with the youngest children. Now they stood in a triangle in the backyard playing catch. I glanced over now and then from where I was replacing a split board on the bed of one of the haywagons. Catching a ball isn't a big deal for most people, but for Tommy it's a major achievement. He would wait tensely, trying to concentrate the dim power of his eyes on the ball in Dad's hands. Dad would swing his arm slowly the first time, a little faster the second, and on the third time he'd release the ball so that it traveled in a gentle arc to Tommy. Tommy's hands would flail at the ball and once in every three or four times, he'd succeed in catching it and Dad and Pam would cheer and clap. Then Tommy would aim the ball at Pam and heave it, his poor depth perception making an accurate throw almost as difficult as a successful catch. Pam would usually have to chase the ball across the grass. Then she'd throw it to Dad and the process would begin again.

They'd been playing for maybe twenty minutes and I'd finally fitted the board to my satisfaction when Jim came rushing out of the barn. "Dad, Dad, I think something's happening!"

Dad had just started to swing his arm for the second time, but instead of bringing the ball back down, he let it go with a sudden hard thrust. The ball sped straight and fast. Tommy didn't even move and the ball hit the corner of his glasses, ripping them off his face. He screeched in terror. "Sweet Jesus," Dad gasped, and ran to where Tommy now lay face down, screaming. I sprinted to their side. Dad sat him up. Tommy had his hands over his face and was still screaming. "Tommy, I'm sorry! Let me see, son. Please let me see." He got Tommy's hands down. The nose piece had gouged into the side of his nose and a long trickle of blood ran down his face from a deep cut. The flesh beside his right eye was already swelling. He'd have a hell of a shiner.

All the other kids and Uncle Fritz, alerted by Tommy's screaming, were there in a minute. Mom pushed between the twins. "What happened, Paul?"

"Tommy got hit with the ball. Jim distracted me and I threw it when Tommy wasn't expecting it. And I guess I threw it too hard."

I could see Mom was furious, but she didn't lay into Dad. She examined the damage to Tommy's face tight-lipped. He was sobbing now. "You're going to be okay, Tommy. Now hush, let Mommy get a good look. This is going to need stitches, Paul. One of you girls get a damp washcloth and a towel . . . and my coat and purse," she called after them. She lifted the little boy, cradling him against her heavy body. She gave us a withering glare, then turned and headed for the car. Pam retrieved Tommy's glasses and ran after them. She was crying too.

In a few minutes they were off: Connie and Pam in the back seat with Tommy, Judy and Mom in front. We were left standing there awkwardly. "Oh, hell," Dad said. "Damn it to hell!"

For the first time I noticed Jim was gone. "Dad, where did Jim get to?"

"What? Oh, shit! I bet he thinks I'm blaming him. Fritz, see to that cow, will you? Jim thought something was happening. Come on, Rick."

Time was crucial now. If we got to Jim before his rage built to the flash point, perhaps we could avert a tantrum. If we didn't find him fast, we'd all be in for one hell of an evening. Dad muttered, "Damn that kid anyway, startling me like that." I started to say that I didn't think it was Jim's fault, but Dad could have been reading my thoughts. "Ya, ya, I know that's stupid. It wasn't his fault. It was all mine. What a dumb-ass thing to do. Damn! . . . You check the machine shop. I'll look around out back. And be careful with him."

Jim was sitting on the workbench in the machine shop. He was scowling and rocking back and forth a little. I knew the signs and they were all present now. "How you doing, Jim?"

He glared at me. "It wasn't my fault!"

"Nobody said it was. Dad just told Mom what happened. It was an accident. If anyone's to blame, it's Dad, and he knows it."

"I heard what he said! 'Jim distracted me.' That means he's going to blame me and so is Mom!"

I felt like telling him that he was being dumb, making a mountain out of a molehill and all that sort of thing, but I knew better. "Well, I think you'll find out different. Don't you think we'd better check on that cow?"

He looked interested for a second, but then his face darkened again. "I don't care about any old, stupid cow. No one will want me around anyway when the calf comes."

"Well, I'm sure gonna want you around." We were both startled by Uncle Fritz's voice. We turned to see him leaning casually against the door frame. "You've spent the most time around her, Jim, and I think she trusts you the most. Believe an old farmer, that's important at a time like this."

"Is anything happening?" Jim asked.

"Not just yet. I think maybe she fooled you a little, but she's more dilated and getting real restless. She's mighty scared, boy, and I think she could use a friend real bad."

That did it. Jim was off the workbench, through the door, and running for the barn in an instant. "Nice going, Uncle Fritz," I said.

He smiled. "I know where that boy's heart's at. Someday, your pa is going to have a hell of a fine man to hand this farm over to."

Uncle Fritz's comment gave me a little twinge. After I left the farm, Dad and Jim would grow closer while I grew apart from them, from Mom, from everyone here. Life on the farm would go on. The kids would grow up. My parents and Uncle Fritz would grow old. When I came home for a visit, I'd be a bystander, my soft city hands no longer fit for the chores, my clothes too nice, my farming skills long rusty from disuse. And for a moment now, I envied Jim the very different life he would lead.

Mom, Tommy, and the girls returned while we were milking. Dad left me and went outside. He came back a few minutes later, silent and brooding. I waited a while before I asked, "How is he?"

"Oh, Tommy's okay. He's got a patch over that eye and a beautiful shiner, but they didn't have to take any stitches.

They put one of those butterfly bandages on his nose. . . . But your mother is mad as all get out. Really read me the riot act. She said if that ball had hit on the lens, Tommy might have lost the sight of that eye. And he's got enough problems that way already."

"Dad, those glasses of his are safety glasses and thick as Coke bottles. I don't think that ball could possibly have broken them."

"I know. I tried to tell her that. Not that I don't feel damn bad about the whole thing, but she's making a major disaster out of it. Hell, I'll bet I had three shiners like that when I was a kid."

I nodded. "Ya, I've had a couple."

He smiled half-heartedly. "Ya, like the time you tried to take on that Olson boy."

I winced, remembering. "Ya, he cleaned my clock, that's for sure. . . . And you and Mom finished the job."

"Well, it cured some of that temper of yours." He laughed and then was silent again.

We worked for a few minutes without speaking. "Dad, I don't think I'd worry too much about it. It'll blow over."

He nodded. "Sure, it's not the first time I've been in the dog house with your mother. . . . But it worries me that she's taking it so hard. She gets so damned uptight every once in a while that it seems like anything, big or little . . ." He shook his head. "Well, that's the last cow. Let's get things washed up."

Jim stayed in the barn with the close-up heifer while the rest of us went in to supper. Everyone was subdued. All the kids knew that there was a cloud between Mom and Dad. Uncle Fritz didn't try to cheer us up either, but ate silently. Tommy was ornery, reaching up to feel his eye frequently and fussing when Mom tried to get him to eat. I hurried through my meal on the excuse that I had to relieve Jim and got out of the house as quickly as possible. It wasn't often I looked forward to returning to the barn.

Jim was leaning over the rail of the pen stroking the heifer's nose. She gazed back at him with what really did seem like trust in her huge brown eyes.

"You can go in to eat now. I'll take over here."

"That's okay. I'm not hungry."

"You know Dad will just make you go in to supper when he gets here."

He groaned. "Ya, I guess. But you call me right away if anything happens."

"Sure." He left and I sat down on a hay bale to wait for Dad and Uncle Fritz. The barn was warm and the animals quiet now that the evening milking had been done. The cows swept up big mouthfuls of hay and chewed earnestly. Every now and then, one would stick her nose into her drinking cup, the end of her muzzle depressing the plunger so water rushed into the cup. A milker drinks about twenty gallons of water a day and the water pipeline is one of the critical systems in the barn. We'd already had one broken pipe in the last month and cleaning up had been an awful job. Fortunately, we'd been able to fix the pipe quickly and hadn't had to hand water the stock. That really would have been murder.

One of the barn cats rubbed against my legs, then hopped into my lap, and curled up. Signa wandered over from her corner, sniffed at the cat, then flopped down at my feet with a grunt. I found myself getting drowsy and smiled ruefully. Here was Rick, the dedicated city boy and future architect, sitting in a barn with a cat on his lap and a dog at his feet, contentedly dozing off. And I'd be spending the rest of the evening and perhaps a good deal of the night in this barn waiting for a calf to be born. Boy, would Bill have fun if he could see me now!

The heifer struggled to her feet again and then slumped back down. She had done that several times since I'd sent Jim into the house. Suddenly a torrent of water gushed from her hindend. I jumped up, the cat fell from my lap on Signa's back and there was a quick exchange of hisses and growls. I paid no attention to them. I was shocked. I mean, I knew about the sack around the calf rupturing and the resulting loss of fluid. But I hadn't expected it by the barrel!

I went shakily to the phone and rang the house. "Dad, the water just broke. At least I think that's what happened. There seemed like an awful lot of it."

"Okay. We'll be out just as soon as we're done with coffee. Don't panic. The water usually breaks about an hour or so before the calf comes. How far apart are the contractions?"

"I don't know. I wasn't paying much attention."

"Well, you'd know it if there was anything to worry about. Do you want me to bring you a cup of coffee?"

"No, that's okay. Just hurry."

He laughed. "Nothing to worry about. I'll send Jim out. I'm sure you two can handle things for a while."

The hell we can! I thought. I went back and reseated myself on the hay bale. Signa and the cat had made peace quickly and the cat sat a couple of feet from the dog cleaning a paw. Everything was peaceful again. Even the heifer seemed less restless, staring at me with big, calm eyes. Steady, I told myself. If you can handle the traffic in downtown Milwaukee at rush hour, you can handle this.

Uncle Fritz stuck his bare arm deep inside the heifer. It was almost 11:00. I was tired and couldn't help yawning every couple of minutes. Jim and Dad stood close to Uncle Fritz, watching him feeling carefully around. I wish the damn calf would quit stalling and get born, I thought. "No problem," Uncle Fritz said. "The calf is coming head first. It won't be too long now."

Dad straightened. "Good. I think we're about to lose Rick."

I shook off a yawn in mid-course. "I'll make it."

"You don't have to stay, you know," Dad said. "We can handle it."

"I've stayed this long, I might as well see the rest."

Dad rumpled Jim's hair. "How about you, Jim? Morning's going to come awful early. You want to turn in?"

"Are you kidding? I wouldn't miss this for anything!"

Dad and Uncle Fritz laughed and I yawned again. The heifer gave a half-moo, half-groan. "That's it," said Uncle Fritz, kneeling again. "Let's get serious now, girl." The contractions were intensifying, coming about a minute apart. More fluid and mucus oozed from her gaping vaginal opening, and after several more contractions, two small hooves slipped into sight. "That's it. Come on, girl," Uncle Fritz encouraged her. Jim squatted near the heifer's head, petting her neck and stroking her nose. She panted and moaned softly.

Dad glanced over at Jim. "Be careful. She may toss her head. She's gentle and she's your friend, but she's having kind of a rough time of it right now."

"Put your arm around her neck," Uncle Fritz said. "Then if she tosses her head, you'll just ride with it. Otherwise you're bound to catch it in the chops, boy." Jim obeyed.

The forelegs of the calf emerged inch by inch as the heifer pushed. Uncle Fritz took them firmly and pulled gently. "I'll give you a hand, old girl. Now push. That's it. Push." The nose of the calf came in sight and then, as the shoulders stretched the vagina wider with each contraction, the rest of the head emerged. The heifer gave an agonized groan and pushed even harder. The shoulders of the calf seemed stuck for a long minute, then the cow's vagina stretched an extra centimeter and very quickly the calf's long, slippery, black and white body slid through. Uncle Fritz pulled its hindlegs free and laid it in the straw before him. Quickly, with the ease of long practice, he spread the calf's mouth wide and cleaned the mucus from the windpipe with his fingers. Dad said, "Jim, better get away from her now." Uncle Fritz lifted the calf gently and placed it close to the mother's head. The heifer sniffed at her child, then busily started licking it clean.

"Now don't go near her for a while, boys," Dad said. "She's got a new calf and she's going to be very protective." He turned to Uncle Fritz, who was standing beside us wiping his arms and hands with a rag. "Well, what do you think?"

"It's a good-looking calf. At least eighty pounds, I'd say, but it's a bull."

Dad grimaced. "I thought so. Bad luck. . . . Well, at least the heifer's all right."

"Ya, she came through it good. Took a while, but the first one's often like that. Too bad it wasn't a female, but the veal market ain't too bad. . . ."

"We'll talk about that later," Dad broke in, looking quickly over at Jim, who'd gone closer to the heifer and her calf and was watching the cleaning process with fixed attention.

I was surprised to find that my fatigue had disappeared. The excitement of seeing the calf born had left me wide awake. The others felt the same, apparently, because no one made a move to go to bed. Dad and Uncle Fritz sat and smoked their pipes and watched the calf gradually become aware of his surroundings as his mother licked his coat dry. Of course, the men had hoped for a female. A calf that would eventually become a milker was much more valuable than one that could only be sold for veal or castrated and raised for beef. Since natural breeding is virtually a thing of the past, there is no place for a bull on most dairy farms. Still, the men did not seem particularly disheartened. After a few minutes, Uncle Fritz said, "You never get tired of seeing it, do you, Paul?"

"No. It's always a thrill. It was the first time I saw it and it still is. What did you think, Rick?"

"I enjoyed it. It didn't make me want to become a vet or anything, but it was pretty neat."

Uncle Fritz grinned. "I don't think you have to ask Jim." Jim was impervious to everything that was being said, utterly fascinated with watching the heifer and calf.

My fatigue was beginning to return, but I was unwilling to leave their company yet. Uncle Fritz and Dad got started telling stories about calving and I listened.

My eyes were beginning to droop when Jim let out a horrified "What's that?!"

We looked over. A thick glob of bloody mucus was oozing from the hindend of the cow. "That's the afterbirth," Dad said. "Don't worry about it. We'll let the heifer eat some of it. There are chemicals in there she needs. We'll throw the rest away. Signa! Get away from there!"

Signa, who had approached the pen stealthily, leaped back, and then trotted back to her corner, where she sat grinning at us. Uncle Fritz laughed. "It's always been a wonderment to me why all farm dogs seem to think the afterbirth is really good eats. Seem to like it almost as much as rolling in cowshit. And they wonder why they can't come in the house." He whistled and Signa trotted over and laid her head in his lap. The heifer had stopped licking the calf and was now cleaning herself. "Poor Signa," Uncle Fritz said, scratching her ears, "you almost got away with one that time."

I was a bit grossed-out by the turn in the discussion, so I stood up and stretched. "Well, that's it for me. I'm going in."

"Ya," said Dad, "it's about that time. We'll have cows to milk before you know it."

In the morning everyone came down to see the new calf. He was pretty uncertain on his legs and only wobbled around a little before lying back down in the straw, but the kids loved it. The heifer watched us nervously, but when Jim came close, she stuck her head over the rail and let him scratch her muzzle. The other kids were all very excited and wanted to get a closer look at the calf, but Uncle Fritz shooed them back. Mom took Dad's hand and he smiled broadly at her—the first calf born on their farm, a big event. Tommy's accident of the afternoon before, Mom's anger, and Dad's remorse seemed forgotten now.

I stood back a little from the others. The calf was cute and it was fun to see the kids so excited, but Uncle Fritz's mention of the veal market stuck in my mind. There's going to be trouble when Dad has to tell Jim about that, I thought.

My old high school had its spring break a week after the

local schools and I'd long since announced that I wanted to take a few days off to visit Milwaukee. I'd gotten over a lot of my early distaste for the farm, but I still longed for the city and my friends. When I'd asked Mom and Dad, I could tell they didn't like my idea much, but they'd agreed and I'd started making plans.

I would bathe about two dozen times to get the manure stench off and then I'd catch the bus south. Bill could pick me up at the station and we'd have a long talk the first night, make some plans for the fall (I still hoped to talk him into getting an apartment with me), and then we'd have a good round of the spring parties over the next few days. I'd call up one of the girls I knew to go with me—a little female companionship would be damned nice for a change. I might even stay around for the first day back at school after vacation to see some of my teachers and the kids I'd missed at the parties. I wrote to Bill and called the bus station for the schedule. It was going to be a grand time.

A couple of days before I intended to leave, I was working late in my room at the desk I'd manufactured from concrete blocks and a sheet of half-inch plywood when Dad knocked on the door. He came in and set a cup in front of me. "I thought the diligent scholar might need some coffee."

"Thanks."

He sat down on the bed. "What are you working on now?"

"Physics. It's kind of hard without seeing the demonstration, but I'm getting it."

"Good, good." I could tell he wasn't thinking about schoolwork. He paused, sipping from his own cup. "Fritz and I walked out into the fields tonight. They'll be dry enough to plow in a couple of days."

Oh, hell, here it comes, I thought. I looked down at my hands lying on the open physics book. The last few weeks had changed them. The early blisters had been replaced by calluses and now they, in turn, were cracking, dirt embedded in the cuts so deep that not even the hardest scrubbing could completely clean them. I rubbed my palms together and felt their roughness. They weren't a city boy's hands anymore, but a farmer's. "I suppose you'd like me to stay."

Dad sighed and got up to look out the window over the drive. The yard light lit up the barn and the outbuildings where the silent stolid machines stood ready to roar into action and turn this muddy brown farm into acres and acres of rich green corn, oats, and hay by midsummer. "I don't want to ask you to. I know that you'll be a man soon . . . no, you're a man now and you have to make your own decisions, but, well, I guess you know the situation. The old man who owned this place hadn't bought a new piece of equipment in years and now we have to make do with the old stuff until we get on our feet. What's worse is that the fields didn't get plowed last fall, so we've got extra work this spring. It's rough, Rick. But once we get these crops in, I know we'll be all right." He paused, sipping from his cup.

I knew what my answer should be, had to be, but God, it was tough. Never again would all my friends be in one place. After graduation they'd scatter like grain—some to work far away, some to the service, most to colleges all over the country. Some would even be getting married and having children. This was my last chance to see them all and the pain of missing it hurt down deep inside. For a long moment a terrible resentment rushed almost to my tongue. Why should I sacrifice my happiness? Hadn't I come up here when farming was the last thing I'd ever imagined doing? Didn't I go to church just to spare Mom a little pain? Why was it always me who had to give something up? Hadn't I been the big brother to a whole family of adopted kids? Hadn't I sacrificed my rightful place so they could have a good home?

The last thought shut off the rage. I was deeply ashamed of it. These were my brothers and sisters! I didn't give a damn if they didn't have the same blood running in their veins. They loved me and I loved them. And I loved my folks. They'd worked and sacrificed most of their lives for us. They were damned good people. I put my hands together and squeezed hard, trying to force out the resentment. I was surprised at what just a few weeks had done for their strength. Then I turned and tried to give Dad my biggest smile. "It's okay, Dad. It wasn't any big deal. There'll be other times. Don't fret about it."

He turned from the window and looked hard into my eyes. Then he grinned. "You're a rotten liar; it *was* a big deal. But thank you. Thank you, son." For a second he seemed almost overcome with emotion, but he checked himself. At the door he said, "Come down to the kitchen. Your uncle and I are going to have a drink, kind of buy off the gods. Luck for a good May."

Downstairs he poured a little whiskey in a glass for me and added a lot of water. Instead of farming, Dad started talking about fishing, his other favorite subject. Perhaps he was worried that talk of farming would make me feel even worse about giving up my trip. Uncle Fritz fell in with it and soon they were recalling some of the fine times we'd had in years past fishing on summer weekends. "Damn it, Paul," Uncle Fritz shook his head, "we take farming too serious sometimes. As soon as we get this crop in, the three of us ought to take an afternoon and go fishing. I know some good spots around here. Makes the work a lot easier if you take off a little time now and then."

"Ya, you're right. We'll do that one of these days. Take Jim too. I need to spend more time with him. What do you think, Rick?"

"Sounds good to me." They went on talking and I just listened, sipping my drink slowly to make it last. Down deep I still felt a great disappointment about missing my trip, but mostly I felt happy. I'd been asked to make a sacrifice, a man's sacrifice, and I'd made it no matter how much it hurt. Being an adult felt both good and bad, but mostly good right then.

6

IT LOOKED LIKE rain the next morning and for a while I thought perhaps I'd get to go on my trip after all. I tried not to hope for it, since I knew the plowing couldn't wait much longer, but a part of me still rebelled and wished that the dark clouds would open and drop a torrent of mud-producing rain.

Midmorning I walked into the house leaving, as always, my muddy boots on the porch. I was pouring some coffee and talking with Judy when there was a crash and a series of thumps on the stairs. We ran and found Mom lying at the bottom of the stairs, her heavy legs sticking out from the shadow of the door into the room. I knelt down beside her and helped her sit up. She was badly shaken. "Where are you hurt, Mom?"

She flexed her arms and moved her head about experimentally. "As far as I can tell, just my rump."

Judy and I helped her stand. She's so heavy that even normally she'd have a little trouble getting up from such an awkward position. Judy kept asking her if she was hurt. Connie, Pam, and Tommy were there, too, by this time, all asking her the same. Mom held her hands up for quiet. "I'm all right, kids. Your clumsy mother just slipped on the stairs. Nothing to get riled up about." She laughed and everyone joined in.

"Mommy, you sounded like a bomb. Boom, Boom, Boom, Boom." Tommy giggled and got her around a fat thigh. "Boom, Boom." All the others started telling where they'd been and how the noise had frightened them. I just watched her as we started gathering up the load of towels she'd scattered in her fall. She really didn't seem to be hurt, so I went back to the kitchen, finished my coffee, and walked outside.

A few patches of blue were beginning to peek through the overcast. So much for my trip, I thought.

By lunchtime the sky was clear except for some puffy, innocent-looking clouds that drifted over in a warm breeze. It was the first day I'd really felt the promise of warm weather, and after I finished eating, I sat on the porch for a few minutes enjoying it. Judy and Connie were out in the pasture getting a horse-riding lesson from Uncle Fritz. Arrow had had a sore foreleg in the winter and Uncle Fritz had forbidden any riding until the ground was dry and there was less danger of the gelding slipping and reinjuring himself. But now with better weather and spring vacation coming to a close, Uncle Fritz had given in to the twins' pleading.

Jim and Pam came out of the house. Jim headed for the barn, his head down, hands stuck deep in his pockets. Pam sat down beside me. "Why aren't you two out with Uncle Fritz and the twins?" I asked.

"Oh, Uncle Fritz said that two kids were enough and Arrow might get nervous with more around. He said he'd give us a lesson later."

"I bet Jim didn't like that."

"No, he's sulking again." She rested her chin in her hand and sighed.

"I don't think Uncle Fritz will forget about you guys."

"No, I guess not. . . . I asked Jim if he wanted to throw a Frisbee around while we waited, but he said he was busy. It doesn't seem like he ever has time for me anymore. All he cares about is farming and that stupid calf."

"Don't worry, he'll get sick of the chores, sooner or later." The calf might be another matter, I thought. "Where's your shadow?"

"Tommy? Mom's giving him his medicine. He has to lie down for a while afterwards."

I tried out Bill's Count Dracula accent. "Zo it looks like ve are alone."

It didn't work. She just sighed again and said, "I guess. . . . I just don't see why the twins have to be first all the time. . . . Maybe it's because they're adopted."

"Oh, Pam, that's silly. You never used to talk this way. Since when did it make any difference to you that they were adopted?"

She shrugged. "I don't know."

"Well, I think you ought to stop thinking that way. . . . You know they were about your age when they lost their parents. I think you ought to be grateful that nothing like that has ever happened to you." I remembered guiltily my own ungrateful thoughts of the night before. "Let's just try to work together."

She looked at me with her big blue eyes. "Maybe I am being silly about the adoption thing, but I wish they'd stop hogging everything. I mean, Dad gave Arrow to all of us, not just Connie and Judy. I don't see why I can't be out there too."

"Well, maybe Uncle Fritz is right. Arrow hasn't been ridden in a long time and he needs a chance to get used to his new owners. Why don't you just trust Uncle Fritz. I'm sure he won't forget." I changed the subject. "Have you heard from Linda?"

"I got a letter Wednesday. She said she'd have to wait a while before she can ask her parents if she can come for a visit. She said they're still mad at her for what she did to the cat."

"What did she do to the cat?" I shuddered to think.

Pam giggled. "She dyed it orange."

"My God! Why?"

"She said it seemed like a good idea at the time. She was

tired of being the only red-haired one in the family. She thought the cat looked pretty good."

"Pam," I said in mock seriousness, "I think maybe we ought to rethink this business about inviting Linda here. I'm not sure Mom and Dad can handle it. I mean, can you imagine what might happen? She might decide to start dying all the animals around here." I had Pam laughing now and I kept her going by describing a farm with every animal dyed a different set of colors. But it was time for me to get to work, so at last I stood. "Well, if I know Linda, she'll find a way to convince her folks. They'll probably be delighted to get rid of her a few days. Want to come down to the barn with me?"

"No, I think I'll sit here and look sad. That way Uncle Fritz will have to give me a chance."

"Not bad," I said. "Are you taking a course in sneakiness at school."

She giggled. "No, I thought this up by myself. . . . But I do have an encyclopedia report due next week." She made a face. "And we've got to get up and read it to the class. Could you help me with it?"

"What's it about?"

She looked over enviously at the twins. "I thought I'd do it on horses. The encyclopedia is about as close to horses as I get these days."

"Sure, I'll help. Remind me when you're ready." I started for the barn, then detoured to the pasture. I was sure Uncle Fritz wouldn't forget, but it wouldn't hurt to tell him the younger kids were a little blue about not getting to ride the horse yet. Judy was getting up on Arrow. She put her left leg in the stirrup and, as Uncle Fritz boosted, swung her right leg over. She just kept going, sliding off Arrow's right side and hitting the ground with a thump. God, it was one of the funniest things I'd ever seen. The rest of us started laughing like crazy. Arrow turned his head to look down at Judy with placid curiosity.

Blushing, Judy got up and dusted off the seat of her jeans. "You pushed too hard."

We tried to stifle our laughter. Judy started around Arrow's back end. "Oops. Hold on there, horsewoman," Uncle Fritz called. "There are about twenty reasons for not going around the output end. Mainly getting kicked in the fanny or gassed to death. Don't know which is worse. Come around the nose. That's it." Judy was still blushing. "Okay. One of the first rules of hay-burner riding is to always get back on after you get throwed."

"I didn't get 'throwed'! I slipped off."

"Same thing. Ready?"

"It sounds like a stupid rule to me," she muttered, but stuck her left foot into the stirrup again. Holding on to the pommel with all her might, she let Uncle Fritz boost her into the saddle. I winked at Connie, who grinned. After a little persuasion, Arrow moseyed off with Judy clinging to his back.

"Be a little time before she's ready for that there Kentucky Derby," Uncle Fritz commented.

Connie and I laughed. "Don't forget the little kids, Uncle Fritz," I said. "Pam's eyes are burning holes in you right this minute."

He grinned, glancing Pam's way. "I ain't forgotten 'em." He beckoned to Pam who jumped up and dashed our way.

"I'll send Jim out in a few minutes."

"Sounds good."

I left the master and his pupils and headed for the barn.

After supper I sat on the porch for a few minutes watching the last of the sunset. But it was a little too cold to sit for long, so I strolled out toward the machine shop, where I heard the voices of Dad and Uncle Fritz. They stood in the tumbledown building behind the shop looking at the ancient combine, pointing now to one part, now to another. I was fond of the old red machine. It looked a bit like some kind of prehistoric monster missed by the glacier and sitting lost in its dreams of a time long past. No one had run it in years and now boxes, shovels, a section of rusty stove pipe, and several old tires leaned against it or lay about its half-deflated wheels.

Uncle Fritz was shaking his head. "I tell you, Paul, it's not worth messing with. You'd spend more time trying to fix it up than you'd ever save in money."

"Well, we've got more time than money."

"Maybe we do, but almost everyone hires out their combining these days. It's a lot quicker and a lot cheaper in the long run."

Dad nodded and knocked out his pipe against the rusty side. "Ya, I know. Right now I just hate to spend money on something we can do ourselves."

"I know how you feel, but it's months before we have to use it anyway. There'll be money by then."

"I hope you're right, but at the rate we're spending it now, I wonder if there'll be enough to pay the bills. If we could get this beast running for just one season, we could buy a couple of cows with any extra money." He shrugged. "But if the doctors say Tommy needs another operation, then we may not have enough for combining or cows."

"Aren't we going to be able to sell some hay or something?" I asked.

Dad turned. "Oh, hi, son, I didn't see you there. Well, yes, there'll be some extra hay, oats, too, probably." He rubbed the stubble on his brown, windburned cheek. "But that depends on the weather. Everything depends on the weather."

There was a long pause while no one said anything, then Uncle Fritz shrugged his shoulders. "Well, you're the boss, Paul. We'll fix up the old combine if you think we should. I've got a few hundred left in the bank, you're always welcome to that."

"Thanks, but I don't want to spend every penny you've got. We'll just see how it goes. If everything holds together and the weather stays good, we might be able to borrow against the crop and sell this beast for scrap."

"Either that or hold on to it as an antique. Ain't no one going to buy it to use, that's for sure."

"We'll see." Dad looked at the sky and then his watch. "Well, I'm going to bed. We start plowing bright and early."

Uncle Fritz nodded. "I guess I'll go into town for a beer. Be a while before we get much time off again. You want to come, Rick?"

"Sure, if you're not going to stay too long."

"Nope, just a beer or two."

We got in the pickup and drove down the road to the highway. A couple of farmers were already in the fields, the lights of their tractors cutting across the long furrows in the dark. I shrugged deeper in my jacket and reached over to flip on the heater. It was getting cool again.

"Engine sounds good," Uncle Fritz commented, cocking his head.

"Yes, it does." I'd tuned it on Sunday, supposedly the day of rest, but I'd wanted something to do outside the noisy house. I was proud of the quiet hum and new power of the engine. My mind drifted back to the combine. "That combine is really in bad shape, huh?"

"I think so. You'd have better luck baking a chocolate cake with cowshit."

"There you go again."

"Just habit." He grinned. "Here we are."

I pulled over next to a dingy bar with a poorly lit sign that read "Irma's." Country music crept out the door mixed with the noise of laughter and loud talk. Inside, it was dim and smokey. Uncle Fritz waved to the heavyset, gray-haired woman behind the worn bar. "Hiya, Irma."

"Hi, Fritz. Where you been keepin' yourself?"

"Down on the farm. Where else?" She laughed and Uncle Fritz went down the bar greeting several of the men with handshakes or slaps on the shoulder. He introduced me to each of them and I shook their calloused hands and said, "How do you do?" Some of them were short and stocky, others tall and raw-boned, and still others small and slender like Dad and Uncle Fritz. They were all tanned even in the springtime, more from the burn of winter winds than the sun. Almost all were middle-aged and some well past it. There didn't seem to be a lot of young farmers.

98

We played pool with two of Uncle Fritz's friends. I played okay, although I hadn't shot any since early in the winter. Uncle Fritz was better, and between us we beat them two out of three games.

On the way home he was in a good mood and talked on about the plowing and planting. I asked a few questions to be polite, but mostly I let my mind wander. All the smoke in the bar had given me a headache and I went right up to my room when we got home. In bed, I figured the time left—over six weeks gone, four months left. Not too bad. The counting had become a nightly ritual for me.

I still had a little bit of a headache when I came down in the morning. I hadn't slept well and for once I was up early. Dad was in the bathroom, so I passed my parents' bedroom to get some coffee in the kitchen. Mom was standing in the bedroom with her back to me. She'd just taken off her nightie and I was surprised and embarrassed by her nakedness, but also shocked to see the huge purple bruises on her back and buttocks. The fall on the stairs had been worse than I'd thought. I turned around as quietly as I could, retraced my steps, and made some noise like I'd just come down the stairs and gone into the living room for something. Her door snapped shut quickly and I went into the kitchen to make coffee.

After milking we started plowing. I rode with Uncle Fritz the first hour until I thought I could handle it alone. Still, even with three tractors going, the plowed patch seemed to grow painfully slowly. The farm is 240 acres: 100 for hay, 10 for pasture, 50 for oats, 80 for corn. The 130 acres for oats and corn had to be plowed, disked, and dragged before the soil was ready to plant. In addition, Dad had rented 40 more acres down the road where he hoped to raise a cash crop of corn.

We plowed all day, stopping only to eat a quick sandwich. After milking and supper we went back at it. About 9:00 Dad hit a large rock and snapped two shear bolts on his plow. While he and Uncle Fritz went in to replace them, I stayed out alone in the wide fields. Surprisingly, I was enjoying it. It was crystal clear and even without the moon the night was bright. You never see the stars in the city like you do out here, and I was thrilled by the vastness of the sparkling sky above me. I was reminded of the phrase "the vault of heaven"—it's like that in the country with the stars painted on the gigantic arch of the sky, like tiny lights hanging in an immense, dark cathedral where the ceiling disappears high in the shadows. It was midnight before I went in to the dark farmhouse standing in the circle of the yard light against a horizon filled with stars and the distant lights of other farms.

The next three days were hard on all of us, but the weather was holding and we pushed as long into each night as we could. My initial enjoyment of the plowing faded into fatigue, but we'd fallen into a rhythm with the work and I shut off my thoughts most of the time I rode on the tractor.

The fifth morning dawned with huge, puffy clouds rolling over the horizon, tumbling gigantic shadows across the fields. Dad was anxious during the morning milking. Heavy rains could slow us and even spoil much of the work already done.

We were about half finished with the milking when Jim started to leave. "Where do you think you're going?" Dad snapped.

Jim turned hurt eyes on him. "To get ready for school, Dad."

For some reason Dad had forgotten. "Oh, yes. I'm sorry, son. I wasn't thinking." Jim started to leave again, but Dad said, "Come here a second, son." Jim came close and stood uncertainly. "Jim, you're such a big help around here, I just forget sometimes that you have other things to do." He put a hand on Jim's shoulder. "I'm very proud of the way you pitch in. You're growing into a man." He turned him and gave him a little swat on the butt. "Now get to school and study hard. Since bigshot over here is going to college in the fall, I expect you to graduate about five years early."

Jim laughed. "Okay. We'll see you guys later." He ran out.

Dad went back to work. I said, "That was nice of you, Dad. I think that made him feel real good."

"Ya. Cripes, I don't know what was wrong with me, forgetting he had to get ready for school."

"It's called hardening of the arteries, Paul," Uncle Fritz called. "It happens to all of us. By the way, which end of these beasts do you milk? I've kinda forgotten."

We laughed. Dad shook his head. "I don't know what we'd do without you, Fritz."

"Say, Dad," I said, "what are you going to do about that calf? Jim's going to take it awfully hard if you sell it for veal."

"Ya, I know. I've been thinking a lot about that. We already have a half-grown steer for beef, so we can't really afford keeping the calf. In another week or so we'll just have to ship him out. Jim and the other kids will simply have to accept it."

"I guess so." I didn't like the idea much either.

"Any day now we should have another one coming due," Uncle Fritz said. "If we're lucky and get a female, maybe Jim won't feel so bad."

"That's a thought," Dad said. "Make me feel better too. We need all the milkers we can get."

We came out of the barn early. Dad glanced at the sky. "Damn, I hope we don't get rain."

The kids were coming out of the house to to go the end of the drive to wait for the bus. At the door Mom was giving Pam final instructions on Tommy's medication. This would be a big day for Tommy. Pam's fourth-grade class was having its annual little brothers' and sisters' day and Pam was taking Tommy. "Now you sure you've got it straight?" Mom said.

"Yes, Mom. You've already told me three times."

"All right then. Now you just call if you have any questions. You've got the kitchen timer?"

"Yes, Mom. Don't worry. Come on, Tommy." They ran off to catch up with the older kids.

Mom stood worriedly at the door watching them. "Don't forget to set the timer," she called.

"We won't," Pam yelled. Mom shook her head slightly and went in.

"I don't envy that teacher any," Dad said. "Boy, is this going to be one hell of a day for her with all those little kids in addition to her usual brood."

"I think Ellie's gonna be sufferin' just as much," Uncle Fritz said. "She looked like she'd just sent them all off to that army the Frenchies got."

"The French Foreign Legion," I said.

"Ya," Dad said. "I expect Ellie's going to worry all day about her littlest. She'd better get used to it, though. When he goes off to that special school in Mason next year, he'll pretty much have to fend for himself."

We took off our boots on the front porch and went into the kitchen. Dad put his arms around Mom, who was standing at the stove cooking our breakfasts. "Well, mother, how does it feel to be without any kids at home? Want to sneak off for a bit?" He gave her a squeeze.

"Stop that! You'll make me spill something." She giggled. "And what do you mean, 'no kids'? I've still got you three." Dad gave her another squeeze and blew in her ear. "Stop that." She raised a spatula threateningly. He let go of her, laughing. "I don't know what I'm going to do with you," she grumbled, trying to sound genuinely exasperated. "Let a man your age grow a mustache and suddenly he thinks he's the world's greatest romancer."

"Oh ho." Uncle Fritz laughed. "You still got a little fire in the old furnace, huh, Paul?"

"Ain't no snow on my roof, yet." Dad sat down at the table.

Mom was blushing. "Talk, talk. That's what he's good at."

"Hey, you guys!" I said. "There are still some tender young ears around here!" There was general laughter. Wow, I thought, this country living produces changes in everyone.

All through breakfast Uncle Fritz, who had seemed particularly tired the night before, was smiling and animated. But Dad was in a hurry to get about the work and didn't give him a chance to tell any long stories this morning. We skipped a last cup of coffee and went back out into the cool morning.

While Dad and I drove our tractors into the field that adjoins the farm, Uncle Fritz drove the other a quarter mile down the road to start disking the forty Dad was renting from old man Renkins, a retired feed dealer. I hoped to join Uncle Fritz after lunch to finish it.

It was pleasant working despite the coolness of the shade whenever a cloud crossed the sun. I love spring when it's too cool yet for the bugs to be out, yet warm enough to take off the heavy winter clothes and feel the lightness of free movement. I was in a good mood when I swung in toward the farmhouse around 10:30. Dad was in the yard working on his tractor motor. He waved me over and I shut off my tractor and walked through the muddy furrows to him. "Trouble?" I asked.

"Not really. Just want to adjust the carburetor. Lend me a hand and we'll sneak in for a cup of coffee in a minute."

I sat on the tractor, starting it when he wanted to listen to the motor, turning it off when he had to reach in too near to the spinning fan. It took maybe ten minutes and Dad had just stood back with a grunt of satisfaction when a black Buick swerved into our drive. I recognized the heavy driver with the red face and thick cigar as Mr. Bergstrom, the farm implement dealer from town. "Hey, Paul," he yelled through the open window, "is that your tractor down the road?"

"What tractor?"

"An International 806. It's stuck up against a telephone pole with its tires spinning."

Dad dropped the tools and sprinted to the car. "Take me there!" I barely had time to catch up and jump in the back before Mr. Bergstrom had the tires spitting gravel. We careened out the drive and down the short length of road. I caught sight of the red tractor almost immediately. It tilted at a crazy angle with its rear wheels slowly digging into the brown earth of the ditch and its blunt nose pushing steadily at the tall, unbending telephone pole. The car came to a hard sliding stop beside the pole and Dad was out running along the weaving path left by the disk. I paused just long enough to reach up and shut off the tractor engine, then I was off after him, overtaking the panting Mr. Bergstrom, who was jogging over the furrows in his slippery city shoes. Dad can run a lot faster than I thought he could, and he was still twenty yards ahead when he dropped to his knees. In a few more steps I saw Uncle Fritz lying half hidden in the furrow. Then I was there. Dad was shaking Uncle Fritz and sobbing out his name. I could see Uncle Fritz wasn't breathing and I grabbed his chin and hair, jerked his mouth open, and started giving him resuscitation. I'd seen a film on it in health class, but I felt horribly ignorant as I fought to remember everything. I hardly had enough wind at first because of the running. His mouth was cold and slimy against mine, no feeling of warmth or life.

In a few minutes I knew it was no good. He didn't respond, my breath simply went in and bubbled out. Dad tried pressing on Uncle Fritz's chest above the heart, but he didn't know how and I had to try to tell him the little I knew about cardiopulmonary resuscitation between breaths. Mr. Bergstrom had come limping up and now squatted a little way off trying to get his breath back, the cold butt of the cigar still clamped in his teeth.

Finally, Dad leaned back on his haunches, tears streaming down his cheeks. "It's no good; there's no heartbeat, no pulse, no nothing." He bent forward, hiding his face in his muddy hands.

Mr. Bergstrom said, half to himself, "He was probably here a couple of hours. He'd barely started disking."

I tried to help Dad carry Uncle Fritz, but he shook me away violently and stumbled across the brown field toward the road with the small body cradled in his arms. I started to run to catch up, but Mr. Bergstrom put a meaty hand on my shoulder. "I think this is something he's got to do himself. Better leave him alone, Rick."

We followed behind, trudging across the wide field under a sky that was turning a deep gray as the clouds collided and mixed. Rain pattered and ran in tiny streams in the mud as we reached the road and looked down toward the farm where Dad walked still carrying Uncle Fritz.

That night I walked out into the field and looked up at the stars. The clouds had broken at dusk leaving a beautiful, fiery sunset that flooded the fields with gold and turned the western wall of our house a rusty pink. I tried to think back on the day, tried to order all the events that had happened since Dad had laid Uncle Fritz's body gently on the porch and gone in to tell Mom.

She'd come slowly to the door, Dad behind her protesting gently, "Ellie, please. There's nothing you can do. . . ."

She looked down at Uncle Fritz and gave a long shuddering sigh. For a long moment I thought she'd lose control, but then she said very quietly, "He's got to be covered up." She went into the house. In a minute she was back with a quilt. Mr Bergstrom and I covered Uncle Fritz's body.

Dad put an arm around Mom. "John," he said to Mr. Bergstrom, "would you make the calls, please?" Mr. Bergstrom nodded. Together Mom and Dad went inside. We heard the door to their bedroom close softly.

I stood alone on the porch while Mr. Bergstrom used the kitchen phone. The rain pattered on the roof. Near Uncle Fritz's right foot a drip fell every few seconds. I watched numbly as the drops soaked the corner of the blue-checked quilt. Finally, I walked slowly over, lifted Uncle Fritz's feet, and folded the quilt underneath. I stayed there squatting by his feet. Mr. Bergstrom came back through the door and stood leaning against the porch railing. He took the cigar butt from his mouth and looked at it distastefully, then threw it out into the drive. It landed in a mud puddle and floated on the surface, surrounded by the gentle splashes of the raindrops. "The ambulance will be here in a few minutes. They'll send a sheriff's deputy too." He stood gazing at the porch ceiling.

I tried to speak for the first time since we'd come back from the fields. Control, I thought. You must be in control now. My voice was okay, a little hoarse, but okay. "What will happen then?"

Mr. Bergstrom looked at me, his heavy face worried. We hardly knew each other. I'd been surprised he'd even known my name. Somehow it didn't seem fair that he was having to take so much responsibility. "I'm not really sure. The ambulance crew won't be able to do anything . . . so I guess they'll call the coroner. He'll take charge then."

I nodded. Down the road I saw a sheriff's car coming our way, its flashing lights somber in the rain. There was no emergency, only the chores of death to do. I was grateful that he didn't have his siren wailing.

The deputy was a tall man in his thirties—handsome, grim-faced, official. He nodded to us as he came up the steps, knelt down, and uncovered Uncle Fritz's torso. He felt for a pulse, then pinched one of Uncle Fritz's fingers. The skin stayed white. He shook his head. "He's been dead for a long time." He covered the body and stood. "I don't see any sense in having the ambulance come out." He looked at Mr. Bergstrom. "They'll come if you want them to, but it'll just be a waste of money."

"Rick is the relative. I'm only a friend."

The deputy looked at me. "They might as well stay at home," I said.

The deputy nodded and went back to his car. He talked on the radio for a couple of minutes, then came back to us, carrying a clipboard. We told him what had happened. He was polite, efficient, detached. When he'd filled out the last question, he asked, "Have you called a funeral director yet?" We shook our heads. "I'd recommend you do that now." He went back to his car and sat working on his report.

"Do you know a funeral director you'd like me to call?" Mr. Bergstrom asked.

"No, I don't think Mom or Dad knows one either."

"Jim King from Mason buried my mother a couple of years ago. He's an honest man."

"I guess he'll be okay."

Mr. Bergstrom went in to call and I stood alone again on the porch with Uncle Fritz. A few minutes later a tan Ford station wagon drove into the yard. A small, cheerful-looking man got out carrying a black doctor's bag. The deputy met him and they talked briefly before coming over. "I'm Dr. Larson, deputy county coroner." I introduced myself as we shook hands.

His examination of the body was quick, thorough, professional. Dad and Mr. Bergstrom came out on the porch and we all watched the coroner work. Dad looked a hundred years old. He wiped his eyes every few seconds with a handkerchief. The coroner asked him a few questions about Uncle Fritz's medical history and Dad got the answers out okay.

Finally, the coroner covered the body again and stood. "Mr. Gebhardt apparently suffered a massive coronary arrest." He looked at each of us in turn and there was sympathy in his small blue eyes. "It was very quick, a sudden massive shock to the system with death following almost immediately. He suffered very little pain."

Dad nodded. "Thank you, doctor. Rick, perhaps these gentlemen would like a little coffee. I'm going back to be with your mother. Call me when the funeral director comes."

Both the doctor and Mr. Bergstrom protested that I shouldn't bother, but I wanted something to do. While I made the coffee, I tried not to think too much. Massive coronary, the doctor had said. Heart attack, nothing fancy. A common death for a common man.

When I went back outside, the deputy's car was gone and a long, black hearse stood in its place. A few neighbors were standing in the drizzle talking to Mr. Bergstrom. The funeral director and his assistant were conferring with the coroner beside the hearse. I felt awkward holding the pot and the cups with no one near to drink any coffee, so I set them down in a corner and went to call Dad.

I wasn't gone three minutes, but when I came back to the porch, they were already loading Uncle Fritz into the hearse. He lay strapped to a wheeled cot and covered by a white sheet. The quilt Mom had brought out lay neatly folded on the floor of the porch. My God, the efficiency of it all! The deputy, the coroner, the funeral director—all of them were so damned efficient! Uncle Fritz had been reduced to a thing to be examined, reported on, moved. . . . Everything that had happened to us, to him, was just another commonplace event. Soon there would be another police report on file, another death certificate signed, another funeral scheduled, another grave being dug in the cemetery. . . . I started to shake. No, damn it! You've got to hold on, I told myself. Don't lose it now. There's too much to do. Think about that other stuff later.

The funeral director came up the steps. He was tall and craggy, eyes deep and gently sorrowful. He looked ageless and eternally reassuring. Something inside me snarled. I did not like this man. He smiled gently and extended a hand. "Rick? I'm Jim King."

I took his hand unwillingly. His handshake, like everything else about him, was carefully calculated. "My parents are inside."

I took him in to the living room where Mom and Dad sat teary, but possessed, then went back to the porch. The neighbors drifted off. A couple of them came up and expressed condolences. But although they'd known Uncle Fritz, they hardly knew me and there wasn't much to say. Finally, Mr. Bergstrom walked over. He shook my hand. "Tell your mother and father how sorry I am. I knew Fritz for twenty years. He was a good friend."

"Thanks for all your help, Mr. Bergstrom." I walked with him to the car. I couldn't think of anything more to say.

He opened the door and paused for a moment. "Call me if

108

there's anything I can do. If you need anything, just call." I thanked him again and he got in, started the car, and drove out of the yard slowly and disappeared down the road toward town. And I was alone.

I went to the shed where the rusting combine sat heavy and broken and tried to cry a little, but the tears just stood in my eyes and wouldn't fall. Signa came and looked in, wagged her tail, and trotted off on the trail of a rabbit. From the barn the sound of the cows stamping and shaking their heads in the stanchions came drifting in through the door to where I sat in the shadow of the combine—a shadow that seemed to me like the outline of a dozing mastodon dreaming of a world sheathed in ice.

After the funeral director left with his assistant and Uncle Fritz's body, I went into the house. Mom was in the bathroom combing her hair and washing her face. Dad stood with his back to me, looking out the living room window. He turned. "The school bus will be here soon." I nodded. "We have to figure out how to tell them."

"Dad, I'm not sure"—my voice choked—"I'm not sure I can handle that." I tried to stifle a sob. He came over and put his arms around me. "I mean there's milking and chores and I just don't know if I can do them if . . ."

"I understand," he said, his own voice nearly cracking. "Leave the kids to us. Go lie down or take a walk. We'll tell them."

Mom came out of the bathroom. "I think you men better have something to eat," she said quietly. "It's been a long time since breakfast."

We ate what we could, then I went out to the barn to feed the stock. When the school bus came, it could have been any other day. The kids got off the bus laughing and hurried to the house to change. I was afraid that Jim would poke his head in to see what was going on in the barn, but he went into the house with the others. In a way I knew I should go in too, but I couldn't handle it. I just couldn't.

I started the milking by myself. Judy came out when I was about half through. She was crying, but she didn't say anything, just started carrying the buckets to the bulk tank. After a while she got out a few words, "Dad says he's sorry, but he's got to be inside with the kids tonight."

"How are they taking it?" I didn't look at her directly, afraid I'd start crying and not be able to go on with the work.

"Okay." She choked back a sob and nodded fiercely. "Ya, okay. Just fine."

I didn't say anything for a while. Connie came in and I gave her something to do. I wasn't feeling brave or grown-up or anything except hurt and confused, but when we were finishing I tried anyway. "I guess we've got to help out more for a while. Mom and Dad need it and we're the oldest." They looked at me with red eyes and nodded. Neither one of them is very good-looking, but at that moment they struck me as beautiful and strong and alive. "Let's go help with supper," I said.

Now as I stood looking up at the stars, I thought of the quiet supper and of the silent, grief-swollen faces. I hadn't thought of Uncle Fritz then. My thoughts had hardly been of him all day and I bit my lip now, ashamed of the self-pity that had seemed to take more space in my mind than any true grief for him. I stared across the field, the tears in my eyes making the stars and the far-off yard lights glisten and shimmer. My thoughts stumbled about looking for something to grab on to, something to hold tight to until the turmoil of my emotions settled. My tractor stood where I'd left it that morning, a dark hulk carved against the millions of stars. I went to it, climbed aboard, and twisted the key. The engine drummed to life. I flipped on the headlights, dropped it in gear, and together we bumped off across the rough field, the disk dragging behind, breaking down the chunks of soil for the spring planting.

I disked until the first rays cut across the sky and then went in to milk the cows, who knew nothing of death or mourning or time off for tears.

We buried Uncle Fritz three days later in a small Lutheran

cemetery not far from the farm. I'd stayed home with the kids
the night before when he was laid out in the funeral home, so
it was a surprise to me when I saw the church almost full for
the funeral.

Mr. Bergstrom and his wife were there near the front with
Irma and a lot of the men I'd seen that night at her tavern.
Irma was dressed beautifully and dabbed at her eyes with a tiny
square of white lace. The pallbearers were all old friends of
Uncle Fritz's, several of them lifelong hired hands like himself
who looked uncomfortable in the suits they'd found deep in
closets or trunks and had asked the farm wife to press. A faint
odor of mothballs drifted from the rarely used clothing to me
as they rolled the casket down the aisle.

My initial reaction to the funeral director had been unfair.
He organized everything skillfully and quietly. What I'd taken
for hypocrisy and calculation now seemed professionalism.
When the casket was properly placed, the wreaths arranged,
and the pallbearers seated, he slipped to the back of the
church. He stood with his hands behind him in an attitude of
kind but detached respect: a picture of stability, grace, as-
surance.

The minister was an aging little man, a retired army chap-
lain now finishing his career in a quiet farming community. I
was distinctly thankful that he didn't run on, but read a simple
service, pausing only long enough to talk briefly of Uncle
Fritz's love of the earth and his family and how he'd died as he
would have wanted to, preparing the soil for another year and
another crop. It was well said, and I let my own dislike of
churches drop for a moment and looked over to where Mom
and the girls were sitting, heads bowed, soaking in the strength
and comfort of his words. Dad sat at the other end, his head
up, his eyes blinking rapidly now and then. He had his arm
around Jim, who kept turning to look up at him. Tommy,
standing between my knees, peered about through his heavy
glasses with the grimacing squint he always has when he's
trying to figure out a new and confusing event. Once he piped

up, "Where's Uncle Fritz?" But I hushed him and he shuffled and twisted for most of the rest of the service, finally announcing in a loud whisper, "I've got to pee-pee." My God, I thought, the world does go on. I looked over to see if the twins were going to be any help. They weren't, so I got up as quietly as I could and led him out.

The driver of the hearse was leaning against the fender by the open rear door smoking a cigarette. I asked him where the bathroom was, but he didn't know, so I led Tommy around the corner and let him urinate in a clump of bushes. From the noise inside I could tell the service was nearly over, so we waited on the sidewalk in the late April sunlight. The crocuses had fought through the hard soil and shone in little bright clumps along the side of the church. I watched them flicker in the breeze, stopping my thoughts as much as I could.

The interment was short and simple, but the lunch back in the church basement seemed to go on forever. I took the first opportunity to suggest to Mom that I take the younger kids home and she agreed.

I was already back in the fields finishing the disking when the rest of them got home.

7

NOBODY TALKED MUCH around the house for the first couple of weeks after the funeral, but children forget quickly, and Mom, Dad, and I were dragged along into their ever-important now. I still had a twinge every time I saw the third tractor standing lonely by the machine shop, and often at night I'd catch myself looking to see if his window shone with the light of the bare bulb inside. I'd spent many evenings with him and the dog in his close little room, listening to his endless collection of stories on farming, hunting, fishing, and the past. How I missed those times now.

To forget, and also because we had to, Dad and I worked even longer hours in the fields, finishing the disking and dragging, and getting in the corn and oats. Mom and the twins came out to help with the evening milking now, and sometimes we left it all to them, bumping across the fields on the tractors as the light grew dim and the barn lights came on. Mom even came out once or twice to help with the planting, but driving the tractor bothered her back and Dad sent her in to mind the kids and finish the house.

She painted the kitchen on a morning late in May and the

smell was still strong at supper time. Since Dad and Mom had gone into town for a conference with Jim's teachers, the twins were in charge of fixing the evening meal. To escape the paint fumes, they proposed a picnic before milking. It seemed a particularly good idea since it might cheer up Jim, who had spent the hours since school moping in his room. I helped the twins get the charcoal started then climbed the stairs to check on Jim.

The weeks since our move to the farm had been good ones for Jim. He loved the work and took particular pleasure in caring for the calves. By now all the cows had given birth and both Jim and I felt like old hands at midwiving. The last three calves had all been females, much to Dad's delight, but the little male remained Jim's favorite. He'd named the calf Onions, for some unknown reason, and I was concerned by how attached to it he'd become. Dad had wanted to ship the calf to the meat processor when it was only a couple of weeks old, but Mom had convinced him to put it off.

"Let's wait until Jim's out of school for the summer, Paul. He's having problems concentrating on his schoolwork and I don't want him sitting in class brooding about Onions."

"The longer we keep that calf, the harder it's going to be for him to give it up."

"I know, I know." Mom sighed. "But a tantrum will cause less damage in the summer. He looks forward so much to seeing Onions and the other calves when he gets home from school. I just don't want to change that right now."

Dad shrugged. "Ya, maybe you're right."

That conversation had taken place a couple of weeks before and I'd agreed with Mom. Jim had never been much of a student, and since we'd moved from the city, he'd paid even less attention to school. Around home he purposely avoided the subject. When Mom or Dad asked how he was doing, he'd mutter, "Okay" and disappear as quickly as possible. Mom and Dad tried to keep him at his homework, but Jim had a fertile mind for excuses. Now, it had apparently caught up with him. I knocked on his door.

"Go away."

"Come on, Jim, let me in. I just want to talk."

There was a pause, then I heard him get up from the bed and come to the door. The lock clicked and I waited for him to open the door, but instead he went back to the bed. I opened the door slowly. He was lying with his face turned to the wall. "What do you want?" He tried to make it a growl, but it came out more like a whine.

"Nothing much," I said heartily. "I just wanted to tell you that we're cooking hamburgers outside and ask if you wanted one."

"I'm not hungry."

"But you love charcoal-broiled hamburgers. . . . You're not going to feel better by not eating." There was a long pause. He didn't move or speak. I sat down on his chair. "Maybe after milking we can run into town and get some ice cream."

"When Mom and Dad get home they aren't going to let me go anywhere ever."

"Oh, it can't be that bad."

"It's worse." He started to cry.

"Come on, so what if you're not the greatest student in the world? You can get by."

"Nobody else in the family has any trouble."

"Well, we haven't been all that great." I tried to think of something more comforting to say. "Besides, you're a good farmer . . . better than I am. . . . I mean, I'm afraid of the cows, you're not."

That seemed to calm him a little. Finally he said, "Some of the guys in my class already drive tractors."

"You will soon. We've only been here a couple of months—you've got to be patient about some things. . . . Now, go wash your face and come get some supper. Okay?"

There was a muffled "Okay," and I got up. At the door I paused. "Really, Jim, it'll be all right. You'll see."

He came down a few minutes later. Everyone tried to be cheery, but he was still gloomy. He didn't eat much and spent most of his time looking down the road. When the family car came into view topping the little hill a couple of hundred yards north of the driveway, he jumped up. "I've had enough, I'm going for a walk."

Dad parked the car and helped Mom get some groceries out of the back seat. He came over smiling cheerfully—and a little falsely, I thought. "Well, well, first picnic of the year, huh? Looks good." He paused and looked around. "Where's Jimmy?"

"He went for a walk over that way." I pointed. "He's a little upset."

"Is it really bad, Dad?" Connie asked.

"No. No. Nothing to worry about. Why don't you girls grill me a hamburger? I'm going to help your mother with these groceries." He walked toward the back door.

"It may not be bad, but I don't think it's very good," Judy said solemnly.

"I wonder what Jim's teachers told them." Connie's voice betrayed her eagerness to be in on the secret.

I shrugged, finished my hamburger, and headed for the house.

Dad was standing on a chair putting cans in the cupboard as Mom handed them to him. "Dad, Jim was more than a little upset this afternoon. He was crying before supper and when he saw you coming, he jumped up and left."

"Ya, I figured as much." He put a couple of cans on the top shelf. "Is that it?" he asked Mom.

"That's all, the rest goes in the refrigerator."

Dad stepped down and slid the chair back to the table. "How hard was he crying?"

"Not too bad. It wasn't one of his tantrums. How much trouble is he really in, Dad?"

"Well, he doesn't seem to be in any disciplinary trouble, so that's good, but he isn't doing very well in his class work. His teachers say he doesn't concentrate in class and his assignments are slapdash, if he turns them in at all."

"Is he going to fail?"

"Looks like it, unless he goes to summer school." I winced. Jim wouldn't like that. Just about all he talked about was the fun he was going to have during summer vacation. "Anyway," said Dad, "we have to break the news to him gently."

The back door opened and we heard the kids coming in. Mom said quickly, "Don't say anything to the kids until we talk to Jimmy."

I nodded. The twins came in with hamburgers, beans, and salad for Mom and Dad. I slipped out and went looking for Jim.

He was sitting on a crate beside the big old-fashioned combine in the building behind the machine shop. Signa was sitting by him and he was digging through her fur searching for burrs. The dog looked up at me, her mouth open in a grin and her tail sweeping back and forth on the hard dirt floor. Signa is a good dog, gentle and affectionate, if not real smart. When you throw a ball or a stick for her, she only looks up at you and wags her tail. As hard as Uncle Fritz tried, he'd never been able to train her as a cow dog. Signa's interests rarely extend beyond rabbit hunting and dinnertime, but she's good with the kids.

"So there you two are," I said cheerfully. "Are you going to give her a bath next?" Jim didn't answer or look up. Signa wagged her tail a little faster. "Well, it's nearly time for milking. You coming?" Jim shrugged, still not looking up. "I talked with Mom and Dad; they don't look upset or mad."

This time he met my eyes. "Did they say anything about what happened at school?"

"Nothing specific," I lied. "I guess you'll have to ask." He nodded dully and went back to inspecting Signa's coat. "Well, I'm going to start milking," I said and left. At least he seemed okay so far.

I had things pretty well started when Dad and the twins came in. "Did you see Jim?" he asked.

"Ya, he's out back sitting next to the combine. He seemed all right."

"Well, we'll wait and see if he shows up." He began working on the other row of cows.

A few minutes later Jim slouched in and came over to help Judy and me. Since he usually works with Dad and Connie, it was obvious that he still wanted to avoid hearing about the conference.

It was warm enough to have the doors open and a spring breeze brought the smell of wet, greening fields to freshen the air of the long-closed barn. Everybody worked steadily, not wasting any time on talk.

We were almost done when Jim whispered, "Are we still going to town for ice cream?"

"I guess not. Mom brought some home."

"Oh." He looked even glummer. His talk with Mom and Dad couldn't be delayed much longer. I felt sorry for him and wished I could cheer him up, but I couldn't think of anything to say that wouldn't give him false hope.

After we got out of our barn clothes, Jim, the twins, and I joined Pam and Tommy in front of the TV. Because Tommy's eyes are so bad, he watches with an open-mouthed, wrinkle-nosed squint. He isn't allowed to watch very much, but there was a Peanuts special on and Mom had apparently given him permission. He asked Pam questions constantly, trying to make sense of what were often confusing images to his feeble eyes.

Peanuts specials aren't my preferred entertainment, but it would be over soon and then there might be something better on. Besides, I was curious about the upcoming conversation between my parents and Jim. Perhaps that was a little ghoulish, but I couldn't help it. Jim sat a little apart from the rest of us, almost like he was hiding in the shadows.

Mom came into the living room. "Jimmy, your father and I would like to talk with you," she said gently.

He groaned. "Can't it wait until the show's over? It'll only be a few more minutes."

She looked uncertain for a moment. "Well, all right, but as soon as it's over, come into the kitchen."

He sat for the rest of the program tensely gnawing on a thumbnail. At last all the Peanuts characters stood waving and shouting good-bye, then a commercial came on, and Jim got up. All of us, with the exception of Tommy, tried to look as if we were completely absorbed in the little drama about mouthwash. Jim stopped by me and whispered, "Will you come with me, please?"

I wished I had gone up to my room or into town. This didn't concern me and I didn't want to be involved. Besides, he didn't have anything to be frightened of—our parents aren't exactly ogres. Still, I got up without a word and followed him into the kitchen.

Mom and Dad must have guessed that he'd asked me to come, because they didn't say anything about it. I poured myself a cup of coffee and sat on the stool next to the oil heater.

Dad began. "Well, we had a nice talk with your teachers this afternoon. They all said good things about you: that you were cheerful and well-mannered and didn't disrupt the classes. Your gym teacher said you're doing very well." He paused. Jim was looking at his hands and his lower lip stuck out a bit.

"They all said you're a very nice boy, dear." Mom reached over and patted his shoulder.

Mom and Dad exchanged glances. Dad took the plunge. "But they also said you were a little behind most of your classmates. Now we're not saying it is entirely your fault. It's not easy changing schools in the middle of the year, and we know you've had your mind on other things besides school—I mean with getting to know the farm and your uncle's death and so on. . . . We're probably a lot to blame for expecting you to do so many chores. Anyway, your teachers say you're going to have to go to summer school or fall a year behind your class." Jim started crying, big tears running down his cheeks and falling from his chin. "Now, son"—Dad put a hand on his knee—"it's only for a few weeks and then you'll have the rest of the summer off." His voice was almost pleading.

Mom tried. "Jimmy, we'll help. Your dad, Rick, and I can help with your homework. You'll still have lots of time to play." He was sobbing now, head down on folded arms.

I tried. "Hey, I know lots of guys who went to summer school. They always said they had a great time. Nobody works very hard and they do lots of fun projects."

"Then why didn't you ever go?" he bellowed, glaring at me. His face was red and puffy and he continued to cry in short, gasping sobs.

"Jim, please," Dad began, but Jim brushed away his placating hand and jumped to his feet.

"I'm not going! You can't make me go! I hate school and I'm never going back!" He rushed from the room and we could hear him stumbling up the stairs. His door slammed.

Mom got up and went to the foot of the stairs. Dad sat with his head in his hands. "Damn," he said softly. "Oh, damn it to hell."

Jim's door burst open and he started yelling. His voice had climbed until it was nearly hysterical. The words were mixed up and hard to understand, but it was the same as all the times before: He hated everyone and everything. No one loved him. Everyone else got all the breaks. No one had ever loved him. And on and on. The door slammed again and we could hear the muffled thump, thump, thump as he beat and kicked the wall.

Dad got up and walked heavily to the stairs, but Mom raised a hand. "No, Paul, not yet. Let him go a few minutes. I know when and how."

Dad came back to the kitchen and slumped in his chair. "He's been so good," he said. "I thought maybe we'd finally made it through all that."

"I know, Dad. It's not your fault."

He shook his head, his lips compressed. "I should have figured out a better way, some way so he wouldn't feel persecuted."

I looked into the living room where the other kids stood wide-eyed and frightened. Jim's door crashed open. Now his voice was almost incoherent with violent obscenities coming through the clearest. Pam clapped her hands over her ears and Tommy started bawling loudly. Connie put an arm around him and knelt trying to comfort him.

"This is a bad one," I said softly. Dad nodded. He looked small, old, and defeated. "Dad, maybe I should take the kids into town for a Coke or something."

"That's a good idea, Rick. No one is going to get any sleep for a while."

We stayed over an hour in town. No one talked about it—we'd all seen it before. It was after 10:00 when we got home, Tommy sleeping in Connie's lap and the rest of us tired and sad.

Dad met us at the door and tried to be jolly. He told Pam and Tommy that they could have an "adventure" sleeping on the couches in the living room. Tommy said he'd be scared, so the twins said they'd get the air mattresses and sleep downstairs too.

The house was quiet and we all moved around stealthily, whispering and walking on tiptoe. Dad kissed the kids good night and went back to the kitchen. I used the bathroom and went quietly to bed.

Long after I had turned off my light I could hear the faint noise of Jim crying and the soft, comforting words of Mom as she rocked him back and forth in her lap.

When I came down the next morning, Mom was already

standing over the stove frying pancakes and bacon. Usually we just have coffee and toast before milking. The twins don't help in the morning since they have an understandable revulsion to going to school smelling of manure. Dad sends Jim in midway through milking to change and eat, and after the kids get on the bus and the last cow is milked, we come in for a leisurely breakfast with Mom. But this morning breakfast would be ready early, so I sat down to wait.

In a couple of minutes Mom put a plate piled high with pancakes in front of me. She looked very tired. "Did you get any sleep at all last night, Mom?"

"Oh, I dozed a little. He finally fell asleep about three."

"How is he?"

"I think he'll be better today. I'm going to let him sleep as long as he can. Then I'll try to talk to him. It's hard not to let him have his way when he gets like this, but we just can't."

"Mom, why haven't you ever sent him to a psychiatrist?"

"We haven't been able to afford it, dear. He did see the school psychologist a few times, and I talked to him about Jim."

"Ya, I know that, but I never thought he knew much."

Mom lifted her shoulders and let them drop. "Well, maybe he didn't. But Jim has made a lot of progress. You remember how he was when he first came to us." I nodded, thinking back to the time when Jim's tantrums happened three or four times a week. "Anyway," she continued, "we'll just have to get through it. He respects you more than almost anyone, so maybe you can talk to him too."

I nodded again. "I'll try." The perils of being an older brother. Well, I couldn't escape that.

Dad said something similar to me during milking, but the work in the barn and the fields kept me away from the house all day and I didn't see Jim until after supper. He was sitting looking out the living room window, his nearly untouched meal on a tray before him. I dropped into a chair. "Whew, long day." He didn't reply. "Say, Jim, how about going into town to see a movie?" He shook his head. "It's supposed to be a good movie. Burt Reynolds is in it."

"I don't got no money."

I started to correct his grammar, thought better of it, and said, "That's okay. I'll pay for your ticket."

He turned. "Did Mom and Dad tell you to do this?"

"No, as a matter of fact they didn't. I'd like the company and I thought it might make you feel better."

"Are the twins coming?" I shook my head. "Well, okay, I guess." His voice sounded like I'd just invited him to a hog butchering rather than a free movie.

The movie wasn't bad—not real heavy on plot, but lots of action. Jim seemed to enjoy it too. On the way home, he talked about it for a while before lapsing back into his brooding. I thought of trying to talk to him about school, but decided against it. Why spoil his evening? It was better for him to have a little fun now.

He surprised me by bringing it up himself when we were only a couple of miles from home. "You think I ought to go, don't you?"

"Well, I think it's better than falling a year behind your class."

"Maybe I just won't go to school at all."

"I don't think they let kids do that, Jim."

"Why not? It's my life."

I shrugged. "Well, all I know is that the law says you have to go."

"Maybe I'll go live in a cave."

I knew he wasn't serious, it was just the blues talking, but I didn't laugh. "I don't think they'll let you do that either."

"That figures, they never give us kids any breaks," he said bitterly.

"I know how you feel; I've felt that way a lot of times."

"You have?" He sounded genuinely surprised.

"Sure. You're not the only one who ever had to do something he didn't want to."

"Like what?"

It was my turn to be a little surprised. "Well, haven't you noticed that I don't exactly love farming?"

"Maybe a little, but if you hate it, why don't you leave? You're old enough."

I shrugged, unable to give a clear answer. "Well, I'll be going in the fall."

"Why not now?" he persisted.

"Because I want Mom and Dad to succeed at farming. Now that Uncle Fritz is gone, they can't make it without me."

"What's going to be different in the fall?"

"Hey, what are you doing? Training to be a lawyer or something?" I said irritably, and to my surprise he laughed. After a moment I started laughing too. My little brother had me in a corner. When we were done laughing, I continued soberly, "That's the deal we've got. Anyway, by the fall things should be better. You kids will be older and able to help more too. It's the getting started that's rough." I turned into the driveway.

Dad was sitting at the kitchen table when we came in. Apparently everyone else had already gone to bed. "How was the movie, boys?"

"Pretty good." I told him a little about it.

He listened attentively, then turned to Jim, who was rooting around in the refrigerator. "How did you like it, Jim?"

Jim answered with his mouth full. "It was okay."

Dad glanced at me. Did he want me to tell him Jim was better? I thought so and nodded. Jim came back to the table lugging a platter of ham, a bottle of milk, and a head of lettuce. I was hungry too, so I got the bread and mayonnaise and we sat down to make sandwiches.

After a couple of minutes, Dad ran his fingers through his hair and spoke again. "You know, I was just sitting here thinking about school. My dad never got beyond the sixth grade. He had to quit then and work to help support the family. Even when he was a very old man he was still bitter about that. Your Mom and I were lucky, we made it through high school, but your Uncle Fritz had to quit after eighth grade because of the Depression."

"Did you always like school?" Jim interrupted accusingly.

"No, I didn't always like school, but I'm glad I stuck with it. I'll bet that Rick feels the same." I nodded. "Jim, it's only eight weeks half days. . . . I really think you ought to go." He was trying too hard now, the anxiety starting to make his voice tight. "I mean, you can't just go off and live in a cave."

"We've already discussed that," I said.

Jim started giggling and Dad looked in confusion from one to the other of us. "Well, if you find a way to do it without starving or freezing to death, let me know, because there are times I'd like to join you." We all laughed at that. Then Dad said, "Tell you what, Jim, if you go and do well, some week-end we'll leave the cows to Rick and go to Milwaukee for a Brewer game. Just the two of us. What do you say?"

"I'd rather learn to drive a tractor."

"Well, I don't know about that. You're still pretty young and . . ."

"Some of the guys in my class do."

"Hmmm, well, I would have to talk to your mother about it." Jim looked crestfallen and Dad added hastily, "But I'll do my best." Jim brightened. "Either way, you'll go to summer school?"

Jim grimaced. "I guess if I have to."

"Good boy!" Dad clapped him on the shoulder and winked at me. We'd made it.

The regular school year ended the last week of May. After my missed trip earlier in the spring, I'd started thinking about going down to Milwaukee for graduation instead, but now that was impossible. Without Uncle Fritz, Dad couldn't possibly spare me, so I never brought it up. Mom and Dad must have known how I felt, because they took me out to eat at a fancy restaurant that Saturday. The three of us sat in our Sunday clothes, feeling a little odd, eating by candlelight and drinking a bottle of wine. After dessert, while we were drinking our coffee, Dad took an envelope from his coat pocket and handed it to me. "I wish it could be more, son, but . . ." He shrugged. "Anyway, we're very proud of you. You did real good."

Inside the envelope was a check for fifty dollars. "Thanks, Dad, Mom. That's very generous." They smiled.

Dad leaned back, puffing contentedly on his pipe. "Well, Ellie, we got one kid through high school, only five more to go. Think we'll make it?" She laughed. Dad went on more seriously. "I hope Jim can stick to it this summer . . ."

She cut him off. "I don't think we should talk about that tonight."

Dad nodded. "Ya, you're right. This is Rick's evening. . . . Well, son, are you looking forward to school in the fall?"

I said, "I sure am," trying not to put too much emphasis on my words. We talked about college then. I started telling them some of my ideas about architecture, getting more enthusiastic the more I talked. "It has to do with both efficiency and beauty. They go hand in hand. Beauty has its value, but efficient use of space is beautiful too. Now if we had a milking parlor instead of that cramped, old barn, we'd have a better environment for the animals and a more comfortable environment to work in. We could milk more cows just as fast and our profits would more than make up for the investment."

Dad laughed. "Listen to the boy. I'd have trouble talking the bank into lending me money to buy a decent spare tire for the pick-up, and he wants me to build a milking parlor?"

"I'm not saying that, Dad. I'm just trying to point out that the farm could be a lot more efficient if some principles of architecture were used."

"I know, son. I'm just having a little fun with you. Go ahead."

I went on to explain how I thought the buildings could be

remodeled and additions made, how new systems and equipment would increase our productivity, how we could change to producing grade A milk instead of the less profitable grade B, and so on. I had a ton of ideas. I'd been thinking more than I realized. Dad got into the spirit of it and pretty soon we'd spent several hundred thousand dollars on paper. Of course, it was all dreaming. We didn't have the money and weren't likely to be in any position to borrow it for a very long time. Still, it was fun to talk about it, anyway. About the fourth time the waitress came over to ask if we needed anything else, Mom said, "I think you men better continue this at home. They're going to charge you rent for office space pretty soon. Besides, the kids will be wondering what became of us."

We gathered up the sketches we'd made on the backs of envelopes from Dad's pocket and rose. Dad winked at the waitress. "Sorry. We got talking." He left her a generous tip.

Riding home, I thought, Well, perhaps it wasn't as exciting as being in Milwaukee with my friends, but it was pretty darned nice.

For Jim's sake, the other kids tried not to seem too happy about being out of school, but that was almost impossible. Pam really blew it the last day of school. That afternoon I was running the tiller through the garden under Mom's direction. Tommy had discovered earthworms and had started a collection in one corner of the garden. He was getting pretty dirty, but at least he was out of the way. When the school bus pulled up, Pam was off first and came running down to us. "Mom, Mom, I got all A's." She waved her report card.

"That's very good, dear," Mom said, looking past her to Jim. He stood a little way off, arms limp. Behind him the twins were looking uncomfortable.

Pam stopped. "What's the matter?" she asked, then looked at Jim. "Oh," she said in a small voice. There was a pause. No one could think of anything to say. Jim gave us all a hateful look and stomped into the house. Pam started to cry. "I didn't mean to hurt him!"

"It's okay," Mom said, hugging her. "You've got a reason to be proud. . . . Rick, better go see to your brother."

Jim was in his room, pulling on his barn clothes angrily. I leaned against the door. "How's it going?" I asked. No reply. "I don't think you should be mad at Pam, Jim. She's just . . ."

He spun. "Look, I don't give a shit how many A's she got! I don't give a shit what anybody got on their stupid report card! I'm going to summer school so Dad will let me drive a tractor! So just keep your nose out of my business, huh?"

"Hey, sorry I'm alive." I turned and went down the stairs, leaving him stuffing his shirt violently and haphazardly into his pants.

Judy and Connie were in the kitchen. Connie started to say something, but I hushed her and poured a half cup of cold coffee. In a minute we heard Jim coming down the stairs. He strode through the kitchen, not looking at any of us, out the door, and across the yard toward the barn. He was probably going to visit the calves.

The twins looked at me. I lifted my shoulders. "He's mad as hell, but I don't think he's going to blow."

Unexpectedly, Judy started crying. Connie said, "Please don't, Judy."

"Sometimes I just can't stand it! Everybody's got to be so careful. It's like walking on eggs! You can't even be happy about getting out of school!" She sobbed.

"Hey," I said, "it's no big deal. Relax."

"It's okay, Rick," Connie said. She had an arm around Judy. "She just had kind of a rough day. Forget them, Judy. You don't have to see those jerks all summer."

"What's going on?" I asked.

"Don't worry about it," Connie said. "Some guys were just giving her a hard time at school. Just teasing. Go back to work. We're okay."

I went outside. In the field to the north, I could see Mom and Pam walking hand in hand, Tommy tagging behind. I felt like beating my head against the wall. Hell, if it wasn't one kid unhappy and crying, it was another! Couldn't we make it through a single day without somebody being upset about something? And what about me? Hadn't I just missed my high school graduation, a day I'd been looking forward to for years? I shut my eyes and took a deep breath. Now you're getting into it, too, I thought. What are you going to do, Rick? Throw a tantrum? Cry? Yell at someone? . . . No, I'm going to try to act my age, settle things down, and get back to work.

I returned to the kitchen. Connie and Judy were still there. Judy was drying her eyes and snuffling and Connie was talking quietly. She stopped when I came in. "Hey, guys, I don't know what's going on, but I think everyone is pretty uptight. Let's try to get through with milking and supper early and then we'll all go to the drive-in movie in Mason. Give Mom and Dad the night off. What do you say?"

"That sounds good to me," Connie said. "What do you think, Judy?" Still snuffling, Judy nodded her head.

"Now I'll talk to Jim. One of you guys talk to Pam. And tonight none of us will talk about the school or the farm or anything that's going to upset anyone. We'll just go and have a good time. Okay?"

They nodded and I left the house. I'd probably spend a pretty good chunk of the check Dad had given me, but maybe it would keep peace in the family for a night. Going to the drive-in with my brothers and sisters. I laughed wryly. Hell, last summer I'd been to drive-ins a couple of dozen times— sometimes with a carload of guys and some beer and other times with a girl, but never with my brothers and sisters. It wouldn't exactly be the same—especially not the same as that night with Peggy. . . . I shook my head. Oh, well, in the fall . . .

Jim had a week off before summer school began and, as each day passed, he grew gloomier. I wished that Mom and Dad were sending one or all the girls to summer school too. None of them would have minded very much, but extra hands were needed at home and in these slim times even the small summer school fees would strain our budget.

Jim particularly resented Pam's freedom. Although she was expected to help around the house some, her main responsibility was looking after Tommy, and that was almost the same as having the whole day free to play. He half-heartedly tried to join them a few times, but the painful prospect of going back to school in a few days robbed play of much of its enjoyment. Helping Dad and me had lost some of its charm, too, it seemed. Dad worked particularly hard at cheering him up, but the only thing that seemed to retain its old joy for Jim was caring for Onions and the other calves.

A letter from Pam's friend Linda made matters worse. One of Pam and Tommy's small chores was watching for the mailman and bringing in the mail from the box by the road. The mail usually arrived just before noon and Dad sorted through it over his lunch. On the Friday before summer school started for Jim, Pam came running in just as everyone was sitting down at table. "I got a letter from Linda!" She tossed the rest of the mail on Dad's lap and ran to her chair. She tore open the letter and started reading avidly.

I glanced at Jim. Linda had never been one of his favorite people—she was a tease and Jim didn't handle teasing well. He was watching Pam read with anger and envy written all over him. "How did the Brewers do last night?" I asked Jim.

"How the hell would I know?" He snarled.

"Jim!" Mom glared at him.

"Mom, Linda says she can come up at the start of July!" Pam yelled. "Can I tell her she can come? Please, Mom."

"Yes, dear. Of course you can. Now calm down. Hand Tommy his soup."

Jim sat hunched over his meal.

Later that afternoon we worked in the barn. Jim was supposed to be helping me clean stalls, but he was paying more attention to Onions and the calf's mother. "Come on, Jim. Those two should be outside with the rest." He groaned and straightened from where he'd been leaning over the calf pen rail scratching Onions's nose. Signa padded up behind him and gave his leg a friendly sniff. Jim kicked at her and the dog jumped back with a startled yelp.

"Jim, for God's sake!" I was surprised! He'd never done anything cruel to any of the animals before.

He gave me a hurt look, then turned and hugged the dog. "I'm sorry, Signa. You and Onions are the only friends I've got." The dog licked his cheek, forgiving and forgetting in an instant. I watched them, then turned back to cleaning the stalls. Shit! What could I say to him? He felt like hell and there was nothing I could do to make him feel better.

"Dad, I've been thinking that maybe we should hold on to Onions."

For a few seconds I didn't think he'd heard me. He finished tightening a bolt, and started checking several others.

I started to repeat myself, but he snapped, "I heard you!" After a minute he stepped back and stared malevolently at the haybine, another piece of our decrepit equipment that needed replacement. He wiped sweat from his forehead with a dirty hand, then turned to me. "Onions is never going to give an ounce of milk!"

"I know that, Dad. But we could raise him for beef."

"We don't need beef for ourselves and by the time we fed him to marketable weight, he'd cost more than we could get for him. The beef market's shot to hell."

"Maybe that'll change."

"Not likely. The cycle is down. Prices are going to be bad for a long time." He got his pipe going and stared moodily out across the fields. The afternoon sun was a pale circle in the haze. This was our first really hot day and no wind stirred to make it less oppressive.

"Dad, Jim is going to . . ."

Dad spun. "Damn it! I know what you're getting at. I know Jim is going to take it hard, but we don't need Onions! We can't afford Onions!"

I looked down. "How are you going to tell Jim?"

Dad returned to his study of the horizon. "I'm not going to tell him until the calf is gone. When Jim is settled down in a couple of weeks, I'll call the meat processor and have them pick up the calf while Jim's in school."

"But, Dad!"

"Do you have a better way?" he said sharply. "Do you think it would be better if I let Jim pet and kiss that calf good-bye?" I didn't say anything. Dad sighed, took off his cap, and ran his fingers through his thinning hair. "Look, Rick," he said quietly, "I'm concerned too. But Onions is an animal and this is a business. Maybe I should have shipped that calf out before Jim got so attached to it, but it's too late to worry about that. Soon Onions will have to go. I don't like it either, but that's the way it has to be. . . . When Jim gets home that day, I'll explain it to him. I expect he'll be upset, but he's got a good understanding of farming and he'll get over it."

"Ya, I guess." I was still far from convinced.

I finished washing the last of the pails and left the milk-house. Another weekend had passed and a new week started. Jim had trudged down the drive to the school bus for his first morning at summer school. Dad had gone to the bank again and Mom had left for Mason with Pam and Tommy for yet another appointment with the eye doctor. And I had the Monday-morning blues. I'd worked all Saturday and in the evening driven into town looking for some excitement. I should have known better. There wasn't any. Sunday morning I'd sat bored in church, once again resentful. I'd planned to go fishing that afternoon for the first time since last summer, but it had rained. Now it was Monday again. What a bummer!

"Rick, is that you?" Connie called from the next room when I came into the kitchen.

"Who did you expect? Paul Newman?" I poured a cup of coffee.

"Don't be smart. Come in here."

Her voice was tight and I went. The twins were standing in

Mom and Dad's bedroom, staring into one of the dresser drawers. "What's up?" I asked.

"Look what we found."

I moved closer. "It's a blood pressure sleeve."

"We know that, stupid," Connie said. "What's it doing here?"

"I don't know," I said and picked it up gingerly. "What were you guys doing poking around?"

"We weren't poking around," Connie said angrily. "We came in to change the bed and the drawer was open. Whose is it anyway?"

"I don't know." My mind was working. I put the sleeve back into the drawer carefully. "Finish the bed and we'll talk." I returned to the kitchen and sat at the table. That fall Mom had taken on the stairs—something about that had always bothered me. The twins came in and sat down. "My guess is that it probably belongs to Mom," I said. "People with weight problems often have high blood pressure."

The twins exchanged glances. "And they get dizzy, too, don't they?" Connie said. "Like when Mom fell down the stairs."

I nodded. "Ya, I'd been thinking about that too."

"And they have heart attacks!" Judy said and started to cry.

"Hold on, hold on. You're jumping to conclusions," I said.

We sat there for a couple of minutes. Judy kept crying while Connie tried to comfort her. I was at a loss for anything to say. Hell, I was scared too. Connie turned to me. "Why didn't she tell us?"

I shrugged. "I guess she didn't want to worry us. Or maybe it's not a big deal."

"I wish we'd never left the city," Judy choked out.

"Oh, come on. That has nothing to do with it. Mom was overweight in the city, she's overweight here. . . . Uncle Fritz would have had a heart attack if we'd been here or not. Let's not make a disaster out of this. Mom's taking her blood pressure. She's not having a heart attack." We sat in silence for a couple of minutes more. Just what we needed—more problems. "Look, let's not say we saw it. Let's just try to be cheerful and help out, . . . not let Mom work too hard. . . . And if there's anything you guys could do to help Mom stay on her diet, that might be a good idea too." They nodded. Judy was still teary.

I thought about it as I started working on the haybine again. I was worried not only about Mom's blood pressure problems, but about Judy's reaction to finding out. She let things bother her too much. She'd always been like that a little, but it seemed worse now. Connie was flightier and Judy better about getting work done, but when something went even a little wrong, Judy got emotional. They'd been so close for so long, I'd rarely thought about them separately, but their differences had become more marked in the last few months. For one thing, they no longer looked so much alike. Connie's complexion was clearing up and she was taller and more graceful. Not that she was becoming beautiful or anything, but something about her manner made her seem older and more attractive than Judy. She was at least more cheerful, not a worrywart like Judy. Oh, hell, I thought, trying to think about something else. We'd all make it through somehow.

8

DAD GLANCED AT his watch for about the tenth time in so many minutes. The truck from the meat processor was very late and Jim would be home from school soon. We'd been up on the roof of the house most of the morning reshingling a couple of spots where rain had begun to leak in. The sun was hot and we worked in light shirts. If we stopped for a minute to rest we could look across our fields, thick now with rapidly growing crops, to the barns, outbuildings, houses, and silos of the nearby farms. Farther away the rolling land and patches of forest hid the shorter buildings of more distant farms, but you could count the barns and silos out to the horizon. I guessed seventy or eighty silos were visible from our roof. More maybe. I'd have to count sometime. Perhaps even dig out the binoculars and really take a survey.

It was nice working on the roof in the sun. If it hadn't been for the impending crisis involving Onions, I would have been truly happy. At least all the kids were out of the way this morning: Jim at school and the rest off at a church youth group picnic and swim. I'd driven the twins, Pam, and Tommy to the church about 10:00. Although none of them had the affection for Onions Jim had, it was just as well they wouldn't be here to see the calf hauled away.

Dad looked off down the road again. "There he is at last." I turned to look and saw the meat processor's truck turning onto our road. Dad stood and started for the ladder. A loose shingle slipped beneath his boot and for a terrible second he fought for balance, then his feet went out from under him. I lunged, my mind blank except for the need to grab him. He landed hard and slid. My right hand caught his collar, my other hand gripping the peak of the roof and my feet bracing against the shingles. Every muscle in my body screamed! God, he was too heavy! Dad twisted, his left hand reaching back to catch my forearm. A hammer, a box of shingle nails, and a half dozen shingles hit the ground twenty feet below. Our eyes locked and for the first time in my life I saw terror in my father's eyes. I was praying, "God, give me strength!" He was fighting to gain traction with the toes of his boots. I was stretched out as far as I could—both my arms felt as if they would tear away from my shoulders. Clawing with his free hand, Dad got a little purchase and I leaned back with every last ounce of my strength. His boots regained their grip on the shingles and, at last, I could let him go. Probably no more than ten or fifteen seconds had passed, but they'd seemed like an eternity. We lay gasping with the effort.

"Christ," Dad muttered, "that was stupid. I'd make a hell of a farmer with a broken spine."

"Better farmer than a roofer, I'll bet."

He laughed shakily. "Damn. I've never liked heights much anyway. I'll dream about this for a while." He slapped my knee. "You okay?"

"Ya, I'm okay. Scared the shit out of me, that's all."

"You aren't the only one." We lay there breathing deeply for another few seconds. "Let's not tell your mother. Okay?"

"Ya, okay. Take it easy this time."

"Right." He stood again and made his way cautiously down

the slope of the roof. I followed carefully, my legs a little wobbly.

The truck swung into our driveway and stopped near the barn. The driver got out and lowered the ramp at the back of the truck. While Dad led him into the barn, I gathered up the hammer and shingles that had dropped from the roof and started picking up as many of the nails as I could find in the grass. I didn't want to see any more of Onions's departure than I had to. I just hoped the school bus would be a little late.

Mom came to the back door. "What was all that commotion up on the roof?"

"Oh, nothing much. I just knocked off some shingles and stuff."

"Well, be careful." She was watching the open barn door.

In a couple of minutes the driver came out leading Onions on a short length of rope. The calf followed unwillingly and at the ramp he balked. I could hear his mother mooing plaintively from the barn. Reluctantly, I went over and helped Dad and the driver boost Onions up the ramp into the dark, dirty confines of the truck. He was the only animal in the truck. The driver, a tall thin guy in his late thirties with dirty overalls and dirty spectacles, tied off the rope to a hook. He came back out and raised the ramp. As the light was abruptly cut off, Onions gave a terrified bellow. We could hear the frightened rasping of his hooves as he pulled frantically at the rope. His mother continued to call helplessly from the barn.

"Sorry I'm a little late," the driver said. "The truck was full up and I had to go back to the plant."

"That's all right," Dad said, glancing anxiously down the road.

"Just a second, I'll get your receipt." The driver went to the cab of the truck and spent what seemed like a very long time getting the receipt filled out. Onions continued to fight the rope, then was suddenly, despairingly, silent. His mother's forlorn moos came less often. The driver returned, handed the receipt to Dad, then leaned back against the side of the truck, and lit a cigarette. "Beautiful day. See you guys are up doing a little roofing."

"A little," Dad said.

"I used to work for a roofing company. Pretty good work when it's not too hot and you're working with shingles, but I tell you, in the middle of the summer working with hot tar, ain't nothing worse. I remember once when we were doing the roof of the new school down in Mason . . ."

"Excuse me," Dad said. "I don't mean to be rude, but we've got quite a bit of work to do and, well, we really don't have time for stories right now."

The driver looked a little offended. "Well, sure, sure. Didn't mean to hold you up." He crushed his cigarette beneath a boot and turned for the cab. "You'll get your check in a week or so."

"Thanks," Dad said. "You have a good day now." The driver didn't reply, but got in, started the engine, and rolled off. Inside the rear Onions bellowed a last time.

The trail of dust from his truck was still drifting across the nearby fields when the school bus pulled up from the opposite direction. Dad had gone back into the barn and I was trying to find the rest of the spilled shingle nails.

Jim came running up waving some papers. "Rick, look what I've got!"

I avoided meeting his eyes. "What's that stuff?"

"They're entry forms for the Labor Day fair in Mason. If I join Four-H, I can enter Onions in the calf judging. Then when he's grown I could enter him again as a steer."

I had a sinking feeling. "I don't know, Jim," I said doubtfully.

"He's a good-looking calf! Dad says so. And so did Uncle Fritz."

"Ah, well, Jim . . ."

"But I've got to do something! Any day now, Dad's going to send Onions to the meat processor. Most farmers don't keep their bull calves this long. I read that in the newspaper we get from the co-op."

I was beginning to feel desperate. "But you'll still have to give him up sometime."

"Oh, I know. But I'll have a lot of fun raising him, and Four-H looks like a really neat club. Onions will enjoy it too. I mean, it's better than having him cut up when he's still young."

"Well, I guess . . . Why don't you go in and change and then we'll talk some more."

The back door opened and Mom came out with a basket of wash to hang on the line. "Hi, Mom," Jim shouted, squeezed by her and the basket, making her grunt, and disappeared inside.

"Mom, have we got a problem!" I explained quickly.

She listened, her face in a frown. When I finished, she said, "Damn!" It was the only time in my life I'd ever heard her swear. She dropped the clothes basket and we rushed for the barn.

Inside she hurriedly told Dad Jim's plan. The intensity of her words left no doubt what she thought we should do. Dad listened, his jaw set hard, but Mom can be very convincing. By the time she finished, he looked uncertain. We stared at each other. Then he said, "Damn!" and headed for the phone.

"What are you going to tell Jim?" I asked Mom. "I mean, he's not going to be happy to find out that we shipped Onions without telling him."

"I'll handle that. If we get Onions back, he'll be too happy to care. Here he comes now. Stay here."

The people at the meat-processing plant weren't real happy when Dad told them that he'd changed his mind about selling the calf, but they agreed to try to contact the driver at one of his other afternoon stops. Dad and I went back up on the roof. Jim stayed below sitting in the swing with his gaze fixed on the road. I didn't know what Mom had told him, but he seemed okay. Onions would be saved and nothing else mattered now.

When Jim shouted that the truck was coming, Dad swore under his breath. "That driver is going to be ornery, especially after I interrupted his story. I think there's some beer in the refrigerator. Why don't you get us each a can." He stood. "Careful now."

"You bet. I learned my lesson this morning."

The driver didn't waste any time. When I came out of the house with the beer, he was already pulling Onions down the ramp. Jim was overjoyed. He took the rope and trotted off leading the calf. Onions was pretty happy too. Dad was talking earnestly as I walked up, but the driver seemed to be ignoring him. He raised the ramp with more force than necessary, then turned to gaze sullenly at Dad.

". . . So that's the reason I was anxious to see you go this noon and why I changed my mind about the calf. . . ." Dad's voice trailed off. He proffered a ten-dollar bill. The driver took it without thanks.

"Would you like a beer?" I asked the driver.

He stared at me a moment, then at the beers in my hand. "I guess." I handed him one and another to Dad. We opened the beers and stood around not saying anything. The driver leaned against the truck and lit a cigarette. He took in a deep drag and let it out in a long sigh. Then he chuckled, "Oh, hell, it's too nice a day to be in a pissing contest." He grinned at Dad. "I got kids too. It ain't always easy."

"We really are sorry about the trouble we caused," Dad said.

"Ah, forget it. The kid's happy, that's the main thing." He glanced at his watch. "This time it's me who's got to hurry." He drank his beer in three big swallows and handed the empty can to me.

We thanked him again for bringing back Onions and watched as he drove out the drive. He honked the horn and we waved. "Strange guy," I said.

"If you had his job, you'd probably be a little strange too. . . . I'm sure glad he took the business with Onions okay. For a couple of minutes I had my doubts."

I thought for a moment. "Ah, Dad, do you feel okay? I mean that fall on the roof was pretty scary."

"Oh, I got a bruise or two, I expect. Haven't bothered to check yet. Nothing serious."

"Well, I don't mean that exactly. I mean do you get dizzy sometimes?"

"Me? No, there's nothing wrong with me. Just clumsy, that's all."

I nodded. Perhaps I should ask about the blood pressure sleeve in Mom's drawer. No, better to let it go for now. "Well, I'd better go pick up the kids."

June lengthened. We were all very busy. Pam and Tommy found that they had barely started to explore the wonders of the farm and were on the go from morning until night. There were cats to be fed, caressed, and counted again and again. Signa padded loyally behind the kids in their wanderings, except at midday when she retired to the shade for a siesta.

Jim had school to get through every weekday morning. The afternoons he devoted to helping with chores and tending to Onions. (Onions would undoubtedly be the most doted-on calf in the state by Labor Day.) Only rarely did he find time to play with Pam and Tommy, but that no longer attracted much notice. Even Pam didn't seem to mind anymore. She was counting the days until Linda arrived.

The relationship between Mom and the twins wasn't smooth this summer. It was no one's fault, really. The twins were good about helping with the morning and evening milking, getting meals, doing the wash, and so on. The conflicts usually came over other things. They'd been given principal responsibility for the garden, and their idea of what constituted a well-tended garden and Mom's differed considerably. When they were supposed to be weeding it, they were more likely to be found taking turns riding Arrow. Pam and Tommy wanted their chance, too, but after a few short circles, they were usually ignored. That griped Pam in particular. She was forbidden to ride Arrow without supervision and, as soon as Mom chased the twins in to do their chores, all further hope for a ride was gone for that afternoon.

A couple of times I spoke to Connie and Judy about trying to cooperate with Mom a little more and being a little more thoughtful with Pam and Tommy. They took it with scowls and excuses, but each time they tried a little harder for a couple of days. I didn't really feel it my place to interfere too much. Hell, I had my own work and my own problems. Besides, I sympathized. They did try hard and they did do a lot. I got sick of all the work, too, and wished I had more of a social life. But there wasn't much to do in town and, with the work, not much time to look for fun anyway. Still, I'd be going away soon, so I didn't have as much reason to bitch. They were only fifteen and it was harder for them.

Mom always had one unfailing way of getting the twins to work: "Look, if you girls don't get serious, you can just forget about a driving lesson this afternoon!" That would always do it. The twins would be sixteen in August and now had their learner's permits. Every afternoon when one of them piloted the Plymouth out the drive with Mom riding nervously along, Dad would wince and shake his head. Then he'd say something like, "I'm sure glad your mother took that chore. I'll pay the insurance bills, but I'll be damned if I'll volunteer for kamikaze duty. The old ticker couldn't handle it." He patted his chest.

Connie, more relaxed and more confident, caught on faster than Judy. That made Judy mad and she'd try too hard, falling even further behind and scaring the hell out of Mom with her clumsiness behind the wheel. It seemed that Judy had begun to compare herself to Connie in almost everything—always finding herself second best. Connie was better with Arrow, better around the cows, better in the kitchen. And worst of all,

Connie looked better. Judy would try to compete for a while, then give up and let Connie have the lead. But she was stubborn about the driving and stuck doggedly to it.

Connie didn't seem to notice her sister's frustration. She just continued blithely on, making everything look easy. I mentioned the changes I'd noticed in the twins to Dad once, but he shrugged it off. "Judy's going through a difficult stage, but there's nothing to worry about. She'll catch up." And he went back to work.

I guess I was so tired most of the time that June that I hardly appreciated how much Mom, with the sporadic help of the twins, had done to renovate the dingy interior of the house. From the supper table we could now look into rooms where cracked paint had given way to flowered wallpaper and nicked, dirty woodwork to varnish that glowed like brightly shined shoes. I couldn't help on the remodeling much now because of the work in the fields, but Dad tried to set aside an hour after supper every night to do some of the fixing Mom and the girls couldn't handle. Still, I could tell that the extra work and the additional draw on the budget were a strain on him.

Once on the porch as we were coming in to supper, I asked Dad if some of the remodeling might not be put off until we had more time and cash, but he hushed me with a quick movement of a calloused hand and led me back outside. "Your mother needs some things." He thought for a second, running a hand through his hair, then went on. "She needs her church, a lot of love, and a bright house. It all boils down to security, I guess. Now if I can help by working a little on the house when I'd rather be sitting on my duff, or spending some money on wallpaper that I'd rather spend on something else . . . well, I'll do that. She's handled everything this spring pretty well. I was very proud of how she got through Fritz's death. But now it's important that we don't let her get into one of her moods. If she can look around every day and see some improvement in the house, that'll help. Do you see what I'm getting at?"

"Ya, I guess I hadn't thought of it that way. I'm sorry."

"You don't have to be sorry. I can't expect you to under-stand all these things. Your mother tries not to let it show when she's depressed. Sure, all you kids know when she's feeling lousy, but I don't think you understand just how down she gets sometimes."

"But, Dad, why did you buy the farm, then? It seems like an awful gamble if the most important thing in Mom's life is security."

"Oh, you bet it was a gamble, but I thought it was worth taking. We both did, and still do. I don't think she was ever really happy in the city, not in all the twenty some years we lived there. I didn't mind it as a young man, but as I got older, it started to bother me too. Now if we can get a good operation going here, I think your mother won't get depressed so often—maybe hardly at all. . . . But things are still very much in the balance. If we can let her know she's appreciated and not let her worry too much, I'm sure things will work out." He paused and lit his pipe. Then he shook his head and smiled wryly. "My God, that woman can worry about anything. Sometimes I think she enjoys worrying. Maybe that's why she wanted so many kids—something or somebody always to worry about. . . ."

The back door popped open and Pam ran out, trailed, as usual, by Tommy. She came skipping across the lawn. Tommy followed, trying to imitate her, but finally had to gallop to catch up. "Mom says, Come and get it or she'll throw it to the pigs!" Pam hollered.

"Daddy, where are the pigs?" Tommy asked.

"That's only a saying, silly," Pam said.

Dad caught Tommy and swung him up in his arms. "Why don't we get some pigs?" Tommy asked when he was seated in the crook of Dad's left arm.

"We don't need pigs," Pam said. "We've got cows."

"Would you two take care of the pigs if we got some?" Dad asked.

"Sure," Tommy said.

144

"Ugh, I'll stick to cats," Pam said.

Dad laughed, dropped an arm over Pam's shoulder, and we went in to supper.

It was a pretty normal supper. After grace the twins dominated the conversation. Jim tried to give the daily report on Onions, but got interrupted by Connie with the daily driving-lesson news. Judy fiercely denied her mistakes, blaming them on the car or the road. Tommy was more interested in talking about pigs than eating. Pam was pretty much silent until I got the floor for her by asking for the most recent cat total. Through it all Dad played the good-natured referee while Mom kept the dishes passing and helped Tommy.

I watched her closely without being too obvious. She started with her usual small portion, but helped herself to seconds. She hesitated over each dish, then took only a small amount, but it added up to a full plate in the end. When Pam and Tommy had eaten all they wanted, she finished their meals. I doubted if she even thought about that. She didn't eat dessert, but I knew that later she would break down and have her share. When I thought about it, it seemed Mom's snacking had been worse recently.

It also struck me how silent she was. I'd never really thought much about it before. She took little part in the conversation except to occasionally correct one of her kids' grammar or to cool down an argument. Otherwise, she spent her time on the logistics of the meal. But she must be happy, I thought. Her life is her family, always has been. And here we all are— seated around her table on the farm she always wanted. We're all healthy and, except for the routine squabbles, happy. She shouldn't be depressed.

Sure, I'd known for a long time that Mom got depressed a little now and then, but Dad's talk about her vulnerability bothered me a lot. Was it really that bad? Was there something more involved? After supper I'd get Dad alone and ask some questions.

But I didn't get my chance right away, since Mom was hot to get some paneling up in the living room and Dad had promised to do some measuring and cutting. With Jim's help, he didn't need me, so I walked back down to the barn to finish a few chores.

More than an hour passed before I came out of the barn. Dad was leaning against one of the tractors smoking his pipe and drinking a glass of iced tea. It had been unusually hot in the last two weeks and this evening heat lightning played along the western horizon. "Hi, son. Get them bedded down for the night?"

"Ya, they're all tucked in."

"Good. Well, I've been thinking about the hay. If we don't get rain tonight, I think we can start cutting tomorrow. It may be a little early yet, but the corn's going to need cultivating soon and I want to get the hay out of the way first."

"The weather's been good, hasn't it?"

"Could hardly be better. If it keeps up like this we shouldn't have any trouble getting three crops of hay and real good corn and oat harvests. . . . If it stays this way. Can't worry about that. Nature'll take its way."

We talked for a while about the schedule for the next couple of months, but part of my mind was still on Mom. After a pause in the conversation, I asked, "Dad, I've been thinking about what you said about Mom. . . . This may sound stupid, but does she eat a lot because she's depressed, or is she depressed because she eats so much?"

He laughed his wry laugh. "The chicken and the egg. Which comes first? I don't know. A lot of things are wrapped up together."

"But if she could just stick to her diet for a while, I think she'd feel better."

"I'm afraid habits aren't that easy to break." He looked at me steadily. "You think your mother is homely, don't you, Rick?"

"No," I protested, "it's not that . . ."

He cut me off. "You don't have to make excuses. She's fat,

there's no doubt about that, but, well, that's not what I see when I look at her. I see a woman with so much love, she can't find enough places to put it all."

"I know, Dad. I didn't mean to criticize her."

"No, of course you didn't. I wish she could do something about her weight. I wish she could be happier more of the time, but that's not the way she is. . . . At least not right now." I was about to say something, but he went on. "You know, she went to a psychiatrist about her nerves and her weight a couple of years ago."

"No, I didn't know that."

"Well, she did." Dad sighed. "I think it helped a little, but not much—especially considering what he charged. She's not as nervous as she once was, but she hasn't been able to stick to a diet any better. She'll lose a few pounds, then get in one of her moods and gain it all back and more. One step forward, two back." He laughed without humor.

"But do you think the farm will help in the long run?"

"Ya, I really do. But until we get going, it's going to be hard on her." He relit his pipe. "I sure miss Fritz. He always knew how to cheer her up. I'm too sour a lot of the time."

"I think you do pretty good, Dad."

"Well, thanks. I try, but I forget how important it is sometimes." We didn't say anything for a couple of minutes. Dad watched the heat lightning morosely, his pipe forgotten in his hand. The yard light clicked on and a cloud of insects gathered immediately around the bulb. Down the road, the bullfrogs set up their chorus along the marshy banks of the tiny stream. When one hopped into the culvert to cross beneath the road, his booming croak nearly drowned out the others until, emerging on the other side of the road, he rejoined the humbler frogs.

The back door swung open and Pam and Tommy came out. "What are you two doing up?" Dad yelled. "It's way past your bedtimes."

"Mom said we could check on the cats once more," Pam called and went skipping on to the barn.

Tommy was still trying to get the skipping down, but his feet kept getting mixed up. He stopped and studied his feet, then turned his head to squint at us. "You're doing fine," Dad said. "Just keep trying." Tommy resumed his awkward progress toward the barn. Dad chuckled. "Those two sure love it here."

"Ya, they sure do."

For a minute he seemed very deep in thought, then he sighed. "But sometimes I think maybe we shouldn't have taken Tommy. . . . I mean, I love all my kids, but Tommy is going to be a load on your mother for the rest of her life. Maybe more of a load than she can handle. . . ." He gazed moodily at the horizon and then said almost in a whisper, "But, God, I love that kid. To think he'll go blind and never see all this as a grown-up, it's almost . . ." His voice caught and he had to clear his throat. "Sometimes it's almost more than I can stand."

"I know, Dad."

Dad looked at me, his eyes brimming with pain. "Just think, when he's a man, he'll be blind. He'll remember how he saw things as a child, but that's all the sight he'll have." He looked down at the toes of his boots, fighting back the emotion that had almost overwhelmed him.

"Dad, isn't there any hope?"

"Ya, I guess." His voice was still thick and he had to clear his throat again. "Ya, there's still a little, I guess. Not much, but a little. . . . We're going to let that new medicine have some time to work and then take him to the university hospital in Minneapolis late in July or early in August. Maybe they'll have some new ideas."

"I hope so." I couldn't think of anything else to say. The conversation sagged. For several minutes we stood lost in our own thoughts. Before Pam and Tommy's interruption, I'd been about to ask about Mom's blood pressure, but now I was more hesitant. This was the first I'd heard about the trip to Minneapolis. Was there something more to it than Tommy's eyes? When Judy and Connie had first shown me the blood pressure sleeve, I hadn't been too worried, but it had con-

148

cerned me more as time passed. A dozen times I'd thought of asking Dad about it, and a dozen times I'd decided against it. If they wanted to keep it a secret, what right had I to pry? But tonight I had to know. "Dad, about the blood pressure . . ."

He looked at me quickly. "So, you know about that."

"Ya, a couple of weeks ago the twins were in making your bed. Mom had left the drawer open and they saw the sleeve. They showed it to me. We figured maybe it was better not to mention it, since you two seemed to want to keep it a secret."

"Ya, well, it's not really a big deal. Your mother's blood pressure is a little high. It's bound to be with her weight. She's supposed to keep track of it on a chart for a month before she goes back to the doctor. Then he'll be able to figure out what kind of medicine she needs, if any. Don't worry about it."

"If it's no big deal, why is she keeping it a secret?"

He shrugged. "I don't know. She gets these ideas sometimes. She thinks it would scare the kids too much. The memory of Fritz's death is still pretty fresh."

"Dad, are you sure that's all there is to it?" My words came in a rush, my voice rising. "She's not getting dizzy and falling down and stuff like that, is she?"

"Hold on! Take it easy! Now I told you not to worry. It isn't any big deal! Her blood pressure has been high for years. They're just thinking of giving her some medicine. There is no other problem, Rick. Believe me. Okay?" I nodded. He laughed softly and shook his head. "Cripes, you're just like your mother sometimes. Make Pikes Peak out of a molehill. You should have talked to me instead of letting this eat on you. You're going to be an old man before your time if you keep worrying so much." I was about to say he was pretty damn good at worrying too, but he saw it coming from my expression and laughed again. "But I shouldn't preach. We're all worrying too much these days—looking for a disaster on every horizon. We've got to stop doing that or none of us will last until the Fourth of July. Let's worry about the things we can change and ignore the rest. Let things flow a bit. Everything will work out." He slapped me on the shoulder. "Okay?"

For some reason I was a little put out. I was glad more wasn't wrong with Mom, but the secrecy seemed insulting. "Well, I think she ought to talk to Judy and Connie about it. They were pretty upset."

"Ya, she probably should. I'll mention it to her. No one meant to get anyone upset. . . ." He remembered the pipe in his hand and got it going again. "And I didn't intend to get you all upset tonight, son. I feel better for talking. I hope maybe you do too. Really, everything's going pretty well. Let's just try to keep your mother from worrying about everything and everybody."

"Well, she doesn't have to worry about me anyway."

"Actually, she worries about you quite a bit."

"Why does she worry about me?! I'm doing all right."

"Oh, she worries about you going off on your own." He took a long meditative puff on his pipe. "And, I guess she's afraid that you're so unhappy here, you won't come back very often."

"That's silly. I'll be okay. And I'll always come back, you know that." I thought for a second. "Do you worry about me, Dad?"

"Me? No, not so much. I know you'll do all right. . . . I'm more sorry than anything, because I know this isn't where you've wanted to be these last few months."

"It's not so bad. It was at first, but I'm getting used to it. It's okay. Really, Dad, I don't mind."

"Good, I'm glad to hear that." We stood for a couple of minutes in silence, then Dad tapped out his pipe on a tractor tire. "Well, I wonder what those kids are up to. I guess we'd better go down and help count the cats or Pam and Tommy will be up all night.

At the milkhouse door he stopped. "Don't you worry about your mother. Except for Fritz things are going pretty good. She'll be fine once we get through the first year."

"I hope so."

"Just try not to worry so much. Okay?"

"Okay."

But I did worry about her, and Dad, too, quite a bit. As a matter of fact, I was spending so much time worrying about other people these days that I rarely thought about college and almost forgot my own birthday.

I turned eighteen on June 19. (I'd always been young for my grade in school, but it hadn't made much difference since I grew tall early.) We've never made a big thing of birthdays in the family, just a cake and a single present, so in the rush of everything that June it wasn't too surprising that I found myself halfway through the day before I remembered my birthday. I wondered if everyone else had forgotten, too, but that night Mom brought out a cake with all the candles and everyone sang. (Mom is still the only one who can sing. If anything, everyone else has gotten worse despite all the open space to practice in.) I knew the present was a book from the heft of the package and I tore the paper to find the title on the thick volume, *Modern Movements in Architecture*. It was a beautiful book full of plans and pictures and I lost myself in it right at the table, even while the kids were demanding to see it too. They were instantly bored when I paused to show it to them and went off about their own affairs.

I read late that night, but it was slow going since I really knew little about architecture beyond my own fantasies. Still, I had a warm feeling just turning the pages. Mom and Dad must have spent a lot of time looking for the right title before ordering it by mail. Books like this weren't normal stock items on the drugstore bookrack and the love their gift showed was infinitely more important to me than all the diagrams and glossy photos.

It struck me when I set the book down finally that I'd forgotten even to think about my dreams in recent weeks. That disturbed me and I searched myself to see if I was still truly interested in becoming an architect, or if it had been only a passing fancy all along. Yes, I still wanted to be an architect more than anything in the world. I didn't understand exactly why, but I knew that I was meant to build walls and raise roofbeams, that if I'd been born seven hundred years earlier I would have built cathedrals and now I would build sky-scrapers. It had just been a busy spring with so much commotion and strain with Uncle Fritz's death and the effort of trying to get the family settled on the farm. Now these thoughts made me restless again and milking in the morning seemed almost as much torment as it had in the early days. By evening I'd wound myself into a knot of confusion. I begged off from supper and took the pickup into town as soon as the last frothy bucket of milk poured into the bulk tank. In town I walked around a bit, then had a hamburger at the root beer stand. The movie was some cartoon thing about animals, and I'd had my fill of animals, cartoon or otherwise, for that day. So I kept walking. If I only had someone to talk to, I thought—a girl friend, maybe. Or Bill. God, I'd like to talk to him now. . . .

Eventually, I found myself in front of Irma's and went in for the first beer of my day-old official adulthood. A couple of the men at the bar recognized me and nodded, asking a casual question or two about the farm. I answered, but sat down near the end by myself, not wanting to get into any conversation that would center on farming. Irma came over and I ordered a beer. I could see when she brought it that she was trying to place me. I helped her out. "You remember me, I'm Rick Simons, Fritz Gebhardt's nephew."

"Oh, yes. Shame about Fritz. He was such a nice fellow. I went to the funeral."

"Yes, I saw you there."

"It was a nice funeral. He would have liked it. The minister said some lovely things."

"Yes, it was a nice talk."

"Sure was. Your family making out okay?"

"We survived. It was a little tough, but we're okay now."

"I'm sure you are. I've been meaning to talk to your mother after church. She seems like such a nice woman."

I didn't know whether to say "thanks" or "she certainly is" or what, so I just nodded and ordered another beer. I did know

152

that Irma made me uncomfortable, s- I made a show of studying the Brewer game on the TV.

I drank a couple more glasses of beer and watched the game, uninterested in it, the beer, or the bar, but unwilling to go back home to bed only to awaken to another round of life on a dairy farm. Still, whenever I let my attention stray from the game, my mind was instantly engaged in seeking solutions to problems on the farm—how to fix this or that piece of machinery, how to improve the hay cutting so that it took less time and effort, how to make one process or another more efficient, and so on, endlessly. I found myself constantly thinking next year we'll do it this way, or in another couple of years we can buy that machine to do it faster. But there wasn't going to be another year on the farm for me. In the fall I was going back to the city. Back where I belonged. Maybe not Milwaukee forever, but a big city. I'd have fulfilled my obligation to the family, helped them get started on the farm. In the fall it would be time to get on with my own plans. And I didn't mean just school and architecture either. I needed to have some fun, some social life, a few friends my own age. I loved my family, but I'd spent eighteen years at home. I no longer resented coming to the farm. I would have preferred it another way, maybe, but I'd learned some things. Perhaps grown up a little. Soon it would be time to leave. I had another life to lead. Somehow I had to refocus on that.

The baseball game was winding up and my excuse for not being more talkative running out. I finished the beer and headed for the door, waving to Irma on the way. "Thanks for coming in, Rick," she called.

"Sure. We'll see you."

On the way home from Irma's I had an accident. Perhaps the beer had made me sleepy or all my tumbling thoughts had distracted me, but when two of the neighborhood dogs broke from a ditch and raced across the road hot after a rabbit, I swerved too far to the right and the pickup slammed into the ditch, the right side crumpling against the embankment and the front end smashing over a boulder, snapping the front axle.

I was stunned but unhurt and, after a long moment of breathing very deeply, found the flashlight in the glove compartment and got out to look at the damage. It didn't take long to see that I'd made a royal mess of things. The pickup was wrecked, perhaps totaled. Apparently no one had heard the noise and after ten minutes of leaning on the front fender furiously cursing my stupidity, I took the flashlight and walked the half mile home past the lonely farms that fronted on the road—the silence of the night broken only by the barking of the farm dogs as my feet scuffed the gravel on the dark road.

In the morning we hooked a chain around the broken front axle and pulled the pickup home behind one of the tractors. Dad didn't yell or scream at me, but I could tell from the tight set of his jaw that he was angry and worried. Surveying the damage in the driveway, he finally sighed and said, "Well, we've got to have a pickup, but we don't have enough money to fix it right. Go up to the junkyard in Carleyville and get an axle. We'll just knock out the dents as best we can and run it like this until we've got more money."

I was watching a slow drip of water from under the front. "I think the radiator is leaking, too, Dad."

He groaned. "Goddamn it, Rick." He crawled under the truck again, looked around with the flashlight, then pulled himself back out. "We'll try to solder it for now." He stood chewing the stem of his pipe and gazing out across the fields.

"I'm sorry, Dad. I really am."

"Ya, well, just get the axle, will you?" He walked off toward the machine shed. I stood watching, hurt and troubled. It had probably been my fault, but, hell, it hadn't been like I was drunk or something—it was an honest enough mistake. But there's no more important piece of equipment on a farm than a pickup, and now ours stood tilted and broken like some great bug with its front legs torn away.

I drove up to Carleyville in the car and found an axle pretty cheap. The man at the yard tried to talk me into one in better condition. "You know, this one went through an accident, too, and it might be a little bent."

"It looks okay to me; I think it'll work."

"Maybe so. I'll let you have it cheap, but no refund if it doesn't. I warned you."

"Fair enough." I didn't want to spend more because it was important to me to use only my own money and I didn't have much. I drove back a little worried, but pretty sure I could make it fit.

After milking and supper we put the pickup on blocks and crawled under. The axle was heavy, rusty, and greasy, and we worked for hours with the mosquitoes and gnats buzzing around our heads and arms, diving in to bite us when we were in the worst positions. Finally Dad muttered, "Okay, let it down." We slid out and stood beside the truck working the cramps out of our legs and arms. I felt sick. So stupid, I thought, I should have paid the extra ten bucks. Finally Dad sighed and said, "Well, it's not going to fit, bent just a hair. Take 'er back up in the morning and get another one."

"They said no refunds, Dad."

He looked puzzled. "How can they do that?" I told him and he looked at me with astonishment, then he exploded. "Well, you are just having a great time! There goes another chunk of money we don't have!" He hurled a wrench into the dirt. He was so mad he was shaking. "If you want to screw off and wreck this farm, then at least do it when you're working, not off boozing in town!"

I was shocked and so deeply hurt as I can ever remember being. I protested, "I only had three beers, Dad. I told you about the dogs . . ."

He cut me off. "Ya, ya, ya, you told me all about it." He turned and stomped off toward the house. I heard him kick his boots off against the porch wall before going into the kitchen in his stocking feet.

At breakfast he apologized half-heartedly. I could see he was still angry, but also angry with himself for losing his temper. It was the money, I knew. We'd always eaten cheaply, lots of chicken, ground meat, and stews out of the cheap cuts, but now I could see Mom trying to stretch the food dollars even further. She spent a lot more time baking bread and we ate a lot of greens, beans, and radishes as they started to come up in the garden. There were also more patched clothes and fewer family trips into town for a movie or ice cream cones. It was the unexpected expense of fixing the truck rather than anything else that had Dad so upset.

Before leaving for Carleyville, I asked Mom for some money, promising to pay her back as soon as I could. She took it from her purse without comment. I could tell she was troubled by the row between Dad and me, but couldn't make up her mind how to patch it up.

I took Pam and Tommy along, partly to give Mom a break and also for companionship since I dreaded seeing the junkman again. But he was off for the day and a young red-haired guy just a year or two older than I was took us out to the back to find the right axle among the hundreds of wrecked, abandoned, and rusting cars. We had just come around a stack of car bodies that had been through the crusher and lay waiting to be hauled off for a melting down when I saw a familiar shape, only shorter and less complete. It was a copy of our mastodon combine. Somehow I'd thought all the rest of the species extinct. But here sat a brother, its wheels long gone and much of the superstructure torn away. I walked around it while the young junkman watched us quizzically. "What are you going to do with this?" I asked.

"Don't know. It's too big for the crusher and no one wants the parts. Nobody has used that kind of thing in years. I guess we'll cut it up for scrap eventually."

I nodded, called to Pam and Tommy, and went on looking for the axle.

That evening Dad and I finished repairing the pickup and afterwards Dad went in and brought out a can of beer for each of us. "Maybe you'd better drink your beer at home until you learn to handle it." He smiled and I knew it was supposed to be a joke, but it hurt anyway. I didn't say anything, just tried to smile, and stood watching the last light fade over the warm fields now thick with the sky-reaching stalks of corn.

9

FOR THE NEXT few days Dad maintained a forced good humor and I, too, tried to make as if nothing had happened. But every time I looked at the battered pickup or drove into town with the new creaks and knocks rattling in my ears, I was ashamed, cursing my own bad luck and everything connected with life on the farm. The worst part was knowing how much the accident had added to Dad's problems. We had always been close before, but now I felt him drifting away from me, lost in a constant round of worries about money, the family, and the future.

Mom, too, seemed distant in these days. The lines on her face were deeper and dark rings started to appear under her eyes on many mornings. I knew she was having trouble sleeping, the worry driving her to the kitchen late at night to eat cookies or cake and to drink coffee that made her even more restless. Part of it was worry over money, but more was fear about the family—that somehow life on the farm, instead of pulling us closer together, was tearing us apart. The fatigue made her snappish, too, especially with the twins, whose frequent attacks of giggling irresponsibility grated on the nerves of my parents.

The younger children weathered the hot summer days better than the rest of us, although Jim hated summer school and waited out the long mornings at his desk in a state of barely restrained anticipation for the noon bell. Once off the school bus, he was back in his element. He'd roar through the afternoons and evenings with an energy I envied. Caring for the calves (Onions in particular, of course) continued to be his special interest, but he was a willing helper with the other chores too. Uncle Fritz had been right—Jim was a born farmer. Only toward bedtime, when Mom or Dad forced him to do his homework, would his energy and high spirits fade. And, the next morning, glum and peevish, he'd drag himself down the driveway to wait for the school bus.

Pam and Tommy did their small list of chores and played. Mom had to caution them often about avoiding the dangerous places around the farm. Tommy's eyesight was fading with the passing weeks and, despite his increased familiarity with the farm and its animals, he was more vulnerable than ever. Mom was particularly nervous when he rode Arrow with one of the twins. Still, the riding was the high point of Pam and Tommy's day, and Mom couldn't find the heart to change that.

The old conflict about equal time on Arrow had surfaced again. Connie and Judy felt that they needed the majority of the time to develop their riding skills and the younger kids should be content with a couple of quick turns around the field. Tommy was satisfied with the arrangement, but Pam was irked. Linda was due to arrive in a couple of weeks and Pam wanted to be an accomplished horsewoman by that time. If Jim had been there to squawk a bit, the twins might have given in, but he'd decided he wasn't very interested in horses and Pam was left to defend her rights pretty much by herself. She appealed to Mom and got some support, but since Connie and Judy were in charge of Arrow, that didn't have any lasting effect. Personally, I was sick of the whole subject.

Yet, despite the petty squabbles and occasional blowups, the work was getting done. The equipment broke down, but we fixed it. The hours were long, but we worked them and wished we had even more time. And the weather, at least, was holding fine with long hot summer days and gentle showers nurturing the hay, corn, and oats in the long green fields.

Dad always brightened after hearing the cheery words of the farm reporter forecasting another good day on the radio that always played in the barn during the morning milking. True, a single hard wind could ruin much of the oat crop or hail smash both oats and corn, but so far the summer gave promise of a bumper crop in the fall.

Farming is a risky business even in the best of times. But our farm was far from modern and, at least financially, these were hardly good times. Everything depended on a successful first year, and as July opened, I found myself working harder than ever for that goal. At first I was just trying to make up for the accident. I'd bust my ass to win back Dad's respect. I'd do everything in my power to get the family through to the fall. Then I could leave with a clear conscience. School, the city, my friends, and my future waited for me. But now I was going to make this farm work if it killed me.

Yet, I soon found myself forgetting about the accident. It had happened. Probably part of it had been my fault, but it was over and done with. Then I began busting my ass for a better reason: I'd never been content to do a mediocre job before, and I'd be damned if I'd do one now.

I hate being involved in something I don't understand, so I started reading carefully the periodicals that came in the mail and going to the county extension office and the library to find more answers. Before long the stack of farming books, magazines, and pamphlets on my desk buried the book on architecture I'd been given for my birthday. But I hadn't really forgotten about the book or my plans. Sometimes, when I wasn't too tired, I'd dig it out and read a few pages before bedtime. I found my interests less lofty these days. Visual beauty no longer intrigued me as much as efficiency. How could a building be designed so work got done with the maximum comfort and speed? How could materials and people be moved with the minimum of hassle? To get a handle on the answers, I needed something specific to work on. I was by now more familiar with a dairy farm than any other kind of plant, so I started sketching and resketching my ideas for the perfect dairy farm. There was a lot more involved in the problem than I'd imagined, and I got thoroughly caught up in it. Often I'd have to force myself to stop reading or sketching so I could get a few hours' sleep before milking.

The more familiar I became with dairy farming, the more I found myself actually enjoying the work. Still, despite the confidence my added knowledge and experience gave me, I knew luck always played a crucial part in farming. Some had it, some didn't. An incident on the second of July brought that home for me.

Mom, Pam, Tommy, and I were driving back from town where they'd shopped for groceries while I was in the hardware store. The day was beautiful—cloudless and hot. The morning's work had gone well and we were done with our errands in town ahead of schedule, so for fun I took the long way home, driving slowly along the back roads. The warm breeze flooding through the open windows brought with it the lush smell of moist rich earth and green growing crops. In the pastures the cows lay in what shade they could find, chewing their cuds in the noonday sun.

A small river meandered across the pastures on our right in gentle curves, brushed the edge of a woodlot, widened then narrowed before running beneath an old railroad trestle, and finally slipped a last few hundred feet to cross under the road and disappear into low, swampy woods to our left. I slowed as we crossed the bridge. Long ago Uncle Fritz had told me about fishing from the trestle. There would be trout in that river, for sure. One of these days, when we get a little ahead on the work, I thought, I'll drag Dad down here for a few hours.

We were coming up on a smallish farm with a frame house

weathered gray by decades of paintless exposure to the elements. I saw the man only at the last second. He was stumbling down his driveway toward the road waving a hand. I braked hard, afraid that his unsteady course would bring him in front of us. At the road's edge he fell to his knees and doubled over, hands clutched to his midsection. I threw the shift lever into neutral, set the parking brake hard, and leaped out. Mom yelled, "You kids stay in the car!" and clambered out the other side.

I knelt beside him. He was a big man about sixty years old. Normally his face would have been handsome, but now it was contorted with pain. "Help me, please," he gasped. The whole front of his worn overalls was soaked with red, more blood squirting from the right hand held against his stomach by his left. I tore off my shirt, not even bothering with the buttons. I pulled his left hand away. The right was torn apart, fore, middle, and ring fingers ripped away at the knuckles and the stump of the hand a hash of splintered bone and raw flesh. Mom cried out in horror. I wrapped the shirt as gently as I could around that ghastly, pitiful hand, pulled the big man's left arm across my shoulder, and with all my strength brought him to his feet. Together we staggered to the car. "Pam, Tommy, get in front," I yelled. They crawled over the seat, and together Mom and I got him into the back. "You drive, Mom!" He slumped against the opposite door and I squeezed in and pulled my door shut. Mom slammed the driver's door, dropped the car into gear and we roared off. The bleeding, my God, I had to stop the bleeding! I searched for the pressure point. Boy Scouts had been a long time ago, but miraculously I found the point and pressed hard. The flow of blood seemed to ease. "Pam, give me Tommy's belt!" There was fumbling and a whining protest from Tommy, then she was leaning over the seat holding out the belt. "Wrap it around his right arm. No, above the elbow. Now put it through the buckle and pull. Good. Okay, I've got it." I released the pressure point and took the belt end. We were traveling fast, a huge cloud of dust kicking up behind. Soon our farm would come into view. I made a hasty decision. "Mom, stop at the end of our driveway. Pam, as soon as she stops, you run and find Dad. Tell him to call the fire station and have them get the ambulance ready. We'll be there in ten minutes. Do you understand?" She nodded.

It seems strange, but I'll never forget the picture that they made in the frame of the rear window: little Pam, blond hair streaming, running toward our house for all she was worth, while Tommy, holding up his pants, galloped awkwardly behind.

Two miles out of town we heard the firehouse siren howl. "There's the siren," I told the man, "we'll have you in the ambulance in a couple of minutes." He didn't reply. He leaned back against the window, eyes closed, face running with sweat. His mouth was open and his breath came in shallow gasps. "Hey, can you hear me?"

His face contorted and he managed to get out a "Ya."

"Okay. Just hang in there."

We were rocketing along. Mom's face was hard with concentration and her hands gripped the wheel. The speedometer needle hovered a fraction below 80 m.p.h. No traffic ahead, thank God. In sight of the town limits she took her foot off the gas and we slowed to a less phenomenal speed. Two turns brought us up in front of the fire station. The ambulance had already been pulled into the street. Two volunteer attendants with a wheeled stretcher rushed to the car. One wrenched open my door and helped me out, while the other leaned in over the injured man.

"Who is it?" the man at my shoulder asked.

"Jack Peterson," the other said, unwrapping the hand. "Holy Christ, half his hand is gone. Got it in a grain auger, surer than hell. He's lost lots of blood. Let's get him out."

With practiced hands they lifted him out and laid him on the stretcher. A third volunteer pulled off Tommy's belt and replaced it with a tourniquet. "Let's go!" They raced for the ambulance. Peterson was up and inside in seconds. Two of the volunteers jumped in to tend him and the third slammed the rear door and hammered three times with his fist on the side of the ambulance. The driver slammed his foot down on the accelerator and with a squeal of tires, the ambulance, lights flashing and siren screaming, roared off toward Mason and the hospital.

For the first time I became aware of the small crowd of people gathered about. I looked down at myself. My bare chest, my hands, and the front of my jeans were covered with broad patches of blood, some still violently red, others already drying a dull brown. I looked at Mom beside me. She was shaking all over. An older woman took her arm. "Come into the house. I'll get you a cup of coffee and your son can wash up." I recognized Mrs. Riedel from church, although I'd never spoken to her. Several people asked me questions as I dully followed the two women to the house, but I just shook my head.

Mrs. Riedel brought me a clean shirt and pants. "I think these will fit. My boy is in the service and won't mind. Go ahead and use the shower."

I did, the hot spray reviving me. I felt a deep sorrow for Peterson. I had never know him before, but now I felt very close to him. His hand was forever ruined. A little bad luck, a single careless move, and that merciless grain auger had ripped off his fingers and ground his hand into a horrible, useless thing. I wept for him as I stood beneath the steaming shower.

Dad, Pam, and Tommy were waiting for us on the porch when we got home. The twins and Jim must have been off somewhere. Dad came over to the car, his face grave, as we got out. "How is he?"

"We don't know yet," Mom said. "Oh, Paul, it was terrible. That poor man's hand was just mangled."

"I tried to tell, Daddy," Tommy broke in, "there was lots of blood and Pammy took my belt and Ricky put it on the man's arm and we were going really fast . . ."

"Hush now," Dad said and put an arm around him. "How are you two?" Mom started to shake again, but not as bad as before. Dad led them off leaving Pam and me.

"Is he going to be okay?" Pam asked.

"I don't know, Pam. He's not going to die, but, well, his hand won't ever be the same."

"Yes, I know. I got a good look." We wandered out toward the pasture. Arrow and several of the cows raised their heads to look at us. Pam didn't seem upset, just thoughtful. "Did I do what you wanted me to?"

"Sure. You did great. The ambulance was waiting."

"I mean in the car."

"You did fine there too."

"I hope so." I looked at her. This pensive mood in my little sister was something I hadn't seen before. She went on after a minute. "You know it was real scary and I feel sorry for him, but . . . but I didn't feel like screaming or crying or anything. I couldn't find Dad right away, so I called the fire station myself. Only after I hung up and went to look for Dad did I start feeling really scared and sick." She looked at me. "Was that wrong?"

"No, I think that was right."

"But when that kitten got stepped on by that cow, I cried right away. And I threw up a little while later."

"I know." I sat on a haywagon and helped her up beside me. The cows and Arrow had gone back to cropping grass. The sun was still hot, but the wind had come up a little and a few clouds drifted over. Peaceful. A gentle summer day in farm country. "I guess when there's something you can still do, you go ahead and do it and worry about feeling bad later. I felt pretty bad afterwards too. . . . I think you ought to be proud of yourself. I'm proud of you. I knew you'd do the right thing when we dropped you off." She nodded and started to cry very softly. I put my arm around her and sat looking out over the pasture where the animals grazed. In the distance barns and silos shimmered in the hot July haze.

The weather was much the same a week later when I came into the kitchen to see if there was anything cold to drink. Connie held out a slip of paper and snapped. "You had two calls. Mr. Bergstrom and Mr. Peterson. Here are the numbers." The twins had had another blowup with Mom that forenoon and now I was being included in the general pout. Connie went back to washing the windows. Outside, Judy stood on a ladder doing the other sides. Their movements were lethargic. At this rate it would take them all afternoon to do the kitchen windows. I found some lemonade in the refrigerator and poured a glass.

Judy and Connie had planned to go on a picnic with some kids from school just before noon. I'd been crossing the yard headed for the machine shop when an old green Pontiac with a half dozen kids inside pulled into the yard. They were in pretty high spirits already. Connie and Judy were taking down the last couple of sheets from the line. The driver yelled, "Come on, Connie! Come on, Boots! Let's go!" Another kid let out a howl and someone else yelled, "Arf! Arf!"

Connie called, "We'll be ready in a minute," grabbed her basket, and ran laughing to the house. I looked hard at Judy. Boots. I'd heard that before, but I couldn't remember where or when. She didn't look as happy as Connie, but she managed to smile and wave at the kids in the car, before getting the last sheet into her basket and hurrying after Connie.

I was digging around in some boxes on the workbench trying to find three or four decent lag bolts when I saw Mom come out of the house and stroll over to the car with a large thermos of lemonade and a pan of brownies. I'm sure she was just being friendly, not going to the car to check out the other kids. I think she was happy that her eldest daughters were going off for a good time. A good clean wholesome time, that is. Somebody in the car must not have seen her coming, because suddenly she stopped and the smile disappeared from her face. Oh, shit, I thought. Somebody forgot to hide the beer. Mom did an about-face and marched back to the house.

Five minutes passed. I found the lag bolts and straightened up the bench a little. The kids in the car must have figured it out, because there was less horsing around now. Finally, a tall kid got out of the front passenger seat and walked hesitantly toward the door to the house. Connie met him on the steps and they talked for a minute before the kid walked solemnly back to the car. The car pulled out fast and Connie scurried over to the door of the barn, glanced in, then headed in my direction. "Rick?"

"In here."

She opened the door. "Rick, I've got to talk to you."

"Okay."

"Did you see what happened?"

"I think I figured it out. Mom saw they had some beer in the car and now she won't let you go on the picnic."

"Ya, that's right. . . . And Don Olson, the kid who was driving, had one in his hand."

"Ouch!" I said.

Connie nodded and scuffed a tennis shoe along the dirty floor. "Ya, she's real mad. . . . But what's with her, anyway? I mean, who ever heard of a picnic without beer? Just because some kids brought some doesn't mean we're going to drink any. And Don is an okay guy. He's not going to drive drunk or anything."

I shrugged. "Ya, well, maybe so. . . . Not much you can do about it now. The kids in the car should have been smarter, that's all."

"Rick, can you talk to her? Tell her you'll give us a ride down there. We'll ride back with someone who hasn't been drinking."

"I think it's a lost cause, Connie. She'll never buy it."

"But you've got to talk her into it, Rick! That guy I was

talking to . . . well, I think he's kind of interested in me. Judy and I hardly ever get away from here and this was our real chance to have some fun. Judy's upstairs crying right now. You've just got to talk to Mom!"

"Hey, look! I'm sorry, but it just isn't going to work! I'm not going to jump into this and get Mom mad at me just to prove it."

She glared at me a long moment. "Thanks for nothing, big brother." She whirled and slammed the door behind her.

I really did feel sorry for them, but there wasn't a thing I could do. Besides, the kids in the car had been pretty stupid and I wasn't sure I thought much of Judy and Connie going with them anyway. Not that I want to sound hypocritical—double standard and all that kind of crap. God knows, I had been to my share of beer parties. Still . . .

But now as I watched them moodily rubbing at the dirt on the windows, I felt more sympathy for them. They really didn't get out much and then only with the family or to go to the church youth group meetings. The picnic had been something very special for them. Too bad it had gotten screwed up. I finished my lemonade and went to the phone.

I dialed Mr. Bergstrom first, completely in the dark about what he wanted. I guessed Mr. Peterson wanted to thank me for helping him out the previous week and I wasn't looking forward to that; it would be embarrassing for both of us.

A female voice answered on the third ring. "Bergstrom Farm Implement Sales."

"Hi. Rick Simons here. Mr. Bergstrom wanted me to call."

"One minute, please."

A pause followed, then Mr. Bergstrom's deep voice was on the line. "Hello, Rick?"

"Yes, sir. I'm returning your call."

"Good. I wanted to see if you had a few hours a week available. I could use someone to clean up around here, polish the equipment, and so on. Twenty or thirty hours a week in all. It won't pay a lot, but I thought you might be able to use the cash."

"Well, thanks, Mr. Bergstrom, but I really don't have the time right now. Dad needs me here. Otherwise I'd say yes."

"Okay. I figured that would be your answer, but I thought I'd ask."

"Uh, Mr. Bergstrom"—I was watching Judy and Connie listlessly cleaning the windows—"I think I might know someone who'd jump at the chance."

"Who's that?"

"Can it wait until evening? I'd like to talk it over first."

"Sure, call me at home or here in the morning. No rush."

"Thanks. Good-bye."

"Bye."

I hung up the phone, an idea forming in my head. If the twins worked in town a few hours a week, they'd probably see a lot of kids their own age. They'd earn enough to buy their own Cokes, movie tickets, and clothes for the fall, and that would help the family budget a bit. Also, they'd be out of Mom's hair a little and that was bound to reduce the strain around the house. Altogether, I thought it was a damn good idea. But it would take some real negotiation to convince Mom and Dad. I picked up the phone again and dialed Mr. Peterson.

His phone must have been right at his bedside because it only rang once before a strong, cheery voice answered. I identified myself.

"Rick! I'm glad you called. I didn't have a chance to thank you last Wednesday."

"No problem. You kind of had your mind on other things."

"Ya, I was feeling pretty punky then. Anyway, thanks. You and your ma probably saved me from bleeding to death."

"It was our pleasure." That sounded dumb, but what could I say? "How's the hand?"

"Oh, pretty screwed up, I guess. My own damn fault, but I'm not the first farmer to get tangled up in one of those meat grinders." He laughed. How the hell could he be so cheerful?

"Well, I'm glad you're in good spirits anyway."

"Ain't no sense in crying about what's done. I'll make do. But, say, I'd like to pay you something. I must have made an awful mess of your car and clothes."

"No, no. We couldn't take anything. I'd expect you to do the same for me. Just get better and you can buy me a beer sometime."

"Okay. I'll look forward to that. Thank your mother for me, and the kids too. I hope I didn't scare them too much."

"No, no. Everything's fine. I'll tell them we talked."

"Okey doke. Thanks again and watch where you put your fingers!" He gave another booming laugh and rang off.

I hung up the phone and shook my head. My God, there are some tough people in this world! I went to tell Mom about him and to sound her out on my plan for the twins.

Her first reaction to the plan was, "Absolutely not!" I argued, explaining the reasons I thought would sell best and offering to drive them in and pick them up. In a few minutes the "absolutely" lost some of its starch. By suppertime I could see she was wavering. She and Dad took a stroll afterwards and on their return they called the twins and me into the kitchen for a family parley. Mom explained the idea and, as I'd predicted, the twins were full of enthusiasm. Dad had to snap, "Settle down!" before Mom could state her conditions. "Now I'm willing to let you girls do it providing you spend an equal number of hours working around here. And I mean working hard. Is it a deal?"

They quickly agreed and Dad added a final provision. "And if I get a single complaint about you two from Mr. Bergstrom, that'll be it! No more job. Got it?" They tried to look serious as they nodded, then charged off to celebrate.

Mom shook her head. "I have my doubts if they're ready for this."

Dad nodded. "Me, too, but I guess they deserve a chance to try."

I was pretty sure they could hack it, but I didn't want to bet any money on it either.

Later the twins thanked me and I called Mr. Bergstrom, who agreed to give them a try. They were to start the following Monday. I felt pretty good about it, but on Sunday evening Judy moped around and went to bed early. I asked Connie what the problem was.

"Oh, nothing. You know how Judy gets."

"Ya, but she should be happy tonight of all nights."

"She's just a little scared, that's all."

"Scared? Scared of what?"

"Oh, she just gets hyper about everything these days. Forget it."

"Is it something about Mr. Bergstrom? He's a nice guy."

"No, nothing about him." She avoided my eyes, then gave an exasperated sigh. "She's just afraid to meet some of the guys in town. They've got a nickname for her and she doesn't like it."

"Boots?"

"Ya, but it's no big deal."

"How did she get it?"

Connie was evasive. "Well, it's kind of a secret. She wouldn't want me to tell. . . . But don't get hyper about it. It'll go away, just let her alone." I was starting to get angry and she saw it and quickly put a hand on my arm. "Please, Rick. We're really grateful you got us the job. Just let Judy get used to it. I'll look out for her. Believe me, she'll be fine. Just don't get her upset right now, okay?"

I shrugged. "I guess." But I didn't like not knowing what was really going on.

From the moment she hopped off the bus, Linda was in motion. She'd never visited a farm before and she had to see and do everything. Within hours she had significantly raised Dad's aspirin intake, Mom's blood pressure, and Pam's spirits.

Linda had sprouted two inches in the last few months, much to Pam's dismay, but otherwise she was the same happy, freckled, frenetic kid I remembered. Uncle Fritz would have called her a "pearl-handled, nickel-plated pistol loaded for bear hunting," and found her impact on the farm vastly amusing. I enjoyed her almost as much as Pam did. The summer dog days had depressed spirits around the farm and Linda was a much needed, if tempestuous, blast of fresh air.

Fortunately, the girls didn't mind Tommy tagging along, although he really had to work to keep up. With Signa padding amiably behind, the three of them explored every corner of the farm; counted, caressed, and fed every cat; got in the way of what anyone else was doing; and generally had one hell of a good time.

Riding good old Arrow was, of course, the feature event. This was somewhat complicated because the twins were now working several hours a day in town, but Mom took their place supervising the riding. She did it with no great pleasure, since she was busy and no hand with horses anyway. But Linda wouldn't be here long and Mom knew how much the horse riding meant to both girls. Linda took to it with her usual energy, but no particular talent, and Pam got a big thrill out of coaching her. Arrow is about as mellow a horse as I think you could possibly find and ambled good-naturedly through his paces while Pam shouted directions to Linda, Tommy echoed her, and Mom stood worriedly watching. Signa, whose mellowness often resembles complete inertia, lay in the shade throughout these exercises, panting happily, and occasionally snapping at a bothersome fly.

Tommy moved into my room for Linda's stay, which was no great joy for me since he's a squirmy little brat when he sleeps. A couple of times I abandoned ship and went downstairs to sleep on the couch, but I really didn't mind. Pam and Linda sat up giggling and whispering half the night at first and three or four times Mom trudged tiredly up the stairs to tell them to get some sleep. But after the first two or three days, they were too tired to talk for long at night.

They really didn't get in trouble until Sunday morning when they got a fit of giggles in church. Tommy, of course, wanted to know what was funny and that added to the commotion. A couple of old ladies turned and looked disapprovingly at us. Blushing, Mom clamped a hand over Tommy's mouth and hissed a few threats at the girls. The rest of us, even Dad, were pink from trying to hold in our own laughter, but we knew better than to let out a peep. Mom might have poisoned us all.

After church Mom stung Linda and Pam pretty good and there was no horse riding for them that afternoon, but they quickly forgot about it and found other things to do.

Perhaps inevitably, the two girls' high spirits soon led to trouble with Jim. All week he'd tried to be both the sophisticated older brother, too worldly for little girl games, and the willing playmate when the games attracted him. The girls saw through his act and started to tease him unmercifully, especially about being the only kid in the family who had to go to summer school. They took to greeting his return with little rhymes, not particularly poetic, but effective nonetheless. He stood it pretty well for a couple of days, but when he got off the bus on Wednesday they had a new one and he blew.

I was coming into the house for lunch after a hot, exhausting morning of haying. Dad had driven the tractor pulling the baler and haywagon while I grabbed each fifty-pound bale coming off the baler and stacked it on the growing pile on the wagon. It took 130 bales to make a load. Back at the barn, Dad loaded the bales on the elevator to the hayloft while I stood at the top, pulling each one off and piling it with the hundreds of others. After two round trips, I was hot, itchy, sweaty, and bushed. As I came out of the barn, I was trying to calculate how many pounds I'd moved in total. The school bus pulled up and Jim got off. The girls were there to greet him in a singsong chorus:

Jimmy, Jimmy
Jimmy's home from school
Did you learn?
Did you learn?
Or are you still a fool?

As I said, not great poetry, but effective; Jim dropped his books and took off after them. They ran screeching and giggling, but I could see from his face that this was no game. I grabbed him as he went by. "Hold on, Jim."

"Let go of me!" He tried to pull away, but I held on.

"Calm down, damn it! They're just little girls."

He kicked me in the shins and started swinging with both hands. "Let me go . . ." he screamed and used every cuss word he knew.

I tried to dodge the blows, but he was wild with fury. I threw him down, planted a knee on his chest, and held both his arms. "Jim, cool down! They were just teasing you!" He writhed on the ground, cussing and threatening. I could see in his wide, blazing eyes the signs of a real tantrum. Damn it, it wasn't going to happen this time! I jerked him up and hugged him tight, my mouth next to his ear. "It's okay, Jim. Take it easy. Just forget it."

He beat my back and neck with his fists, but I kept whispering. Then he was sobbing, holding on to me. "Why are they always picking on me? Why is everybody always picking on me?"

"They're not, Jim. They really didn't mean to hurt you. They're just stupid little girls." What I feared most now was that Mom or Dad would intervene, giving Jim an audience for a full-fledged tantrum. "Come on, forget it, screw them. Let's go to town for a hamburger." I pulled him to his feet. The two girls were staring at us with wide, frightened eyes. I glared at them. "You two don't have to mention this to anyone! Just tell Mom and Dad that we went to town. And the next time you start singing one of your cute little poems, I'm going to throw you both in the horse trough and hold you under for about an hour. Got it?" They nodded. "Let's go, Jim."

We rode into town in the pickup. Jim was still sniffling, but the worst had passed. I tried to cheer him up by talking about the Carleyville Fair. Carleyville is a quiet little town most of the year, but for three days in midsummer the community turns out for what is advertised as "the biggest little fair in Wisconsin." Like scores of other farm families, we had all been looking forward to a real holiday and the fair had been the main source of supper table conversation for days now. If anyone had told me when I lived in Milwaukee that I'd be looking forward to a small town fair with such anticipation, I would have laughed. But I was. The summer had become a long grind of full days with even Sunday afternoons spent in the fields, barn, or machine shop and the prospect of a real day off, even if it was only to go to a fair, had made me as excited as the rest.

Jim responded to the subject and by the time we pulled up at the root beer stand across from Mr. Bergstrom's lot, he was talking excitedly about how he planned to spend the money he'd saved on rides, food, and games. Across the street the twins were polishing a big John Deere tractor. It was a beautiful machine with huge double tires in back and a high en-closed cab, probably equipped with stereo cassette player and radio and, even more important, air conditioner and heater. We waved and the twins waved back, clambered down, and ran across the street to us.

"Hi, are you going to buy us a Coke?" Connie asked with what I'm sure she thought was a disarming smile.

"Can't you pay your own way now? You know that farmers never have any extra money."

"Oh, please. Our purses are inside."

"That's a near excuse. Aren't you going to get fired deserting your duty?"

"Naw, he won't mind as long as we're talking to our darling brothers. Please buy us a Coke."

"Oh, all right. There's nothing I hate more than whining women." They giggled and I ordered Cokes and hamburgers from the carhop.

When the Cokes came they took theirs and with a "Thanks, sweetie," ran back across the street to the lot.

"I wish I had a job like that," Jim groused, "getting a couple bucks an hour just for shining tractors."

"Don't worry, you'll be old enough before you know it."

"How come you sound just like Mom and Dad these days?"

"Sorry. Rubs off, I guess." I turned on the radio. A Brewer game had just started and we talked about baseball as we ate the hamburgers.

Later that afternoon Jim went out for a tractor-driving lesson with Dad. Summer school had only a few days to go and Jim was holding Dad to the bargain. Jim had done well enough to stay with his class, so now he deserved a chance to drive a tractor. With the twins and Jim all learning to drive this summer, Dad looked perpetually worried. I'm sure the memory of my accident with the pickup didn't make him feel any better.

Since it takes at least two to load haybales, I was temporarily unemployed, so I started digging through the junk in the old chicken coop. The next time it rained, we planned to burn it down and I wanted to make sure nothing useful lay hidden under the jumble of old boards, rusting cans, and assorted garbage. Pam and Linda came to the door. "Rick," Pam started hesitantly, "we're sorry about this morning."

I was still angry with them and not about to let them off easy. "You two ought to know better, especially you, Pam."

She blinked back tears. "We said we were sorry."

"I heard you, but you don't have to apologize to me. Say it to him. Or better yet, be nice to him instead of teasing him all the time."

"We didn't mean to hurt him."

"The hell you didn't!" I felt my temper rising and held it down. "Now look, you know how sensitive Jim is and up to now you've had fun trying to rile him up. Now it's time you laid off." They nodded and scurried away.

I went back to searching through the junk. Maybe I'd been too hard on them, but, hell, they had to learn some manners sometime. I flipped over a square of moldy carpet and found a jumble of old tractor parts, some still in their original boxes. Well, I'll be, I thought, this was worth it after all. I bet I can find uses for a lot of these. I started gathering them up.

10

THE DAY BEFORE the fair opened, I spent the morning cutting hay with Dad and after lunch drove to town for some odds and ends we needed to fix up a couple of the outbuildings. Down from our farm, the dirt road crosses another country road a quarter mile from the railroad tracks and the highway. On the corner there's a modest ranch-style house. I'd never paid much attention to it until that day, and then it wasn't the house but the girl out front who made me slow down. She was mowing the lawn in a pair of shorts and a halter top, and even from a distance I could see she had a nice figure. She turned the mower around as I passed and on impulse I waved and she waved back.

In town I forgot half the things I'd come for. It was silly, I know, but on the way back up the highway I pulled over on the shoulder and drained about a quart and a half of water out of the radiator.

She was still mowing the yard when I slowed to a stop and got out to raise the hood. After gazing thoughtfully at the engine, I had just gotten my courage up enough to go ask for water when I heard the heavy drum of a tractor. It was Dad,

perched high on the seat of the big red International. What
lousy damn timing, I thought. He stopped the tractor and
climbed down. I could tell by the set of his jaw that he was
expecting the worst and that the memory of the pickup accident was again fresh in his mind.

"What's the problem, Rick?"

"A little low on water, Dad."

"Shouldn't be. I checked it this morning. I imagine that
damn radiator is leaking again."

"No, the radiator's fine." I drew a deep breath. "I let some
of the water out back on the highway."

Dad's quick. He looked at me with a puzzled frown and
then at the girl who had stopped mowing to watch us. "I see."
He got out his pipe and bit down on the stem to stifle a belly
laugh. He got the pipe going. "Well, I hope you get it running
again."

He sauntered back to the tractor, climbed aboard, and
dropped it in gear. I won't hear the end of this for a while, I
thought. Driving by, he winked at me and farther down the
road I saw him slap his thigh repeatedly and, under the roar of
the tractor, I knew he was howling with laughter.

I waited by the door while she filled a pail with water. She
wasn't all that pretty close-up, but she had a big smile and
beautiful brown eyes and, as I said before, I can't sell myself as
any great prize either.

"Was that your father?" She held out the plastic pail steaming with the hot water.

"Ya, that's him."

"He must have thought something was awfully funny."

"Guess so." She trailed me across the lawn to the truck and
watched as I poured the radiator full. I shrugged mentally. "I
guess he thought it was funny I drained out some of the water
so I'd have an excuse to stop and talk to you."

"Did you really?" She laughed. "That's cute." I blushed,
but her eyes were dancing and red was in her cheeks too.
"Come on, there's some lemonade in the refrigerator."

We sat on the steps talking for an hour. Her name was Lorie and she was easy to talk to. She wasn't a local girl, but had come from Des Plaines, Illinois, to live with her grandparents after her folks split up. She wasn't so smiley when she told me about that and I could tell she needed to talk about things too. But we kept it pretty light, laughing a ·lot and telling stories about the funny things we'd seen around the neighborhood.

The time flew by and when I glanced at my watch I saw that milking was just a little while away. I rose, suddenly awkward again, and choked out an invitation to the fair. She grinned and said "sure"· and we agreed on 1:00 the next afternoon.

On the way home I was happier than I could remember being in a long time, even singing a few bars in my flat baritone. It struck me I'd forgotten even to mention to her that I was only a temporary farmer with a path all laid out for college and a career in architecture. But there would be time to tell her about that later. I didn't even dread the ribbing I was sure to get back home—the cry of "How'd it go, Casanova?" from Dad or the mock cautions about upright living from Mom or the breathless questions from the twins. I could handle all that. Everything seemed bright and clear for once, and I leaned back enjoying it.

Mom, Dad, and the kids went into Carleyville around noon. Pam was slow getting ready, intentionally I think, so they left her to ride in with Lorie and me. I was ready to go well before it was time and I needed something to keep my hands busy, so I went out to the machine shop to finish the inventory of the old tractor parts I'd uncovered the week before in the tumbledown henhouse. Pam tagged along, but soon got bored and went out to see the horse. Linda had taken the bus home the previous Saturday and Pam seemed lost and lonely again.

I usually find it easy to lose myself in a job, but that day I spent more time looking out the window, idly shuffling parts, than I did really concentrating. Pam was combing the horse

and I was just about to call her to go into the house to wash up
when I saw her grab Arrow by the mane and swing up. She
knows that she isn't supposed to ride bareback or without
someone around, but I guess kids get funny impulses sometimes. She wasn't strong enough to get all the way up, so when
the horse shied Pam lost hold and fell hard and awkwardly.
There was something about the angle she landed that sent me
running.

She was sitting holding her arm and wailing. "Where are
you hurt?" I yelled.

"My arm. Oh, Ricky, my arm hurts." I tried to touch it, but
she cried out and started calling for Mom. Finally, I got her
calmed down a little, although I wasn't very calm myself, and
we walked to the truck. She was holding her arm and whimpering and I had my arm around her when she choked out,
"Oh, Ricky, I'm sorry about ruining your date. Jimmy hates
me and now you will too!" She started crying harder.

I'd forgotten about Lorie and our date altogether until then.
I'm not sure what was in my mind. I guess I was mainly
worried about Pam, but somewhere in the back of my mind I
was blaming myself for another accident, something else that
would cause Mom and Dad grief. "It's okay. I'm not going to
hate you. And Jim doesn't either. Be brave now." I helped her
into the seat of the pickup.

On the way down the road I glanced at my watch. It was
nearly 1:00. I'll call Lorie from the hospital, I thought, but as
we came close to her house, I saw her sitting on the steps. She
waved and came almost skipping across the lawn. When she
saw my face, her smile disappeared. It took her only a glance
in the truck and she knew enough. I'm not even sure she paid
any attention to my explanation as she got in. She simply
gathered Pam into her arms, slammed the door, and we were
off.

They became great friends on the way to the hospital,
twenty miles south in Mason, and I really didn't have a chance
to say much to Lorie until we were sitting in the waiting room

watching the examining room door where a big friendly nurse had led Pam. "I'm sorry" was the first thing I said.

"It's not your fault. Don't worry about it."

"It's just another thing I've done wrong." I gazed at the white ceiling with the rows of long fluorescent lights. "Just another thing I've screwed up." Everything came out then and I found myself telling this girl I hardly knew all my troubles and all my fears about the farm, the family, and the future.

She listened, watching me with big, serious brown eyes until I halted, buried in a heap of self-pity and depression.

"I think you think too much." I looked at her, startled. "Really, you worry too much. Your parents aren't going to blame you. It wasn't your fault, it was an accident."

I got up and went to the drinking fountain. The realization of how much and how personally I'd been talking came crashing down on me. "I'm sorry, I shouldn't have laid all that on you," I said as I sat back down.

"That's okay. Don't worry about it. I feel complimented." She took my hand and we sat quietly waiting for Pam to come out. Lorie's hand was firm and warm and I gained confidence from feeling it in my own hand, a hand that was coarse and rough against her smooth skin.

After a while a tall woman came over with some forms for insurance and I filled out what I knew and told her I'd have Mom call with all the other information. She was very nice and also very efficient and soon Lorie and I were again alone, but only a few minutes more passed before the examining room door opened.

The folks at the hospital have a lot of class. They had Pam smiling when she came out. The doctor, a tiny, smiling Asiatic, had his arm around her shoulder and the big nurse was carrying a teddy bear for her.

"Your sister is going to be fine. The X-rays show just a simple broken wrist." The doctor spoke with a refined English accent that sounded funny coming from his Oriental face.

"She'll be back riding her horse before you know it." He chucked her under the chin.

The nurse held out the teddy bear. "She says she's too old for stuffed toys, but maybe she'll change her mind."

"If she doesn't, I'll keep it." Lorie took the stuffed animal and held Pam's good hand. "Does it still hurt?"

Pam nodded, her eyes filling with tears again. "A little, and I'm going to miss the fair and you and Ricky aren't going to have any fun either."

I looked over at the doctor. I seemed to be the only one without anything to say. "She can go for a little while," he said, "but no rides, her stomach may be a little upset." I nodded, thanked him and the nurse, and followed Pam and Lorie out to the truck.

It was a beautiful afternoon, the hot day cooling as the sun fell and high cirrus clouds brushing the sky like wisps of cotton candy. I didn't have much to do except drive, because Lorie spent all the time asking Pam questions about school, Arrow, and just about everything else that could interest a little girl. I was just as glad, since I was busy worrying about telling Mom and Dad and imagining their reaction. I tried to take Lorie's advice about not worrying, but it was hard.

We found Mom and Dad almost immediately. The twins and Jim were off somewhere, probably with friends they'd met from school, and Mom and Dad were strolling slowly down the midway with Tommy between them, enjoying the bright sights and sounds of the carnival. Mom saw us from a distance, dropped Tommy's hand, and pushed through the crowd to us. She knelt in front of Pam, taking her gently by the shoulders. "What happened?"

"I fell off Arrow. It wasn't Ricky's fault. Don't blame him. I shouldn't have tried to get up alone. It wasn't his fault."

"No, of course not." She looked at me. "What did the doctor say?"

"It isn't bad. Just a simple break."

She looked back at Pam and then, by God, she laughed.

"Well, child, you sure picked the day for it! Come on, I'll buy you some cotton candy. You'll have to eat with one hand, though." She led her off, still laughing, her fat arm wrapping the little girl to her thick side.

Dad was beside me, holding Tommy by the hand. Tommy's faint eyes were big behind the thick glasses. "I'm sorry, Dad," I said. "I didn't know she'd try to ride Arrow." Dad cleared his throat and nodded past me. "Oh, ya. Dad, this is Lorie."

"Glad to meet you." Dad extended a hand and they shook, almost like two men, she laughing and saying, "Nice to meet you too." Dad looked at me and then back at her and chuckled. "Quite a strange introduction to the family, eh?"

Lorie was all smiles and laughter. I could tell they hit it off right away. "It's not so bad. I'm thinking of becoming a nurse and this was just practical experience." She squatted down in front of Tommy. "Hi, I'm Lorie."

"I'm Tommy. Are you the hot little number?"

"Oh, Christ," I said and turned away. Dad and Lorie exploded with laughter.

"My phrase, not Rick's, Lorie. We were just giving him the razz last night."

"It's okay; I think it's funny. Come on, Tommy, let's go help your mom and sis with that cotton candy."

We watched them go over to the stand where Pam had her face stuffed in a swirl of pink candy and Mom was fighting to keep from plucking another twirl for herself. Dad got out his pipe. "Seems like a nice girl."

"Ya, I think so, but, Dad, I'm sorry about Pam. I should have reminded her of the rules."

Dad slapped me on the shoulder. "Pam's old enough to remember the rules and she's got no one to blame but herself. I guess kids just have to make some mistakes now and then to learn. You did. We all did."

I didn't understand. "Then why were you so upset about the

pickup accident," I blurted, immediately sorry I'd brought it up.

He pursed his lips. "Well, maybe I blamed you more than I should have. I've felt guilty about that. Still, I'm not perfect either, you know. . . . But this isn't any place for a conversation. Go look after your girl friend. Do you need some money?"

"No, I've got enough. Well, thanks, Dad. I'll leave Lorie with Mom and the kids to come home for milking. I already told her I'd have to go for a while."

"Foolishness. Your mother and I will take care of it. You don't have to take everything on yourself. The twins can look after the kids. You go have fun."

The rest of the afternoon was almost better than anything I could remember. The air was filled with the fragrances of carameled apples, popcorn, and frying chicken and the sounds of kids screaming on the rides, the hawkers calling the unwary to gamble on the games and, over all, the laughter of hundreds of people, young and old, farmers and city folk, letting out their tensions in the bright carnival afternoon. But most of my attention was fixed on Lorie as she clung to my arm laughing, or went dancing away, calling me to hurry up as if there was only this single minute to enjoy the wonders of this booth or that tent. It might only have been a country fair, but she made it more exciting for me than the biggest circus.

Toward suppertime we sat in the bleachers at the edge of the fairgrounds to eat hotdogs and watch the finals of the heavyweight tractor pull. The huge machines grunted against the weight of the sled until the increasing load of the automatically shifted weights turned the grunts to roars and finally to howls as tires fought, smoked, and finally spun on the hot asphalt. Any one of them, given free run to use all its power to gain speed at the beginning, might have pulled the sled into the next county, but the pace vehicle, a tiny garden tractor, crouched under their mighty noses, moving at a maddeningly deliberate speed until the great machines kicked and shuddered from the agony of the unbearable load behind. The crowd cheered and shouted encouragement to the farmers who drove, sweating and grimacing, fighting to get the final ounce of power from their tormented machines. It was hugely more exciting than any drag or stock car race, because these weren't thoroughbred machines with professional drivers, but working machines and workingmen who, the next morning, would turn this power and skill loose in the great green fields of central Wisconsin to bring in another crop in one of the best dairy farming areas in the world. I found myself yelling and urging them on too, happy this day to be part of this beautiful, hot, green, humid land.

The last event was for women only, but it was hardly a powder puff derby. Most of the women were every bit as skillful as the men and bullied their tractors just as far. Almost the last tractor, a huge International Harvester, was driven by a big, grinning woman with her silvering hair wrapped in a bright scarf. Her husband, a lanky, balding farmer, strode along beside the tractor, signaling her to increase or decrease her pressure on the throttle. As the weight on the sled climbed, the tractor slowed and fought to keep traction. A little too much gas now and the tires would spin and the tractor slither to a stop. It had already passed the longest run by a woman driver and was bearing down on the men's record. People yelled and cheered, but the tractor was barely moving now, its nose only a few feet short of the mark as the pace tractor drew away. The husband pumped his arm up and down frantically and the woman put the throttle to the floor. The tractor howled and the crowd roared.

Lorie and I found ourselves on our feet screaming with the rest, "Go! Go! Go!" The tractor jerked forward bellowing like some mad beast, its exhaust pitch black, its tires smoking, and with a final shuddering lunge crossed the mark. We whooped and cheered. People embraced as if the home team had scored the winning touchdown with a second to go.

Laughing and a little breathless, we made our way down from the bleachers and through the crowd. "Rick!" I turned and saw Mr. Peterson a dozen feet away working his way toward us. I shook hands with him awkwardly, my good right to his good left. "How are you, Mr. Peterson?"

"Fine, fine." He grinned. "Is this your missus?"

I glanced at Lorie, who blushed and giggled. "No, we just met yesterday."

"Well, I guess that would be kinda quick." He laughed. I introduced them. "How about that beer now? Buy your girl friend one too."

Before I could think of declining, he was leading us off through the crowd in the direction of the beer tent. I tried to explain who he was to Lorie, but the noise of the crowd swallowed my words.

In the tent people were shouting orders as a half dozen men from the local Jaycees rushed about grabbing cans of beer from steel tubs filled with melting ice. The tractor pull had made a lot of people thirsty, apparently. "Leinie's okay?" Mr. Peterson asked, then ordered three before I had a chance to ask Lorie if she even liked beer.

She stood on tiptoe, leaning against me. "What is this all about?"

"I'll tell you in a minute."

"What?"

"I'll tell you in a minute," I shouted. Mr. Peterson handed two cans to us and we retreated to a quieter corner. "So, how's the hand?" I asked.

"Getting better every day. Hurts some, but I'll live."

I turned to Lorie. "I helped Mr. Peterson out after he hurt his hand a couple of weeks ago."

"Helped out! Hell, he saved my life! If him and his ma hadn't gotten me to the ambulance, I would have bled to death right on the road."

"Really?" Lorie gazed at his bandaged hand in the sling across his chest with interest.

With surprising enthusiasm Mr. Peterson explained his injury and the doctor's prognosis. Lorie nodded, asking a question here and there. "So," he concluded, "it could have been a lot worse." Lorie was about to ask another question when he yelled to a couple just entering the tent, "Sam, Millie, over here."

Sam and Millie were the husband and wife who'd combined to win the tractor pull. She waved a big trophy effortlessly in her strong hand and a number of people started clapping and yelling out congratulations. "Way to go, Millie! . . . Goddamn, here's the queen of the fair! . . . Great driving, Millie!" A wide smile split Sam's face. No man could have been prouder.

"Rick, Lorie, this is my sister Millie and her worthless husband Sam." He laughed and Sam, grinning, made as if to hit him. "This is Rick Simons and his girl. He's the one who got me to the ambulance."

To my embarrassment Millie hugged me while Sam pumped my hand. Sam said, "Well done, boy. We sure are grateful."

Millie released me and held me at arm's length. "Jack told us how wonderful you and your mom were. We are so pleased to meet you."

Others were crowding in now to congratulate Millie on her triumph, and Lorie and I were soon separated from the three of them.

"You ought to be a doctor. You certainly seem to be around when people get hurt," Lorie said.

"Maybe so. I'm sure getting lots of practice these days. My uncle died last spring and I was around then too." I was sorry I'd brought it up so I went on quickly, "Hey, let's get out of here, I can hardly breathe."

"Okay."

We waved to Mr. Peterson, who waved back and shouted, "Thanks again, Rick. Nice to meet you, Lorie." Then we struggled through the mob of beer buyers to the door.

"I just can't understand how he can be so cheerful," I said when we got out of the crush.

She frowned. "I don't know, some people are just that way, I guess. There was a girl in my class who'd spent most of her life in a wheelchair, but she was the nicest and most cheerful kid I knew. I wouldn't have been."

"Me neither. Let's talk about something else. What do you want to do? It'll be a couple of hours before the grandstand show."

"I want to dance. I hear a polka band."

I hesitated. "Well, I'm not much good at that sort of thing."

"Then I'll have to teach you." She laughed.

I was reluctant, but she dragged me into a big tent where the band was playing and attempted to make my big feet find the rhythm. I was clumsy and ill at ease at first, but with her warm arms leading me and her face turned up smiling into mine, my awkwardness soon disappeared.

After a half dozen numbers we stumbled panting and laughing into the fresh air. In the excitement of the moment I kissed her and she kissed back, then pushed away, and we strolled down the midway. We bought sodas and sat at a table to rest. The evening air was cool after the exertion of dancing. After a couple of minutes I said, "You know, I uh . . . hope you didn't think I kissed you because I thought, uh . . ."

"That I was a hot little number?" She kicked me in the shins with the side of her foot. "Jeez, I've never known anybody who worried as much as you do. Relax." She kissed me quick. "And I'm not a hot little number, whatever your father thinks."

I was saved from saying anything else stupid by the arrival of the twins. I'd figured they would find us eventually, but I was surprised that Connie had a guy with her. I recognized him as the kid from the Pontiac on the day of the aborted picnic. He wasn't bad-looking and I could tell that Judy, who trailed a little behind, was green with envy. I introduced Lorie, and Connie introduced Phil.

We sat down around the table and made small talk, but Judy sat a little apart and didn't say anything.

"I thought the kids were supposed to be with you," I said to Judy, not quizzing her, just trying to get her involved.

"Mom decided they should rest awhile, so she took them home when she and Dad went to do the milking." She paused and glanced at Connie and Phil. "But I'll probably get saddled with them when they get back." Her tone was bitter. I felt sorry for her, but with Lorie beside me, I didn't have time to talk with Judy at length.

A half dozen high school guys went by. "Hiya, Phil. Hiya, Connie. How's it going, Boots?" There was laughter. "Go get 'em, Boots!"

That name again. "What's the Boots stuff about, Judy?"

"Nothin'. Just a nickname." She looked at her watch and stood up quickly. "I gotta go and meet Mom and Dad. See you later." She hurried away.

I thought of asking Connie again why they called Judy Boots, but the crowd was beginning to filter toward the grandstand and I turned to Lorie. "Shall we go and get good seats?"

"Sure. Nice meeting you guys. Have a good time."

The grandstand was really only the bleachers, not exactly Milwaukee County Stadium, and the show wasn't much either, but we enjoyed it anyway. A couple of comedians started things off. Their jokes were pretty corny, but we laughed anyway. They were followed by a juggler, a knife thrower, and a nut who walked the length of the stage on forty-foot stilts. The main attraction was a country singing group I'd never heard of, but they weren't half bad. The air was getting chilly now and Lorie snuggled close to me as the group sang.

"Do you like country music?" I asked.

"It's okay every now and then, as long as they're not singing those stupid songs about divorce and cheating and being drunk and lonely. I like cheerful music, not the sad stuff."

"Me too."

"It wouldn't be so bad if my mom and dad didn't both drink too much. And now that they've split up, everyone is kind of sad and lonely. I don't have to be reminded of it all the time."

"I see what you mean. Well, let's forget about it now."

The singing ended a few minutes later and the floodlights came up. Behind the stage, a row of a dozen junked cars stood side by side with a big ramp at one end of the row. The finale was coming up and the crowd buzzed excitedly as the master of ceremonies thanked the singers once again and announced loudly, "Now, ladies and gentlemen, let's have a round of applause for the junkyard daredevil, Red Hamilton. Give him a big hand, folks."

A young guy in a racer's uniform with a helmet under his arm came out on stage. "Hey, I know him," I said.

"You do?"

"Ya, he works at the junkyard up here. I got some parts from him earlier this summer."

"Well, Red," the master of ceremonies said, "how far do you think you'll make it tonight?"

"Well, the conditions look pretty good. There's only a little dew on the grass, so I'd say I'll get out to the ninth or tenth car."

"Any chance you'll clear all of them?"

"Oh, there's always a chance."

"Red, tell me, how fast will you be going when you leave the ramp?"

"Between forty-five and fifty miles an hour."

They talked for a few more minutes about how long he'd been doing this and how many jumps he'd made, and so forth. I said to Lorie, "Gee, he looked perfectly normal when I met him. I didn't think he was insane."

She giggled and snuggled closer. It was getting pretty cool now.

Finally, the master of ceremonies wished Red good luck and the crowd sent him off with another round of applause. The M.C. filled the next couple of minutes by asking the crowd questions: "Well, did you enjoy tonight's show?" The crowd shouted "Yes." "Shall we do it again next year?" And so on.

There was the roar of a car without a muffler behind the grandstand and a few seconds later Red drove a delapidated Chevy onto the infield. He circled the field once, then swung into line with the ramp. He paused, gunned the motor, and charged. The crowd gasped as the car flew off the ramp, sailed through the air, and landed with a tremendous crash on the tenth car.

Men went running to the car and the M.C. worried dramatically, "I hope he's all right, folks. Is he? Yes, he is!" Red, helped from the wreckage, stood on the roof of a car waving both arms in victory. "A big hand, folks, for the junkyard daredevil, Red Hamilton!" The crowd cheered. "Now be sure, folks, to stick around for the fireworks. We have the biggest show ever in central Wisconsin. And there they go." Three skyrockets exploded above as the floodlights went dark.

Like the show, the fireworks were pretty modest. I was, after all, a big-city boy and had seen lots better. Still, with my arm around Lorie and her hand on my knee, I never enjoyed anything more.

I was glowing like the embers of a fallen skyrocket when we got back to her place. Sitting on the step we talked until past midnight when her grandmother turned on the porch light. "Oops," Lorie said, "they're of the old school. I better go in now." I made a motion to kiss her, but she kept me away. "No, not now. Save it for another time."

She winked and was gone so fast I barely had time to ask, "When can I see you again?"

"Come for dinner tomorrow night." And she was gone.

11

LORIE FILLED MOST of my thoughts as Dad and I worked through the last of July and into August, cutting the second crop of hay and getting ready for the big push at the end of the month when the third crop of hay and the oats would have to be brought in.

I saw Lorie almost every night. When I could get away for the full evening, we'd go dancing or to a movie. Often, however, I could only take a short time off because of the work, and then we'd stroll in the fields and talk. Probably Bill and my other city friends would laugh if I told them, but these quiet evenings were the best. We both needed someone to confide in and, as we walked on those summer evenings, we talked about everything that was important to us—our families and their troubles, our own frustrations and disappointments, our plans and dreams for the future.

Lorie's parents had separated early in July and she had come up to stay with her grandparents a week or so later. She still hoped there would be a reconciliation, but the prospects didn't sound good. One evening she summed it up: "I don't know why they can't get along. When they get angry they drink, and when they drink, they get angrier. And then a lot of things get brought up—things from years and years ago, sometimes from even before I was born. It seems so silly, but it's like neither one of them can admit that he or she was ever wrong or forgive the other for not always being perfect. I mean, I'm sure they love each other. Half the time they're like newlyweds, but once they get fighting, it goes on for days. In the last six or eight months it's been constant. I think they separated out of exhaustion."

Another time, when I complained about all the bills my folks had to pay, she nodded and said, "I know. It never seemed like there was enough money around our house either. Four years ago, another mechanic and my dad borrowed a lot of money and bought out the owner of the garage. Six months later, my dad's partner had a heart attack and died. Dad couldn't make the payments by himself, so he had to sell out. In the end, he lost both his job and most of his money. Mom just can't forget it, even though it wasn't really his fault. Every time we can't afford something, she brings it up. Then Dad gets mad and"—she shrugged—"they're off again."

Most of the time she didn't like to talk about her family problems, but I could tell it had been a rough spring for her, probably worse than mine. Still, she was naturally cheerful and refused to let her problems get her down. That was a trait I envied.

I ate about twice a week at her grandparents' and Lorie ate at our house about as often. Her grandparents made me feel immediately welcome in their home, although I was a little taken aback when Mrs. Amundsen surveyed me for the first time and said, "John, just look at the boy! He's practically starving. We'll have to get some meat on his bones."

I blushed and Mr. Amundsen patted his big belly. "And she can do it too. Look what she's done for me!"

"And me too," Lorie added ruefully.

I enjoyed them a lot. Mr. Amundsen had a thousand jokes

and stories and his wife was a fabulous cook, even better than Mom.

Around our house, Lorie was quickly popular with everyone. The first night she ate at our house, dessert was barely over when Lorie hopped up and started clearing away the dishes. Mom objected, but Lorie just laughed and said, "I don't mind." About the third time she came for dinner, she insisted that Mom shouldn't have to worry about cleaning up at all. "Just enjoy your coffee. The girls and I can handle it." And they did. I don't think I've ever seen the twins work so fast or efficiently.

The other kids liked her a lot too. Pam almost worshiped her. They all wanted a share of Lorie's attention and sometimes I'd feel a twinge of jealousy. But she'd take it away quickly by looking my way and giving me a smile and a wink, as if to say, *They're just kids. Be patient, I'll get away in a few minutes.*

Lorie was someone new on the family scene, and she distracted us from our petty conflicts. When she came to dinner, the usual bickering ceased. Everyone seemed more cheerful when she was around. I certainly knew I was. I'd had quite a few casual relationships before and even a couple of girls I could safely call real girl friends for a few months, but Lorie was different. I'd never had a girl I could talk to so naturally.

Of course, talk was far from my only interest. Lorie was willing to have a physical relationship, but only to a point. Then she'd say, "I'm not ready for that, yet, Rick." Or, "Let's wait awhile. Okay?" But it was never a putdown. She was warm and tender and she liked being close to me and, even if I would have liked some things to move a little faster, her companionship was enough.

Not that I'd given up. But, after all, I told myself, you haven't known her very long. Besides, would you really want her to be like Peggy Mathews, ready and willing anytime?

The week of the fair in Carleyville had been kind of a

turning point for all of us it seemed, and for a while everything was more cheerful around the farm. For the first time since we'd moved from the city, Jim was paying real attention to Pam. He acted as if the cast on her arm made her a complete cripple. He guarded her, helped her with everything, constantly inquired how she felt. And although she wasn't nearly as bothered by the cast as Jim made out, she knew better than to reject his attention. They were buddies again, much to her joy. And when Jim was too busy with chores or Onions to lavish much attention on Pam, Tommy was quick to emulate his brother. To be his nursemaid's nursemaid was lots of fun. Of course, Mom had forbidden her to ride Arrow until her arm was healed, but having two doting brothers wasn't a bad trade.

Phil started showing up frequently to take Connie out. He was a tall, gawky, shy kid and didn't linger any longer than he had to. I talked with him a couple of times and liked him. Mom and Dad inspected him, decided he was okay, and let Connie go out, although she had to be in early. Judy, of course, would have given anything to trade places with Connie. Phil might not be Mr. Universe, but he was a hell of a lot better than nothing.

Phil had a part-time job at the feed mill in town and Connie soon arranged the twins' schedule at Bergstrom's so they could ride in with Phil in the morning. That was fine with me, because it spared a half hour for my work. More work in the morning, more time for Lorie in the evening. Judy didn't like it at all, and after a few days asked me to start giving her a ride again.

"Why? What's wrong with riding with Phil and Connie? Isn't he a safe driver?"

"He's fine when he keeps his mind on the road," she said sourly.

"Well, if he doesn't, just tell him to."

"How am I supposed to tell them anything?! They spend all

196

their time cooing and making eyes at each other. I just can't
stand it! I might as well not even exist!"

"Oh, come on. You're being silly. What's a fifteen-minute
ride? Ignore them."

"I can't ignore them! And I won't ride with them anymore!"

"Then I guess you're going to have to walk. I'm not going to
waste my time giving you a ride just because you're jealous of
Connie."

"I'm not jealous!" Judy screamed and fled.

Way to go, dumb-ass, I told myself. Real sympathetic! Oh,
well, I'll talk to her later.

But I didn't. That evening I went to a show with Lorie and
by the time Judy rode off to work with Connie and Phil the
next morning, I didn't think it was worth the bother. I might
have prevented a lot of grief later if I'd talked to Judy, but I
didn't.

Mom had about as much tact as I did. One night shortly
after Phil and Connie left, she looked at Judy's woebegone face
and said, "For heaven's sake, Judy, why don't you have Connie and Phil get you a date?" Judy gave her a mortified look
and ran from the room. Mom let out an exasperated sigh and
went back to putting away the last few supper dishes. Dad
looked at me, eyebrows raised, finished his coffee, and went
out to the barn. Girl and boy troubles—best not to get involved.

Mom's suggestion had seemed reasonable enough to me,
but my guess was that Judy didn't want a date so badly that she
was willing to ask Connie's help. Better to be lonely than to
admit to your twin sister that you couldn't get a boy of your
own. Although, come to think of it, that was pretty damn
obvious! And, of course, I had Lorie, and it probably irked
Judy to see us together too. Maybe Judy's luck would change
soon. I hoped so. Anyway, Mom would probably talk to her
later. Like Dad, I was going to stay out of this one.

The third time I ate at Lorie's, the meal started with the

usual good cheer, but a few minutes later the phone rang. Mrs. Amundsen went into the living room to answer it and didn't return for ten minutes. When she came back, her expression was worried. "Lorie, your mother wants to talk to you." Lorie got up quickly and left the room. Mrs. Amundsen sat and stared at her uneaten meal and then looked up at her husband. "Susan says it's all over. She's filing for divorce."

"Damn." Mr. Amundsen shook his head and said "damn" several more times very softly. Neither of them ate much more, just sat toying with their food.

"Maybe I'd better go," I said.

"No, Rick." Mrs. Amundsen patted my hand. "Go ahead and finish your dinner."

"This will be hard on Lorie," Mr. Amundsen said.

She nodded. "I just don't understand; they always seemed so happy."

"Well, let's not spoil Rick's dinner." Mr. Amundsen tried to sound jolly. "So I imagine you and your dad are real busy this time of year?"

"Ya, there's a lot to be done."

"I'll bet. Never wanted to be a farmer myself. Too damn much work."

We continued trying to make a conversation until Lorie came back in. She attempted a smile, but tears glistened in her eyes. She picked at her food. No one spoke for the rest of the meal.

A while later we walked across the field behind her grandparents' toward the woodlot on the far side. I had my arm around her. Tonight she seemed smaller, almost fragile. I wanted to help, but I couldn't think of much to say. After a few minutes I tried anyway. "I guess the news must be pretty bad, huh? Your grandmother said your mom was going to file for a divorce."

"Ya, it's really the pits. I thought they could work it out somehow, but Mom said she's fed up."

"Why now?"

"They had another session with the marriage counselor to-day and it just turned into another fight. Dad said he wouldn't go to any more sessions because the counselor always sided with Mom. Mom said that wasn't so and if Dad stopped com-ing she'd file for divorce. Dad said fine, because he wasn't spending any more time or money on crap." Lorie paused for a long minute. "So I guess that's it. They're both too stubborn to back down, so now there'll just have to be a divorce." She was almost crying and I stopped and put both arms around her. She leaned against my chest.

"I'm sorry," I said gently. "Some things you've just got to accept. At least they stayed together until you got through high school."

She pushed away and glared at me. "You've always got an answer for everything, don't you?"

"I was just trying to help." I stood there, surprised, looking into her hot, tear-filled eyes. "What did I say?"

"You make it sound like all I care about is myself. I want them to be together for them, not for me. I want them to be together because, despite everything, I know they still love each other."

"Well, I'm sorry. I didn't mean to make you mad."

"Then just keep your friendly advice to yourself." She started crying and stalked back to the house. I tried to apolo-gize a couple more times, but she just shook her head angrily and made no reply.

That night I lay awake for a long time trying to figure it out. I mean, I'd just tried to console her. Sure, she had a right to be on edge, but I didn't understand what had made her so mad. Maybe I had sounded patronizing by telling her that some things just happened and all you could do was accept them. But, hell, what was I supposed to say?

I didn't see her again until late the next afternoon. We both apologized half-heartedly, but several days passed before we really got beyond that. I continued to be very careful when I said anything about her parents and she didn't seem inclined to talk about them much either.

The big trouble started in the middle of a Thursday afternoon. The twins were at work and Jim and I had the place to ourselves, since Mom, Dad, Pam, and Tommy had left early for an appointment with an eye specialist at the university hospital in Minneapolis and wouldn't be back until the next evening. Jim and I were cutting some boards in the backyard to reframe a rotten window in the machine shop. When the phone rang, I said, "I'll get it," and trotted to the empty house.

It was Connie. "Rick, have you seen Judy?"

"No, isn't she at work with you?"

"No, she went downtown at lunchtime and didn't come back. Phil and I were eating at the root beer stand and didn't go with her. I thought maybe she'd gotten sick and you'd come in to pick her up."

"I don't think she called, but let me check with Jim." Jim didn't know anything about a call. Why would Judy skip work? I wondered as I returned to the phone. "No, she hasn't called. Was she okay at noon?"

"Oh, ya, she was fine."

I thought I detected a little hesitation in Connie's reply. "There was someting wrong, wasn't there?"

"Well, I'm not sure. She was kind of upset after talking to a couple of guys this morning, but I didn't think it was very serious."

"What did they say?"

"Oh, that old crap about Boots came up, that's all."

"What does that mean, anyway?"

"Rick, I gotta go now."

"I really think you ought to tell me what's going on with this nickname thing."

"I will sometime, but I've really got to get back to work now."

"Well, okay. . . ." I hesitated. I didn't want to get Connie in trouble with Mr. Bergstrom. Still, I had an uneasy feeling in the pit of my stomach. It wasn't at all like Judy to miss work. Schedules had always been almost absurdly important to her. In the mornings she was always the one who worried about being late for work or the school bus. If anything didn't go according to plan around the house or barn, Judy would get upset. So why was she missing work without explanation? "Well, give me a call when she shows up."

"Okay. Bye."

I hung up the phone. It's probably nothing, I told myself. Judy probably forgot to tell Connie about some errand. Maybe she's getting her hair cut or something. I went back outside to finish cutting the boards.

But it continued to bother me and when Connie hadn't called in an hour, I went back inside and dialed Bergstrom's. When Connie came on the line, I asked, "Has she shown up yet?"

"No. . . . Rick, I'm kind of worried."

"Me too. . . . Look, I'm coming in. Ask Mr. Bergstrom to let you off early."

"Okay."

I hurried for the truck. Something deep inside me kept saying that this was serious—very serious. Of course, Jim wanted to come into town with me, but I told him someone had to stick around in case of phone calls. As I got the pickup started, Lorie rode into the yard on her bicycle and I asked her to come with me. On the way, I told her what I knew and she creased her brow. "You know, I've heard her called Boots a couple of times too. What do you suppose it means?"

"I don't know, but I wish I'd taken the time to find out."

"Well, I don't think you should be too worried about her now. She probably just had something to do and forgot to tell Connie."

"I hope you're right."

Connie was waiting out in front of Bergstrom's. She saw us coming and came to the curb. "Have you seen her?" she asked.

"No, how about you?" She shook her head. "What's this Boots stuff, Connie?"

"It's just a nickname, that's all."

"That's what you always say. Come on, tell us the truth." She shrugged and looked at her feet. "Damn it, Connie, tell us! We don't have time for stalling!"

"Well, I promised I wouldn't. Judy didn't want anyone in the family to know. . . ." She sighed. "Well, it all started last spring. We came out of school a little late and there were some guys on the sidewalk talking. Curt Bingham had his dog with him. Duke is this great big German shepherd, but he's real friendly, and since we didn't know many boys back then, Judy starts petting him so we have an excuse to talk to the guys." Connie looked down to hide a smile. "And, well, Duke kind of gets carried away. He breaks away from Curt and jumps up on Judy and she loses her balance and falls into one of those big snow banks that were still around. Duke thinks she wants to play and he's all over her, licking her face and smelling her crotch and all the time poor Judy's fighting to get him off her." Connie had to pause again to keep from smiling.

I glared at her. "I'm sorry, Rick, but it really was kind of funny. Judy was yelling, 'Get him off me!' and flailing around in the snow with her skirt hiked way up and Duke still thinks it's all just a big game and keeps pushing her back down. Curt tries to help, but he can't get hold of Duke's collar. And Duke's getting more excited all the time. I mean, you know, he's getting kind of aroused. And then, well, he starts humping Judy's leg!"

Connie started laughing. I know now that she was laughing because she hurt so much for Judy and it was either that or start crying, but at the time it made me angry.

"I don't think you ought to laugh, Connie!"

"I know I shouldn't!" she almost sobbed. "God, it was so embarrassing for her! But if you'd only seen it, Rick. Poor Judy's trying to kick the dog away and Curt's trying to get a hold on Duke's collar and somewhere in the middle of everything, Judy's boot comes off. And Duke grabs it and runs away with it! Three or four of the guys take off after him, but Duke thinks they want to play keep-away and starts dodging them. I help Judy up and she's dancing around on one foot yelling about how it's one of her best boots. Whenever the guys stop for a minute, Duke drops the boot and waits for someone to try and grab it. And Judy keeps hopping around yelling, 'Get it! Get it!' But when anyone tries Duke just snaps it up again and takes off. It must've gone on for ten minutes.

"Finally, all the guys are pretty beat, so Curt says, 'Let him go. He'll get tired of it.' So we wait. Almost everybody except Judy, who's about to cry, is laughing and making jokes. Duke stands there grinning at us and wagging his tail. When he finally sees no one is going to play anymore, he starts sniffing the boot again." Connie laughed, but now I could see the memory really hurt her. "And then he lifted his leg and peed all over it! Oh, God, it was awful, Rick! But everyone just had to laugh. What else could they do?"

I looked over at Lorie. She had her face in her hands and her cheeks were red from trying not to giggle. "Knock it off!" I snapped. She straightened, wiping tears from her eyes, and tried to regain her composure. I turned back to Connie. "Okay, what happened then?"

"I went and got the boot. Duke had lost interest in it, I guess, and let me have it. I wiped it off as well as I could and helped Judy get it back on. Most of the kids are trying to be decent about it and not laugh anymore, but Mike Benson won't leave it alone. He's a real shit—always making fun of people who are fat or retarded or in trouble. He hadn't helped chase Duke at all, but just stood there laughing with a couple of his friends. He's kind of the leader of this little group of kids who aren't much good at anything, and they can be real mean when Mike gets them going. Anyway, while I'm helping Judy on with her boot, Mike says real loud, 'Looks like Dukie's got a real hard-on for Judy Simons. Wants to screw her or her boots. Maybe both.' Curt says, 'Shut up, Mike,' and most of the kids think that's a rotten thing to say, but Mike and his little gang just keep laughing and making more jokes about Duke wanting to screw Judy."

She paused. She wasn't smiling anymore. I turned to Lorie. "Still think this is something to laugh about?" I asked sarcastically. She shook her head and put her hand on my arm. I turned back to Connie. "Go on."

"Well, the story got around over the next couple of days and that was pretty hard on Judy. And, well . . ." She shrugged. "Somebody, probably Mike, got the bright idea of calling her Boots. Every time he and some of his bunch saw her in the halls they'd yell, 'Hey, Boots, you and Duke getting it on?' Or some shit like that. And they started barking at her too. The name caught on and by now I don't think a lot of kids know her by anything except Boots."

"Where does this Benson shithead live? I'm going to redesign his face!"

"I heard he quit school and went into the army."

"Well, by God, the next time he's home, I'm going to look him up and . . ."

"Talking like that isn't going to help now," Lorie put in. "What happened today?"

"Well, I'm not really sure exactly. This morning we were out polishing a tractor and some kids drove by and there was a bark or two, but that's not too unusual. Then later when I was inside, I looked out and saw Judy talking to Charlie O'Brien. He had his cousin with him, Brad somebody. Brad just moved to town and he's a real hunk. But Charlie's kind of a jerk, and I think he must have told Brad about last spring, because they both started laughing like hell and I could see Judy was real embarrassed. She spent about half an hour in the bathroom and I was going to talk to her when she came out, but Phil came by and we went to lunch. We saw Judy walk downtown, but that's the last I saw of her."

"Did she say anything to Mr. Bergstrom or anybody else?" I asked. Connie shook her head.

I sat there fuming. Lorie said quietly, "Well, let's start looking. She's probably just moping around somewhere."

We couldn't find her. The three of us checked every store in
town and talked to anyone who might have seen her. Nothing.
We called her friends and even a couple of her teachers. No
one had seen her.

It was nearly 5:00 when we came out of the grocery store. A
young guy coming in called out, "Hi, Connie, where's
Boots?"

I felt the rage boil up in me. I spun to face him, aware that
my hands were clenched. "I'm Judy's brother. You got a cute
nickname for me too? Or maybe you'd like to think one up
right now!"

The kid's smile disappeared. "Hey, I didn't mean anything,
man."

"Then what's this Boots shit?!" Without thinking, I gave
him a hard push.

"Rick, for God's sake!" Lorie cried.

The kid held up his hands, palms out. "Jeez, be cool man! I
got no fight with you."

"Well, you're damn close to having one! I feel like hitting
somebody this afternoon and it might as well be you!"

Connie pushed between us and I felt Lorie trying to drag me
back. "I'm sorry, Jeff," Connie said. "It's just that Judy was
upset by something today, you know, the Boots thing, and
now we can't find her."

He looked uncertain. "Well, hell, I didn't start it."

I tried to pull away from the two girls, but they held on.
Connie said, "I know, Jeff. It's okay. We'll see you later. Rick,
please, let's get out of here!"

I let them drag me along, but not before I snarled at the kid,
"Tell your buddies to back off or I'm going to start breaking
some heads!"

I was too mad to talk on the ride home. Connie was crying.
Lorie rode between us, looking straight ahead and saying nothing.

There were no messages waiting at home. After the hours alone, Jim was beside himself with curiosity. I told him as much as I thought he needed to know and we got about the milking. Connie and Lorie made supper and we ate in near silence. Phil came by around 7:30 and Connie went out to talk to him. When she came back in, she said, "Rick, we're going to drive around and see if we can find her."

"What's he going to do? Howl and see if he gets an answer?" Lorie said, "Oh, Rick."

Connie reddened. "Don't start in on Phil, Rick! He never had anything to do with it. He's not that kind of guy. He's worried and he wants to help."

"All right, I'm sorry. Call if you find out anything. Lorie and I will start in a few minutes. Jim will be here." Jim started to protest, but, holding my temper, I explained. "Look, Jim, somebody's got to stay here. It's a big responsibility. If Judy calls and she's still upset, you'll have to calm her down. Just tell her to wait wherever she is and we'll come pick her up. We'll call in every half hour or so. Okay?"

"I guess if you put it that way," he said without enthusiasm.

So we looked and looked. Nothing. It started to rain hard, a real soaker. I hoped that Judy wasn't outside somewhere. About 9:30 we stopped back at the farm, running from the pickup to the house. Connie had called twice, but had no news. Things have gone far enough, I decided, and called the sheriff's department. They took the information, asked some questions, and said they'd keep an eye out for her. Lorie and I went back out into the storm.

We drove along the same roads again, always hoping we'd see a sad and bedraggled Judy trudging home through the rain. But we didn't. Between Phil and Connie and the two of us, we must have hit every place still open in town a dozen times. Nothing. About 10:30 we stopped at the all-night truckstop again and found Phil and Connie talking to three guys. I recognized the kid I'd almost punched that afternoon. He looked at me a little fearfully. Just give me an excuse, I thought.

Connie turned. "Rick, Lorie, this is Jeff Waters and . . ." She introduced the other two guys. "They're going to go up to Carleyville and check around for Judy."

I looked hard at them, caught between wanting to be angry and knowing I ought to be appreciative. "Ya, okay," I mumbled. It didn't sound very gracious.

The other two guys said good-bye and turned for the door, but Jeff hesitated, then uncertainly extended a hand. "Hey, I'm sorry, Rick. I, ah, just never thought anything about calling her Boots. I'd forgotten even where the name came from."

I nodded and took his hand. "Ya, okay. I'm sorry about this afternoon. I was kind of hot."

"I understand. We'll do what we can."

"Thanks."

He left and I called Jim. No news. Then the four of us discussed what to do next. I was beginning to like Phil quite a lot. He didn't say much, but he seemed genuinely concerned and completely willing to spend the whole night looking for Judy.

At 11:00 Lorie and I headed back for the farm. It was time to call Mom and Dad. I hadn't wanted to upset them since there was nothing they could do from Minneapolis, but I couldn't wait any longer. Jim was at the door waving when we pulled up. "He must have heard something," Lorie said. We ran through the rain.

"Judy just called. She says she's okay," Jim hollered. "She sounded real happy to me," he added as we got under the cover of the porch.

"Where is she?" I asked, stripping off my dripping coat.

"She didn't say, but she said not to worry and that she's staying with a friend tonight."

"Who? We called all her friends."

"She didn't say, but she was real giggly and happy."

"Well, why didn't you ask her?!"

"I tried to, but she hung up."

"Where was she calling from?"

"She didn't say that either, but there was a lot of noise. Music and stuff. I could hardly hear her."

"Well, if she isn't the stupidest, the most inconsiderate . . ."

"Calm down, Rick," Lorie said. "She's safe, that's what counts." She brushed back a strand of wet hair. Phil's car swung into the driveway. "I'm tired. Let's call the sheriff and then you can take me home. Connie can call her friends with the news if she thinks she should."

I was still pretty damned upset, but Lorie was right, at least Judy was safe. But wait until I got my hands on her. . . .

I kissed Lorie good night on her grandparents' porch. Her mouth was cold. "What's the matter?" I said.

She stared at me a long moment. "You know, a couple of times today I didn't like you very much. I didn't realize you had such a temper."

"Well, for Christ's sake," I muttered.

"Oh, I know you were upset, but you didn't have to snap at me when I started laughing while Connie was telling about that dog and Judy. Rick, it was funny. I feel just as sorry for Judy as you do, but sometimes people want to laugh because it hurts too much to do anything else. You must know that."

"Ya, I guess you're right," I said grudgingly. "I'm sorry."

"Well, I believe you and I could have overlooked that, but when you tried to pick a fight with that Waters kid . . . well, I don't know. It just didn't prove anything. It didn't help Judy at all."

"Anything else?" I asked sarcastically.

"Well, as a matter of fact there is! What was the point of saying that bit about Phil and howling? I was really ashamed of you then."

All the anger and frustration I'd felt since the middle of the afternoon was bubbling up in me again. Who the hell did she think she was? But she stopped me from lashing out at her by putting a finger on my lips. "Don't say anything now. Don't make me regret what I feel for you most of the time. Just think about what I said. Good night." She took her finger away and kissed me quickly. "I love you." She turned and went in.

On the ride home my brain wasn't functioning worth a damn. What was I supposed to make of all that?! My girl, the only girl I'd ever really felt a lot for, had just informed me that I'd acted like a jerk half the day, then finished by telling me she loved me. It was too damned complicated!

Phil and Connie were sitting on the couch. Jim had apparently gone to bed. I rustled around in the refrigerator, found a can of beer, and went to sit down across from them.

"Rick," Connie said, "Phil and I have been talking about this Boots thing. We can talk to some of the kids and it'll do some good. I don't think Jeff Waters will call her Boots anymore, but . . . well, some of the kids are just going to keep on doing it."

"Why the hell didn't anybody think of this before?" I growled and took a swig of beer. Connie started to say something, but I cut her off. "I mean, of all the stupid crap to let happen. Jesus! Didn't anyone ever bother to think about how it made her feel? I just can't believe it!"

Phil raised his thin face. His voice was soft and steady. "A lot of us never called her anything but Judy, you know. You can't blame everybody. And most of the other kids probably didn't know what it meant. Maybe it's not my business, but I think you're making too big a deal of this thing."

I was about ready to rip him up one side and down the other, but his deep, calm eyes stopped me. I drank some more beer and tried to get my thoughts steadied. "Ya, maybe. . . . Hey, look, I'm sorry, but I just can't think anymore right now. I'm going to bed. You guys talk it over." I got up.

A few minutes after I got in bed, I heard Phil's car leave and Connie come upstairs. I lay there wishing I knew exactly where Judy was, but I couldn't worry for long before exhaustion made me sleep.

The rain let up a little in the night, but by morning it was coming down hard again. Judy still wasn't home when we finished the milking. The phone rang and I picked up the barn extension. It was Lorie. "Rick, Judy just called me. She's in Hawthorne and she wants us to pick her up. But don't bring Connie or Jim."

"What the hell is she doing in Hawthorne? That's fifty miles!"

"I don't know. Just tell the others she's okay and come pick me up."

"Well, why did she call you instead of us?"

Lorie's voice was irritable. "I don't know that either. All I know is that she wants just you and me to pick her up. It's very important to her. Now tell Connie and Jim she's okay and get over here."

"Hey, I don't understand quite what's going on, but . . ."

"Rick, damn it!"

"Okay, okay, I'll be over in a minute."

I ran to tell Connie I was going to pick up Judy and avoided her questions. As I headed for the pickup, Jim intercepted me. "Where are you going?"

"I don't have time to talk."

"You found out something. Is she okay?"

"Jim, I can't talk now. Look after the place." I jumped in, started the truck, and rattled off in the rain.

Judy was waiting at the counter in the drugstore. Her hair hung wet and straggly down her plump, pimply cheeks. I felt sorry for her. She was truly very plain, to put it politely. What lousy luck for a girl! We sat down across the booth from her. "How you doing?" I asked, trying to keep my voice natural.

She shrugged. "Okay. How's everybody else?"

"Hanging in there." She sat there, not meeting our eyes, slowly stirring the ice in her Coke. "Do you want to go home now?" I asked.

She shrugged again. "I guess."

We rode most of the distance from Hawthorne home in silence. A couple of times I tried to question Judy, but she didn't answer. Finally, when we were about fifteen miles from home, she said, "I don't want to go home like this. Can I take a shower at your place, Lorie?"

"Sure."

"I think we ought to go right home, Judy. Everybody's been worried long enough."

Judy started crying then, her face all screwed up and uncontrollable sobs coming through her gritted teeth. "Let her clean up a little, Rick," Lorie said. "It won't take long."

"She can clean up at home," I snapped. I was boiling. What the hell right did Lorie have butting in—and what the hell had Judy thought she was doing running off in the first place! "I mean, Christ, she won't even tell us where she's been. We've been up half the night looking for her and worried half to death and she wants to stop off for a shower, for God's sake! Where the hell have you been anyway, Judy?" Judy collapsed sobbing in Lorie's lap. Lorie held her tight. I said, "Shit," and pressed down on the accelerator.

"I was with a guy."

She said it so softly I wasn't sure I'd heard her right. "You were what?"

"With a guy!" she yelled, and sobbed the harder.

With a guy! Somehow that possibility had never occurred to me. I slowed the pickup, pulled over on the shoulder, and stopped. The truck was silent except for Judy's crying. "Who?" I finally asked.

"His name was Bob and he gave me a ride and bought me dinner and he was nice to me." She had trouble getting the words out between sobs. "And he didn't call me Boots or yell woof, woof at me . . . so I gave him what he wanted!"

"Oh, Jesus," I said, half to myself, "Mom is gonna die." Judy let out a wail.

"Oh, for God's sake, Rick! Nobody has to know!" Lorie turned hard, burning eyes on me.

"You stay out of this!"

"What's the matter, Mr. Perfect? Haven't you ever done anything you were ashamed of? Look at her. Don't you think she feels bad enough?"

"This isn't your family."

"Well, she called me because she thought she could trust me! And I called you because I thought we could both trust you! Now you drive this truck to my house, or so help me God, we'll both get out and hitchhike."

We glared at each other. Judy said, between sobs, "Please, Rick."

I drove the back roads to Lorie's house and sat stewing in the pickup while Lorie took Judy inside. After a while I got out and stood in the drizzle, pitching pebbles from the driveway at an old bucket in the yard. At least her grandparents weren't home. We'd been spared that, anyway.

After a half hour Lorie came out. I didn't look at her, but went on throwing pebbles at the bucket. "Well, I think she's going to be all right. That guy gave her a few drinks and she's got a hangover, but she'll get over that. Otherwise, I guess he was nice to her."

"Where did she find him?"

"She doesn't want to talk much about it, but I guess she was so depressed she just started walking down the highway. A couple of miles out of town this guy stopped and asked if she had car trouble or something and she asked him for a ride. And, well, he took her to dinner, then a bar, and then a motel. That's all I know except that this morning he realized how young she really was and got pretty nasty about dumping her in a hurry. . . . Still, she's handling things okay. She's darn sorry, but there's not much she can do about it now." I pitched another pebble at the bucket. "At least I don't think you have to worry about her getting pregnant. Her period was over only three days ago, so it's not very likely."

"I'm sure super-nurse has spoken to God about it."

She was suddenly very angry. "Damn it, Rick! Just get off it, huh! Sure, I know there's a chance she'll get pregnant out of this, but it is not very likely. There's a chance she caught something, too, but what do you want her to do about it? Go crying to your mom? That'll just get everybody terribly upset and not solve a damn thing! . . . All Judy can do is wait. If something's wrong, let her tell your mom then, not now when it doesn't mean anything."

I turned angrily to face her. "Don't you think it means something now?! Judy's not even sixteen yet and she's been screwing some guy all night! Somebody she didn't even know until yesterday afternoon! I think that's pretty goddamn serious even if you don't."

She glared back at me. "Don't make a crisis out of this, Rick! Sure I think she made a mistake, but it's not going to kill her or ruin her life unless you make a big deal out of it by running to your parents." She flung out an angry hand toward the house. "What you've got in there is one very scared kid who's got a lot of problems. She doesn't need any more right now. She sure doesn't need a big brother who's going to condemn her and make her even more miserable!"

"Well, I don't think it's too damn cool she's been running around like some barroom slut!"

"Oh, come off it! She's not a slut. She ran into someone who was nice to her for a change, got a little drunk and went to bed with him. That was stupid, but it doesn't make her a whore!"

"I can see you know all about this sort of thing from experience!"

Her face went pink with anger. "Ya, as a matter of fact I do know something about this sort of thing. I sure as hell know enough about men to know you wouldn't turn it down. And you probably haven't. You've tried pretty hard to get into my pants. And I might even have let you one of these days if I hadn't found out what a hypocrite you really are!"

That speech rocked me back almost physically. I stood staring at this person I'd thought I'd known. I had nothing to say. My anger died in a single fiery plunge and I realized what a terrible thing I'd said to her. Tears welled up in her eyes. "And I'm sorry I found that out," she sobbed. She turned away and wiped her eyes with her sleeve. I couldn't say anything, couldn't move. She sniffed and cleared her throat. "I'm going in to look after your sister. . . . Good-bye, Rick. I hope everything works out for you."

Judy came out alone twenty minutes later and we rode home in silence. At the end of the driveway she asked in a tiny voice, "Are you going to tell?" I shook my head.

12

So it was over between Lorie and me. I knew it was more than just a passing quarrel, something that could be made up when tempers cooled. Perhaps deep down, we'd never really liked each other. Perhaps we'd only enjoyed each other's company because no one else was available. But it was over now and I tried not to think about her. Instead I concentrated my thoughts on college and all that remained to be done before I left the farm. I worked like a fiend on the machinery and the buildings. I wanted no guilt, just a clean break with my life on the farm.

Lorie had become so much a part of the family scene that everyone was curious when she no longer came by. I cut off all questions with, "We're just not seeing each other anymore, that's all," and refused to talk more about it. Mom didn't pry, of course. Dad made a couple of subtle offers to talk about it, but I didn't take him up on them, and he dropped it. Jim asked a question or two, then forgot about it. (After all, who needed to worry about that kind of stuff? Onions and the other calves needed pampering and ten thousand other projects were far more interesting than older brother's love life.)

Judy had the best idea of what had happened, but she was avoiding me, and I was just as glad. I wasn't mad at her any longer—felt sorry for her, actually—but I didn't have any comforting words for her. She was spending a lot of time at Lorie's in the evenings and I figured Lorie could play the confidant far better than I.

Pam missed Lorie a lot and if Connie wasn't spending the evening with Phil, all three girls would sometimes ride their bikes over to Lorie's. But mostly Judy went alone. And I was jealous, because as much as I tried to tell myself otherwise, I missed Lorie terribly.

Connie was the most persistent. She'd always been a gossip-hound, and she wanted to know everything that had happened the day Lorie and I had gone to Hawthorne to pick up Judy. But I wasn't explaining anything to her. If Judy wasn't going to tell about her fling, I certainly wasn't. As for my relationship with Lorie, that was none of Connie's business. But she kept trying.

She was on the porch one night waiting for Phil when I came out in my going-to-town clothes. "Are you going to see Lorie?"

"No, I'm just going into town."

"Have you guys broken up for good?"

"We didn't even know each other a month. I'd hardly say there was much to break up."

"Well, you sure saw a lot of each other in that month."

"Connie, give me a break, will you? I don't want to talk about it!"

"Gee, I just wanted to help."

I stopped myself from replying that all she really wanted was the gossip. "Just don't try to help, okay? I don't need it."

I left her on the porch feeling hurt.

The short time when we'd all been pretty happy, with the exception of Judy, had passed. Connie, Jim, and Pam were still in good spirits, but the rest of us were back in the dumps.

Tommy's eyesight was deteriorating rapidly. He could no longer make even the feeblest attempt at catching a ball and now Pam had to hold his hand when they walked through many areas of the farm. Cat counting, one of his favorite pastimes, had become a frustrating exercise. The cats moved too quickly, were too hard to distinguish against the background of hay bales, cows' legs, and barn walls. Pam had to do all the counting now while Tommy sat on a hay bale with two or three kittens in his lap, listening disconsolately to the score.

The doctors in Minneapolis had prescribed even more drugs and the schedule was so complicated that Mom had to use the timer on the stove to keep track. Ten times a day she'd call Tommy from play for yet another dose of medicine. The drops were the worst, so strong that he had to lie on her lap squirming for three minutes each time, while she pressed the tear ducts closed so the medicine didn't wash out of his eyes.

Late at night now, I often heard Mom and Dad talking in the kitchen, making plans for simplifying the arrangement of the house against the time when Tommy's sight would finally disappear. They still hoped that the specialists at the university hospital in Minneapolis might devise a way to save at least a little of the dimming power of his eyes, but the time had come to plan for the worst.

Long after they'd stop talking, I'd hear Mom's nervous footsteps and the rattle of containers in the refrigerator as she dug for something to ease her anxiety. She seemed much older now, dark circles under her eyes and worry lines deepening on her face. Her uneasy nights left her very tired, even as her work increased with the approaching fall. The harvest from the garden—bushels and bushels of tomatoes, cucumbers, sweet corn, and squash—had to be put up, the house still needed work, and, of course, there were always meals to prepare, clothes to wash, and kids to mind.

Dad, too, seemed particularly worried these days. After a summer of ideal conditions, the weather had turned nasty, and Dad slouched into one of his silent moods. He wasn't exactly sour, just quiet and deliberate about everything he did, as if a small mistake would bring the clouds tumbling low and dangerous. A violent thunderstorm or, worse yet, hail could destroy the corn and oat crops. With little financial margin as it was, a single brutal storm could bankrupt us.

More often than ever I found myself avoiding the tension and squabbling in the house. I'd work late in the machine shop and if I couldn't concentrate there, I'd take the pickup and go to town for a beer or two at Irma's.

One Friday evening about ten days after my fight with Lorie, it seemed everyone was particularly bitchy at the supper table. Tommy squawked continually about the food, even though beef stew was usually one of his favorite meals. I could see that Mom was already getting pretty irritable when Pam decided to reopen the issue of riding Arrow, cast or not.

"Mom, can I start riding Arrow again? I'll go real slow and Jimmy says he'll help."

"Absolutely not!" Mom said.

Jim piped up, "But, Mom, I'll lead Arrow the first few times. It'll be safe."

"You just hush!" Dad said. "You heard your mother."

"But Dad . . ." Pam pleaded.

"You both heard her. There'll be no horse riding for you, young lady, until that cast is off your arm and the doctor says it's okay for you to ride. Now I don't want to hear another thing about it from either of you."

Jim and Pam lapsed into pouting silence. No one said anything for a couple of minutes except Tommy, who continued to announce that the food was "yucky." Connie must have known it was a lousy time to bring it up, but this might be her only chance. "Mom, there's a dance in Mason tonight and Phil and I want to go. Can I stay out an hour late?"

"I think twelve is plenty late enough for a girl your age."

"But Mom I'll be sixteen Tuesday. This is kind of a birthday present."

Mom frowned. "Well, your sister will be sixteen on Tuesday too. I think it would be very nice if you and Phil took her along so she could have some fun too."

"Mom!" Judy yelped in dismay and jumped up from the table.

"You sit right down, Judy!" Dad snapped. She plumped back into her chair and stared at her food. Dad surveyed us with a withering look. "I don't know what's gotten into you kids! Your mother works hard all day and when she sits down to have her supper, all you can do is pester her and complain. I think you're all getting pretty spoiled and unless you shape up, there are going to be some privileges suspended around here!"

God, I was sick of all this. I took a last bite and shoved my plate away. "May I be excused, Dad?" He glared at me, looking for a chance to let me have it too, but I met his look impassively. After a moment he nodded.

I changed my clothes, got the keys to the pickup from the hook in the kitchen, and started for town. But once I was on the road, I no longer felt much like going there. I'd seen the movie, Irma's was a drag, and the youth center would be filled with rowdy high school kids. I drove the back roads for a while, trying to decide if I wanted to go down to Mason. I hadn't been there since I'd broken up with Lorie and now that didn't sound like much fun either. Lorie. Damn! Why couldn't I stop thinking about her?

After a half hour of driving aimlessly, I parked the truck on the side of the road not far from where Mom, the kids, and I had picked up Jack Peterson. I walked down through the ditch and across the field to the old railroad grade. In a few minutes I reached the trestle spanning the creek and sat on the edge. The dark, cracked timbers were still warm from the hot afternoon, smelling of tar and sun and long years standing in the rain. Below my feet the creek eddied in a deep pool before dropping away across the fields to the road and the woods beyond. Behind Peterson's barn I could see his small herd grazing against a backdrop of green hills already darkening in the fading light. A pickup pulled out of his driveway and headed down the road away from me, the dust rising and blowing across the fields in the deep yellow of the sunset. If I'd had Lorie beside me I would have been happy, warm, and at peace like the land. But she wasn't. She never would be again.

And I had to stop thinking about her. Look, I told myself, even if you patch it up with her, there'll be damn little time left anyway. In another few weeks you'll be gone. Just a little more than a month and it'll be good-bye farming, hello future. There is too damn much work and too little time! Forget about her, Rick!

Another few weeks . . . Before long fall would be in the air, the leaves would be changing, and I'd be going away to college. We'd have the oats and the last crop of hay in and Dad would be planning for the corn harvest. And my time on the farm would be done. There was so much I'd like to talk to Lorie about. . . . Maybe, just maybe, there was still a way to start again. . . .

Damn! I was doing it again. I'd only been through this ten thousand times or so. Okay, I'd try one more time to work out what had really happened. And then I'd never think about it again. To begin with, I couldn't blame her for being mad. Hell, I'd virtually called her a whore. And most of what she'd said had been true. I hadn't exactly acted my age that day. Like trying to pick a fight with the Waters kid. That had been just plain dumb! I was no fighter, hadn't been in a fight since Jim Olson kicked my ass in ninth grade. But the afternoon Judy'd run away, I'd been almost begging for the chance to punch somebody. It was damn lucky that Jeff had been cool and Connie and Lorie had been there to stop me. Otherwise, I'd probably have had my butt tossed in jail or gotten stomped by a bunch of Waters's friends. Christ, what a stupid act I'd put on!

And I'd been real slick with Judy too! When she'd been about as down and hurt as I'd ever seen her, I'd started talking about telling Mom. Who was I to be playing the goddamn saint anyway? I'd done my share of craziness. Sure, she'd made a bad mistake: risked pregnancy and God only knew what else. But she'd been desperately unhappy and that had led to some pretty desperate things. And I'd known she was unhappy, but I hadn't done jackshit about it. If I'd tried to help, maybe she wouldn't have run away that day. Maybe she'd have come home instead. But I hadn't tried; I'd ignored her anguish, then kicked her when she was down. Real smooth, Rick!

I paused, fighting to keep the anger down, trying to get my thoughts organized again. Okay, if I admitted Lorie had been ninety-five percent right, why didn't I just go to her, apologize, and hope she'd take me back? That was the hardest part to figure out. Sure, she'd hurt my pride. I could admit that. She'd read me out pretty good: told me I'd behaved like a jerk and called me a hypocrite about sex. All that had hurt, still hurt, but I'd tried to hurt Lorie too. Maybe we could forgive each other for that.

And yes, I'd been shocked by her attitude about Judy sleeping with that guy. But I knew now that Lorie hadn't taken it lightly, that she was very worried about how it might affect Judy both physically and mentally. After all, she'd spent a lot of hours with Judy since. So, okay, maybe Lorie had been around a little more than I'd thought. So what? I'd been around a little too. Peggy Mathews and I hadn't exactly spent our time discussing the fundamentals of architecture. . . . Maybe if the evidence of our past experience had come out slowly, gently, there would have been no problem. But even if it hadn't, that was hardly enough reason to spoil our relationship.

What was the problem then? I didn't know. Perhaps I couldn't go back to Lorie because I was afraid of her now. I wanted the old Lorie sitting beside me on the railroad trestle. I wanted the Lorie who'd seemed gentle and innocent, the Lorie I could protect. I wasn't sure I could deal with the real Lorie—the Lorie who could get very, very angry. And suppose she didn't take me back? Suppose she'd meant just what she'd said: good-bye. That would be a humiliation, a wallop to my ego, that I couldn't handle.

No, it was better to forget her. Remember now and then all the good times we'd had, but otherwise forget her. I was going away soon. I'd get my work done around the farm and think about the future. Hell, next Thursday I had to go to Milwaukee for registration at the university. Let Lorie go on with her life and I'd go on with mine.

But I'd come to this conclusion a few dozen times before, and I still couldn't quite accept my own advice. Disgusted, I got up and walked along the railroad bed in the last of the sunset. The light was falling fast and the crickets and frogs had set up their nightly din. In a hundred more feet I'd cut across the field to the road and walk back to the pickup. What then? I still didn't want to go home. Maybe I'd go into Irma's for a beer.

As I got closer to Peterson's farm, I heard a ring of metal on metal. A pause followed, then a less distinct sound, then the steady sound of metal on metal again. I tried to see where the sound came from, finally making out the silhouette of a big man on the edge of the circle thrown by the yard light. He was splitting wood, positioning each piece awkwardly on the splitting block, hitting it with a short-handled splitting mall, then driving the head of the mall through the wood with a sledgehammer. I stopped and watched. Despite the awkwardness of his method, the pile of split wood was growing steadily.

I hesitated. I could easily walk back up the line a few dozen yards and then across the field without being seen. Still, I liked Mr. Peterson and wouldn't mind talking to him for a few minutes. Better that than trying to fight off further brooding about Lorie.

I didn't want to startle him while he was swinging the mall or sledge. He had enough problems already and I didn't want to be responsible for him hitting a kneecap with an eight- or ten-pound hunk of steel. So, I approached to within twenty

222

yards or so and waited for him to finish a piece and bend for another. "Hi, Mr. Peterson."

He didn't spin around, frightened and startled like a city person. Still leaning over, he half turned and squinted in my direction. "Rick?"

"Yes, sir." I walked closer as he straightened. "I was up on the old track and saw you working. Thought I'd come down and say hello."

"Glad you did. How you been?" We shook, my right hand with his good left.

"Fine. How about you?"

"Can't complain." He adjusted the sling that held his right arm. "The hand's coming along. Can't use it for anything much yet, but I get by." He grinned. "Thought I'd better get started on my woodpile or else it's gonna be a mighty cold winter. Don't want to have to burn the furniture." He laughed his booming laugh.

I smiled. "Guess not. It looks like you're getting a lot done."

"Oh, it's a pretty clumsy way of doin' it, but I can't help much with anything else. Sam and Millie come over to do the milking, so I've got a lot of time to make wood. Enough for tonight, though. How about a beer?"

"Sure."

I followed him into the house. It was pretty bare, but clean and cozy. The furniture was old and the stuffing showed through on the arms of the big easy chair in front of the TV. I saw beyond the half-open door to a back room two carefully organized workbenches, a metal lathe, and a drill press. The house had the musty but not unpleasant smell of long use by a man who'd lived quietly alone. I wondered if he'd ever been married.

Mr. Peterson was talking as he dug around in the refrigerator. "One good thing about getting busted up is all the pamperin' you get. Between Millie and some of the neighbor women, I have to eat about six times a day just to keep ahead of all the food they bring over. Be fat as a hog by the time the snow blows." He laughed. "There they are. I knew I'd hidden 'em somewhere." He brought out two cans of beer and handed me one. "Want a sandwich to go with that?"

"No, thanks. This will be fine."

"Okay, but I'll just have to eat more tomorrow. Let's sit on the porch. Too nice a night to be inside."

It was nearly dark now. We sat in a couple of old chairs listening to the crickets and frogs and sipping the beer. For several minutes neither of us felt inclined to talk. Finally, I spoke, "Mr. Peterson . . ."

"Call me Jack. All this mister business makes me feel like a bank president or something." He laughed.

"Okay. Ah, oh ya, I was going to ask if you knew my Uncle Fritz."

"Fritz? Sure, knew Fritz almost all my life. Even went to school with him, though neither of us ever got very far. . . . Ya, I felt real bad about missing the funeral, but I was down in Georgia visiting my boy. Didn't hear about it till I got back. Felt bad about it. . . . My boy's in the army. Been in close to twenty years now. Could retire in another couple of years, but says he's going for thirty, longer if they'll have him. The army's done real good by him. And I think he's done good by them too. He's a master sergeant with enough ribbons and medals and whatnot to fill half his chest. Real good boy. Got a fine wife and five kids too. Couple of them near as old as you are. . . . Ya, Billy's turned out real good. Don't much care for that Georgia, though. Ever been there?"

I shook my head and then said, "No," realizing that it was now too dark to see much.

"Ya, that old Georgia's way too hot for me. Lots of bugs and snakes and clay soil too. No, thanks. This is God's country as far as I'm concerned."

"Ya, it's pretty nice." We didn't say much for a few minutes, just sat listening to the night. He went inside and brought out another beer for each of us. "Thanks," I said.

"Sure." He half sat on the railing on the other end of the

porch, gazing beyond the circle of light into the darkness. I was about to ask if he followed the Brewers at all when he spoke. "You asked if I knew Fritz. . . ." He laughed softly. "Ya, I sure did. I can remember some of the crazy stuff we did as kids like it was yesterday. Boy, we had some times. For a lot of years we was sort of like Mutt and Jeff. I was tall and skinny in those days and Fritz was short and even a little chunky once. I think we knew every fishing hole and every good spot to shoot squirrels within thirty miles of here. And later I think we knew about every pretty girl too."

I was surprised—Uncle Fritz had never mentioned Jack Peterson in my hearing. Come to think of it, though, he had mentioned a Jack once or twice when he'd told stories about his youth. Still, he'd never let on that his oldest friend lived only a few miles from the farm we'd bought. I started to say something about it to Mr. Peterson, but something stopped me.

After a long pause, he said softly, "Ya, those were the days." He took a swallow of beer, then shrugged. "But, well, I guess we were a little too close, because we both fell in love with the same girl. Fritz met Helen first and they started going out steady. But then he introduced us and, well, we fell for each other hard. . . . We didn't want to hurt Fritz, so we met on the sly a few times, but that was no good. We tried to stop seeing each other, but that was no good either." He shrugged. "Finally, we decided to tell Fritz and ask him to try and understand." He shook his head. "And that was the worst of all. How could he understand? He loved Helen too. He said some pretty hard things that night. I didn't mind him laying into me, but when he started on Helen, well, I told him to leave or I'd beat his head in.

"A few days later I ran into him in town and he wanted to fight. I tried to talk to him, but he wouldn't listen. He took a swing at me and I backed up still trying to talk to him, but he just wouldn't listen. So . . . I knocked him down." He sighed. "I don't think I ever did anything I regretted more. . . .

"Anyway, a few months later Helen and me got married. Fritz had gone out West somewhere. He was gone a year or more and even when he got back, I never saw him to talk to." He stared into the darkness for a long time before he went on. "Not until a couple of weeks after Helen died having my boy. Fritz came by then. Brought a pint of whiskey and we sat down and drank it to her memory. Didn't talk much, didn't cry. We'd both loved her and there wasn't much to say and no tears were going to make any difference. I think Fritz probably still loved her the day he died. I know I always will."

"She must have been very wonderful," I said, and it sounded dumb.

"Ya, she was plenty of woman. No great looker, but good and calm and a real worker. God, that woman could work. Maybe she worked too hard and that's why having Billy killed her." He sighed. "I don't know. It's nearly forty years ago, now. But I'll never forget her."

"I wonder why I never heard Uncle Fritz mention her."

I could see him shrug his big shoulders in the dim light. "I don't know. I guess it doesn't surprise me none. It probably always hurt too much. . . . I don't know how you feel about your young lady, but it's real tough to love someone and then lose her. Fritz loved Helen, but she loved me. And I loved her, but in less than two years she was dead. We both lost her and I guess it hurt too much to ever talk about it much. Fritz and I were never close again. Oh, we'd see each other in town. Maybe once a year we'd get half a load on and laugh about the old days, but we never mentioned her after that day we drank the pint of whiskey together."

"You never married again?"

"Tried it once, but it didn't work. Thought about it a couple of other times for the boy's sake, but never did. I had a maiden aunt who came to live here and between us we raised Billy. She's long dead now and Billy's almost twice the age I was when I married his mother. Times pass." He laughed softly. He looked down at the beer in his hand. "Must be the beer

and them pain pills make me run on like this. Ain't talked
about that since I don't know when. Want another?"

"No, thanks, I'm fine."

He brought me one anyway and went back to sit on the rail.
"But you know, I wouldn't trade those two years I had with
Helen for anything. I wouldn't trade the pain of losing her
either. . . . Because, you see, I'll always know that once in my
life I was loved by a really good woman. And I guess that's
made me a happy man. I've always wished there'd been two of
her, that Helen could've had a twin sister so Fritz could've
known that feeling too. But, well, that wasn't how it was. . . .
And I hope you're loved like that someday, Rick. Ain't nothing can ever take the place of it."

We sat in silence finishing our beers. A breeze had come
up, rattling in the tall corn and swaying the branches of the
trees so that leaf shadows danced like moths on the pool of
light between the house and the barn. I'd never known any of
this about Uncle Fritz. I wondered if he'd ever told anyone
about his pain. I wondered if he might have told me someday.
I took the last swallow from my can and stood. "Well, thanks
for the beer, Mr. Peterson."

"Jack."

"Right, Jack. And thanks for the talk too. I, ah, enjoyed it
very much."

"Sure. Didn't give you much of a chance to talk. Drop by
soon. Next time I won't do all the gabbing."

"I didn't mind at all. I really enjoyed learning more about
Uncle Fritz." I turned on the steps. "Jack, do you think my
mom knows about Uncle Fritz and you and Helen?"

"I couldn't say. Your ma was just a tiny little thing when I
remember her, not more than seven or eight. It wasn't long
after Fritz went out West they sold the farm and moved away.
Maybe he talked about it around the house, but . . . I'd kinda
doubt it."

I nodded. "Well, thanks again. Good night."

"Good night. Thanks for coming by."

I walked back up the road to the pickup. The stars were out and a huge orange moon was rising. I felt quiet inside for the first time in almost two weeks. I'd forgotten how we all had our pain and disappointment; how we all made mistakes and hurt each other even when we tried to love. But I'd been reminded.

Down the road coming the other direction toward the farm, I saw a wavering light. One of the girls or Jim out after dark on a bicycle, I thought. I turned in, parked the pickup, and got out. Judy came bouncing down the driveway.

When she got close, I said, "Hi."

"Hi." She got off and pushed her bicycle into the shed where the kids kept their rolling stock. I waited for her. She came out, saw me, and stood uncertainly.

"Did you just come from Lorie's?" I asked in a friendly tone. She nodded. "How is she?"

"Okay."

"Is she still up? I was thinking of calling her."

"Her grandparents just put her on the bus. I rode in with them. She's going back home for a few days."

"Oh." Disappointment rose up inside me, but I tried to suppress it. Maybe it was just as well. I still needed time to think. "How long is she going to be gone?"

"She said until Wednesday afternoon."

We stood for a moment, then I asked, "Do you want to go to town for a Coke?"

She hesitated. "I guess. . . . Let me go tell Mom."

On the ride to town, Judy sat with her face averted, studying the moonlit fields. I turned on the radio and let her be. When we got on the outskirts, she said, "Let's just stop at the root beer stand; I don't feel like going in any place."

"Why don't we just drive on down to Mason? It's not far."

"If you want to."

In Mason I stopped at a small, quiet café. We took a corner booth and I ordered hamburgers, fries, and Cokes. Judy sat toying with her fork. "How you been feeling?" I asked.

228

She shrugged. "Okay, I guess." She glanced up quickly at me, then looked down again. "My period still hasn't come, if that's what you mean, but it's kind of early yet."

"Well, I kinda meant how have you been feeling, you know, mentally."

She shrugged. "Okay, I guess. . . . Lorie and I have talked some."

"Figured anything out?"

"A few things, I guess." I waited for her to tell me what, but instead she raised her head and asked, "Rick, were you really going to call her tonight?"

"I was thinking about it. Why?"

"Because I really wish you would. I've felt really awful about you guys fighting because of me."

"You weren't all of it."

She was looking at her placemat again. "Well, I was a lot of it." She sniffed and reached up to brush away a tear.

"Don't start crying, Judy. It's okay. Let's talk about something else. Here come the hamburgers, anyway."

Eating seemed to make her feel a little better. When I thought it was safe, I asked, "How about the Boots thing? Are a lot of kids still calling you that?"

"Not so many. Lorie says I've just got to get used to it. . . . But it's still the pits."

"Ya, but I guess she's probably right."

"Lorie says I should try harder to look good. She helped me with my hair."

"Ya, I noticed. It looks nice." I really hadn't, but I figured it wouldn't hurt to lie a little.

"Thanks. She also thinks I should try and get involved in some school activities this fall. Maybe go out for a sport. Phil's on the boys' cross-country team and Connie's going to go out for the girls' team. Maybe I'll do that too."

"I think maybe it'd be better if you tried something where you didn't have to compete with her."

Judy met my eyes and there was something fierce there. "I bet I could run the pants off her!"

"Maybe so. . . . But do what will make you happy."

"That'd make me happy." She toyed with the last of her fries. "Just to beat her at something once." She paused then looked up at me again. "Rick, could you take me driving this weekend? We've got our test next week and I need to get some extra practice. If Connie passes and I don't, I'll kill myself!"

"Well, I think that would be taking it a bit too hard, but, sure, I'll take you driving if Mom says it's okay."

"Then Connie will want to come too."

"Well, I think we can get around that." She smiled for the first time. "Ya, I'm sure we can. Just let me think of the best way."

"That would be really great! Connie's so much better than I am and Mom's always so nervous when I'm driving. I'm sure if I could drive with you for a while, I'd get a lot better real fast."

"Okay. We'll do it then."

On the ride home she was quiet again. At last, she said, "You know, I think Lorie misses you a lot."

"Has she talked about it?"

"Well, not exactly, but I think I can tell."

That's not exactly a guarantee she'll even talk to me on the phone, I thought. "Well, we'll see. I might call her when she gets back."

"Please call her, Rick. I think you guys should talk about some things."

"Maybe we should. We'll see."

Before I went to bed I had an idea and the next morning I explained it to Dad and asked for the afternoon off. We had a ton of work to do, but my idea was a good one and he agreed. Connie went off with Phil after lunch, so Judy and I got away alone without any problem. I drove the car up to Carleyville, giving her all the good driving advice I could think of.

At the edge of town, I swung in at the junkyard, hoping that Red Hamilton would be working on a Saturday. I'd done business with the "Junkyard Daredevil" several times over the summer and we'd become friendly. A couple of weeks before, he'd mentioned casually that when he wasn't working at the junkyard or jumping long lines of cars, he did a little caretaking around the fairgrounds—grooming the track, cutting the grass, and so forth. I thought for a few bucks there was a pretty good chance he'd let me use the track for a while.

He was lounging behind the desk, smoking a cigarette and drinking a Coke. "Hi, Rick. How's it going?"

"Good. How about you, Red?"

"Not bad. On a scale of ten, I'd say seven or eight. What can I do you for?"

"Well, I was wondering if I could get the use of the track for a couple of hours this afternoon. My sister's taking her driver's test next week and she's kind of nervous. I figured maybe if she had a little room to practice, it'd help. We'd be happy to pay."

Red thought for a few seconds. "We don't want to get you in trouble or anything. If it's a problem . . ."

"No, no sweat there. I let my friends in to test their cars all the time. The boss doesn't mind as long as you sign a waiver so there's no hassle on the insurance. I'm just trying to think if anybody's going to use it this afternoon." He turned to a big calendar below a picture of a half-naked girl selling mufflers. "Let's see. Jerry called and said he threw a rod and was thinking of pushing his Ford in the nearest river, so he's out. Brian and Sandy are in Eau Claire racing. . . . Okay. . . . Ya, Frank's out too. Seems like the only one this afternoon is Sax and he won't be in till around four. So it looks like it'll be okay. When do you want to go over?"

"Anytime you can get away."

"Good, I've been looking for an excuse to close this dump up. Let me call the boss." He picked up the phone and dialed. "Hey, Dick, Red. Nothing going on so I'm closing up and going over to the track. I'll leave the sign up. Right. Catch ya."

I went out ahead of Red. He put a sign on the inside of the window and locked the door. The sign read, "If you REALLY need something Red is at the fairgrounds."

"Ah, Red," I said, wishing I'd asked before, "how much is this going to cost?"

"How about five bucks and a six-pack? I'll let you drink half. Sound fair?"

"Sure, that's fine." We climbed in the car.

"And," he said, "if your sister passes her test, she owes me a big, juicy kiss." He leered good-naturedly at her. Judy blushed. "You can get the beer at the bar on the corner." He pointed.

When we got to the track, Red turned to Judy. "Hey, fox, maybe you'd like a real pro to show you how to drive this crate. I'll show you how to . . ."

I interrupted, "No, Red. We're not going to be jumping off any ramps today. We're going for a nice quiet drive."

"Suit yourself." He grinned and got out. "Too bad. Perfect day for it. Nice and dry. Probably make it over at least ten."

Judy got behind the wheel and we rolled off. "Strange guy," I said.

"I thought he was kind of nice."

"He's not your type. Okay, let's concentrate on the driving."

After a half dozen turns around the track, I told her to stop. "Okay, it's all yours. Do it as long as you want. We've got the track for another couple of hours."

"Rick, I can't do it by myself!"

"Sure you can. Solo—best thing for you."

"But, I mean, it's against the law!"

"Well, you don't have a driver's license, so they can't take it away from you. Besides, no one will know."

I joined Red in the bleachers. He was on his second beer. "How's she doing?"

"Okay, I think. We'll see if she can keep it on the track."

We watched as Judy cautiously circled the track a couple of times. "She seems kind of scared of something," Red commented.

"Well, this is her first time alone."

"No, I mean, you know, she looks like she's scared of something more than driving."

"Ya, well, . . ." I told him a little about the competition with Connie.

Red grunted. "Ya, I know a little about that kind of thing. Hand me another beer, will you, man?" I did. "Ya, my brother's real smart. Getting his college degree in business this month. It used to make me feel pretty lousy that he was good at school and all that kind of stuff and I wasn't. Of course, that was before I became"—he did it with a flourish like an M.C.—"THE JUNKYARD DAREDEVIL!" He laughed and took a pull on the beer. "It's such a hustle, man. I reinforce the hell out of anything that might break off and hurt me and I'm so padded and strapped you could drop my car off a cliff and I'd still walk away from it. But I make a good buck and get free beer and a lot of girls pawing me. Shit, my brother should have it so good. . . . I'm going to talk to your sister."

Before I could stop him, he'd bounded down onto the track and signaled Judy to stop. He leaned on the side of the car talking to her for two or three minutes, then waved her on. Judy took the next round of the track ten or fifteen miles an hour faster, but smoothly.

He came back up, sat down, and popped the top on a fourth beer. I was still only halfway through my second. "Mind?"

"No, go ahead." Judy was coming around the track well under control. "What did you say to her?"

"Told her to drive like it was her car and she'd had a license for five years. Told her the biggest thing she had to fear was fear itself."

"You quoted Franklin D. Roosevelt to her?"

"Was that who said it? I thought it was some race driver."

"No, it was President Roosevelt."

"Whoever. Worked, didn't it?" Judy came around again, doing better than ever.

"I guess so. Thanks."

"My pleasure." He lit a cigarette. "Hey, you know, man.

You and me ought to tie one on sometime. I bet we could
teach each other a lot of shit. I'll tell you all about jumping
cars and you can tell me who said what." He laughed.
"Really, man, come up sometime. We'll go catch a few
beers."

"Okay. That sounds good."

Judy stopped the car and got out. "Rick, Red, could we
work a little on parking?"

Red made some marks in the dirt to represent parking places
and we both coached her for forty-five minutes. When Red's
friend showed up with the car he wanted to test, three helpers,
and a case of beer, Red put them off and gave Judy a few more
pointers before shooing us off the track. We stood around
watching them test the stock car. After a few turns, Red waved
the driver into the infield and they started messing with the
engine. The sky was growing overcast again and I knew we
should be getting back soon for the milking, but I was enjoying
the afternoon off.

So was Judy. I could see she was developing a first-class
crush on Red. He saw it, too, and a couple of times yelled,
"Hey, fox, get that wrench for me," or something of the sort.

I'd just about decided that we really had to go when a young
guy about Judy's age jogged on to the track in a running suit.
He came over to where Red and a couple of his buddies were
leaning over the engine. I saw Judy's expression turn dark and
she took a step behind Red's friends. "Hi, Red," the kid said.

"Hey, how's it going, Brad? Have a beer." Red gestured
toward the open case.

"No, thanks. Can I run a mile on the track for time?"

"I dunno, Brad. We're gonna be testing this hunk-a-shit in
a few minutes." I could tell Red was teasing Brad, who was all
the while jogging in place.

"Come on, Red. I'll be done before you can even get those
plugs gapped."

"Well, let me think about it."

"Oh, crap," Brad said, stopped jogging, and went over to get a beer.

Red winked at me. "Got to keep these athletic types loose. Hey, Brad, where's that shithead cousin of yours, Charlie whatshisname?"

"O'Brien," Brad said coming back over by us. He drank the beer in big swallows. I made the connection. This was Brad, the "real hunk" whom cousin Charlie O'Brien had introduced to Judy with the Boots story on the day she'd run away. I sized him up for a little alteration with a crescent wrench.

Red was going on. "Well, you tell Mr. O'Brien that he'd better get his young ass up here and pay for that fender he got from me or the boss is going to dock my pay, and that's going to get me real pissed off."

"I'll tell him if I see him, Red, but I don't like him much more than you do. Shithead's about right. . . . Can I run those laps now?" He started jogging in place again.

"Sure. But, hey, first meet Rick Simons. He's from down in your neck of the woods. This is Brad Culver. God knows why, but he jogs in from the country to run here. Damn." Red sucked a bruised knuckle.

"Hi. How you doing?" Brad shook my hand without paying me much attention. He was anxious to be off running.

Red was back working under the hood. "And his sister is around here somewhere. You'll be going to the same school, I think. Hey, fox, where you hiding?"

Unwillingly, Judy came out from behind the car. "Hi."

"Oh, hi. We met before, didn't we?" Judy nodded. "Ya, ah, right, Charlie introduced us. You're, ah . . ."

"Judy," I said quietly.

"Ya, Judy, that's right. How you doing?"

"Okay."

"Good. Glad to hear it. . . . Say, I hope you guys will excuse me. I'm trying to get in shape for cross-country. If I don't run my mile now, Red's gonna run me over. See you later."

I nodded and Judy said, "Sure." With a wave Brad jogged off. He stopped a few feet away and stripped off the tops and bottoms of his jogging suit. From a pocket he produced a stopwatch and fiddled with it a moment. Then he laid it carefully on his suit, pushed the button, and took off running. We watched him. Good stride, I thought. As he got into the backstretch, I glanced at Judy. She had that same fierce expression I'd seen on her face in the café the night before.

We were a little late for the milking, and Dad, Jim, and Connie had some cold glances for us and a couple of sharp comments. I apologized to Dad later and he didn't make a big deal of it, only asked how the driving lesson with Judy had gone.

The next morning it was raining again. After church and dinner, Dad and I worked in the drizzle on the corn picker, tightening the belts and lubricating the hundreds of fittings. Like all the other equipment, the picker was old and would need a lot of fixing to be ready in time for the harvest.

Around us the fields of what Jack Peterson had called "God's country" lay soggy and dreary. A chill breeze blew the drizzle and I felt a sharp urge to be gone before the seasons changed.

After all the hours working together, we naturally anticipated each other's moves and usually talked about other things. But we'd both been gloomy the past couple of weeks and had talked little. Looking at Dad's grim expression now, I wished I could buck him up, but I still wasn't feeling real cheerful myself. Not as bad as before, maybe, but still pretty down. I'd probably missed my chance with Lorie, even now that I'd figured a few things out.

But, God, I didn't want to start thinking about that again, so I made an effort to get a conversation going about fishing. Dad often liked to reminisce about some of the big ones he'd caught or some of the particularly good water he'd fished. I mentioned taking a good look at the stream that flowed by Jack

Peterson's farm and suggested that maybe we should try it one of these days.

But Dad only grunted and said, "Well, maybe next year." That was as much as he wanted to talk about fishing, and we returned to our silence.

After an hour, Dad called a halt and we retreated to the barn for a breather. He propped himself on a hay bale and got his pipe going. "I've been thinking that once we get the picker fixed up, we might take a look at that old combine," he said.

"Really? I thought you were going to contract for the combining."

"That would make a lot of sense, but I hate like hell to pay somebody else if there's a chance we can do it ourselves."

"Well, whatever you think, but I took a look at it a few weeks ago and there are a lot of problems. Quite a few missing parts, I think."

"Ya, I've looked at it, too, and you're right. But I think we can get it going. . . ." We talked about it for a few minutes, then went back out into the drizzle to work on the picker.

Over the years, I doubt if many couples have had fewer fights than Mom and Dad, but with everyone on edge these days, even they were snapping at each other. When I came in from the shop late Monday night, Mom was sitting alone at the kitchen table. I could tell they'd had another row and she'd been crying. I was tired and just wanted to eat a bowl of ice cream and go to bed, but I felt I should try to comfort her. "What's the matter, Mom?"

"Nothing, dear. I just didn't feel like sleeping."

I got the ice cream out of the freezer and scooped some into a bowl. "Do you want some?" I asked her and immediately regretted it. She didn't need other people to encourage her to eat.

She looked tempted for a second, then said, "No, thank you."

I sat down at the other end of the table. "Well, I think that haybine will work better now."

"That's good. Your father will be happy."

"Dad went to bed early. Did he feel okay?"

"Oh, he was out of sorts. You know how he gets when he's overly tired." I nodded. Recently I'd been pretty cautious about prying into other people's business or giving unsolicited advice, but Mom went on without prompting. "Just before the late news came on, I went to get a snack and he said"—her voice choked—"he said, 'If you'd cut out all the snacking, maybe you'd make some progress on your diet for a change.' And I said, 'Well, maybe you can quit smoking and stop smelling up my house with your filthy old pipe.'" She dabbed at her eyes. "Then he got just furious and stomped into the bedroom and slammed the door. Jim and the twins were still up and they were scared, and I feel just horrible." She lowered her head and sat with her face buried in her handkerchief.

What could I say? Considering my recent experience, it would probably be wrong anyway. "I think we're all just tired, Mom. Things will get better once the harvest's in. Just too much has happened this summer. We all need a rest."

She blew her nose and sat up. "I know, I know. I'm just being silly. Your father was right. I should try harder to lose weight." Her attempt at self-control failed and she started crying again. "It's just so hard when I'm always nervous and worried. Tommy's going blind and we don't know if Pam's arm is going to be okay when they take off the cast. And Jim has his temper tantrums and Judy's always so sad. And I worry that Connie may get in trouble with that boy. Now you'll be going away soon and Paul is always angry and I can't help him enough! It's just too much for me to stand sometimes! Then eating is the only thing that seems to help, but I don't want to be a fat cow!" She sobbed and sat with her head down and her handkerchief over her eyes.

I felt a growing desperation. I had to say something. "Mom, you're not a fat cow. You're a wonderful person. You just worry too much. Things will work out, you'll see. Pam's arm will be fine. It was only a simple break. And Jim's already better. Judy and Connie are doing okay. And Dad will be happier soon. Just don't worry so much. For heaven's sake, don't worry about me. Maybe the doctors can even do something for Tommy this time. But it doesn't help for you to worry all the time." I paused, then plunged ahead. "Mom, you ought to get out more, join that homemakers' club or a bridge club or just go to the movies. You can't spend all your time working and worrying. . . . Why don't you and Dad take a weekend and go someplace? We could take care of the farm."

She straightened again, breathing deeply, trying to regain control. "Your father would never do it. Not for a year or two, anyway."

"Then to heck with him. Go by yourself or take one or two of the kids for company. Hell, I'll even go along and be your porter." She laughed at that despite herself. "Really, Mom, even if you don't do that, I think you should get out at least one afternoon or evening a week. And I don't mean just to go shopping or to the Weight Watchers thing. I mean to have some fun."

"Maybe you're right, dear. But there's so much to do, I can't afford any time off now."

"See, that's what I mean, Mom! You worry too much about getting everything done. Leave some of it undone. The world isn't going to end if you don't wash the dirty clothes for an extra day or if you make a couple fewer jars of pickles."

She smiled. "Yes, dear, you're right. I'll try. Now you'd better go to bed. It's very late."

"Well, you should too, Mom."

"I know. I'm just going to sit up a few more minutes."

Still uncertain if I should leave, I got up, went over to her, and gave her an awkward hug. "Just don't worry so much, Mom. Everything will work out. You'll see."

She patted my hand. "Sure it will. The good Lord will provide."

I didn't argue, since I knew believing that helped her.

But I couldn't take my own advice about not worrying and sat thinking in my room for the better part of an hour before going to bed.

I was scheduled to register for college on the Friday of the third week in August. I got the bus schedule and called Bill. Over the phone he sounded a bit restrained. Not that he wasn't glad to hear from me after the months since spring, he just seemed preoccupied. I tried to figure it out for a while, but then wrote it off as something of little importance. I still assumed he'd find the means to set up the apartment we'd talked about for so long. If not, well, it was no great matter; I'd spend a year in the dorms and get an apartment for my sophomore year. The only thing that worried me about living in a dorm was the lack of privacy and quiet for studying. But I could always go to the library. With Bill's antics I'd probably have to do that anyway if we lived in an apartment. Not that I intended to be a bookworm. I was going to have some fun, too, but not at the pitch Bill planned.

Lorie was still very much on my mind. She'd be getting back from Des Plaines on Wednesday afternoon and I'd be leaving for Milwaukee on Thursday morning. That wouldn't leave much time for a reconciliation, and, besides, I still wasn't sure if I wanted to risk trying to patch things up with her at all. Anyway, it would definitely be better to wait until I got back. I was looking forward to my trip and I didn't want to go in a bad mood after another fight with her. Still . . .

I really hadn't made up my mind yet when Dad, the twins, Jim, and I set about the milking on Wednesday evening. The air had hung blistering hot all day and it was stifling in the barn. The cows were restless, anxious to get back out into the fresh air. Several times Dad went to the door to gaze apprehensively at the sky.

We got back to the house just in time to watch the evening weather report. The weatherman usually clowns around during his portion of the show, squeezing a few laughs from whatever tired jokes he can make about the weather. But tonight he came on dead serious. "Radar shows a large front of potentially dangerous thunderstorms moving across the western half of the state with the possibility of heavy rains and locally damaging winds and hail. A severe thunderstorm warning has been issued by the National Weather Service for northwestern and central Wisconsin." He went on to list the counties involved, but I didn't pay much attention to his voice as I watched the satellite map come on with the heavy swirling clouds aiming a tremendous fist right at our part of the state.

After supper, I packed for my trip, looking out the window every once in a while to see the sky darkening as a great mass of clouds rose over the evening horizon from the northwest. The atmosphere was thick with the threat of the coming storm, part of the tension psychological, part of it real as the electricity gathered in the air. Finished, I walked downstairs and outside to watch the black hammer of clouds reach up toward the zenith. The wind eddied indecisively in the tall green corn and bent the yellowing oats in swirls like lake water. Flashes of lightning lit the clouds, outlining great peaks and valleys against the still blue sky. Only occasionally did the lightning flash through to touch the earth. If that has hail in it, I thought, we are really screwed. Hail or heavy wind will rip this crop apart.

Under the growl of the thunder I heard a strange drumming from the seldom used shed beyond the machine shop. Curious, I walked over and looked in. Dad was slamming his fists against the side of the old red combine and cursing terribly in a low gurgling rasp, the word "hail" coming again and again through his clenched teeth. The sheet steel of the combine reverberated each time he smashed his doubled fists against the rusty side. I was embarrassed, shocked, and deeply moved. I backed away from the door and retraced my steps to the middle of the yard. "Dad, where are you?" I called three times before he came out of the shed with his teeth set hard on the stem of his pipe and his head lowered. The sky above now rolled almost completely black and the wind gusted hard. He looked up and then back at his feet, his hands involuntarily clenching again and again. "Do you think it'll pass?" I asked. He shook his head.

We went to sit under the overhang from the porch roof. My insides knotted with the waiting and the shock of seeing Dad so reduced by the menace of the sky. The first raindrops hit big and hard on the grass and formed instant muddy balls in the dust of the drive. I heard Mom come to the backdoor to watch silently with us. A crash of thunder sent a slash of rain across the yard and then in a minute it passed. I was soaked in the first blast, but I hardly noticed. Mom came out and stood with her hands on Dad's shoulders. We waited. Again the wind hurled a stinging sheet of rain across the yard, and again it passed leaving the air dark and strangling. A blow of thunder louder than any before shook us and rattled the windowpanes on the porch. Then there it was: the first drum of hail on the steel roofs of the outbuildings. "Oh, God . . ." Dad whispered. The hailstones came faster, bouncing high on the lawn and ricocheting off the roofs. Then suddenly they stopped, leaving us gasping, half crying, in the silence. The thunder hit us and again our world was all wind and thunder and slashing sheets of rain. Then again the terrible deafening silence. Four more times the wind ripped open the belly of the clouds and lashed a torrent over us. And each time we waited for the hail to smash our crops and demolish the life we'd tried to build.

Then slowly, minute by minute, the sky started to lighten, then, unbelievably, to clear. The thunder diminished to a distant, complaining growl. Looking to the east, we could see the great front with its huge arc of black clouds advancing toward the far horizon, leaving our sky breaking into patches of twilight blue printed with quiet, friendly clouds drifting lazily after the hurtling storm.

We whooped and hollered and danced in the wet grass then, our sopping clothes clinging to our soaked bodies. The kids came to gaze curiously at us as we pranced and I was reminded of an old movie I'd once seen about rain coming to a Depression dust-bowl farm. But it didn't matter if we seemed to be playing some worn-out scene. This was wonderfully, ecstatically real and we were enjoying the hell out of it. Finally, Mom stopped, wrung out of breath and holding a hand over her racing heart. "Well, I guess that just goes to show how little we really own and how much we owe to Him." She pointed at the sky. I began to protest because I really don't think God gets into planning the daily weather very often, but I thought better of it and just stood there grinning until my cheeks hurt.

After the ecstasy of our narrow escape, I found myself oddly dissatisfied. I needed somebody outside the family to talk to, to be with this evening. Inside the house was bedlam. Mom and Dad were changing and the kids were rushing around getting ready for a surprise trip to town. "Ice cream, Cokes, a movie, anything you want," Dad had hollered.

I went up to change too. They were all piling into the car when I came back out of the house. "Come on, Rick," Jim yelled, and Pam and Tommy both joined in, yelling for me to hurry.

I waved. "You guys have a good time. Maybe I'll come in later."

They all waved and the car splashed off through the puddles on the drive and turned down the road toward town. Should I call Lorie? It really made a lot more sense to wait until I got back from Milwaukee. Maybe it was better not to ever call her again. I strolled to the pickup and leaned against the hood to watch the sunset. In my coat pocket lay the keys to the pickup. Oh, what the hell, I thought.

My courage almost failed me when I got out of the pickup and walked toward her door. Suppose she had visitors, maybe even some guy. I should have called. But I couldn't retreat now without looking foolish. I rang the bell and waited.

She was wearing jeans and a sweatshirt with cut-off sleeves when she opened the door—not exactly glamorous attire, but to me she'd never looked better. I stood there grinning foolishly.

"Hi, truck need water?" she said, smiling slightly.

"No, but the driver could use something to drink. Want to ride into town?"

"I can't now. I'm in the middle of doing Grandma's wash. The power was off for a long time. But come in. We'll find something." I followed her to the kitchen. "How you been doing?" she asked.

"Okay, I guess. A little lonely maybe."

For the first time, she actually smiled. "Me too. I've missed you."

"Even if I am a bully and a hypocrite?" I said it lightly and she laughed.

"Well, you have your endearing qualities too. Besides, you shouldn't take everything I say too literally."

We sat at the kitchen table drinking sodas and talking. Her grandparents were out for the evening and we had the house to ourselves. To my surprise I didn't find the talking difficult. I thought we'd have to go over all the stuff raised in our fight, but neither of us seemed interested now. It was just good to be together again and to laugh and talk of light and silly things.

Later, I helped her fold the clothes and then we sat on the steps. The sun had set, leaving only a thin strip of gold in the western sky. A three-quarter moon was already high in the sky.

"I'm going down to Milwaukee tomorrow to register for school," I said.

"Oh, when will you be back?"

"Sunday night. Do you want to come with me?"

"Ah, the hot little number's grandparents wouldn't approve."

"Too bad. Want to go dancing tonight instead?"

"Sure. Let me clean up and write a note to Grandma."

We went to the disco in Mason and later to a pizza place. It was the best time I'd had in a long time and it was after 1:00 A.M. when I dropped her off. Maybe I'd only be seeing her for a couple more weeks, but they'd be good ones.

13

I KISSED LORIE good-bye at the bus stop while Judy got my suitcase out of the trunk. "We'll see you soon," I said.

Lorie smiled. "You be good. I'm not sure I like you going off to the big city by yourself."

"Don't worry."

The bus pulled in. "I hate good-byes," she said. She gave me a hard squeeze and walked quickly back to the car.

Judy came over and handed me the suitcase. "Have a good trip. Say hello to Bill and the other guys."

"Sure. Good luck on your driver's test . . . and everything else too."

The bus driver hollered, "We gotta get going, son!"

I wasn't surprised when Bill was late picking me up at the bus station in Milwaukee. He would hardly have been the old Bill any other way. I tried to kill the wait by playing a couple of games of pinball and watching the people. Being back in the city was a shock. I'd forgotten what it was like to be around so many people. Their very numbers amazed me. Men, women, and children of every age, shape, color, and dress hurried through the station or sat, bored, on the long wooden benches. The hot afternoon reek of bodies, exhaust, and greasy food hung in the dead air, penetrated by the click of heels, the rustling of shopping bags, the thump of suitcases, the rings and buzzes of the pinball machines, the whines and whimpers of children, the impatient answering snaps of parents, the chug of bus engines, the whoosh of air brakes—all the smells and sounds of the city. I felt myself sucked in, overwhelmed. My hands clung to the pinball machine, my eyes riveted on the bouncing ball I misplayed again and again. Damn Bill for being so late. A sign on the machine flashed TILT and I pushed away, grabbed my suitcase, and headed for the exit. Better to wait out in the blazing sun than spend another minute in here.

Bill came hurrying into the station. Catching sight of me, he almost ran over an elderly man. "Oops, excuse me, sir." He patted the man on the shoulder and received a glare in return. "Hey, Rick, how was the trip?" He pumped my hand, the old familiar grin broadening his already wide face.

"Okay. I'm not used to this, though." I waved my hand around the station.

"Not used to what? Oh, you mean all the people?"

"Them and the noise and the smell."

"Oh ya? Hmmm." He glanced around. "Looks like any bus station to me, grimy, smelly, and noisy. So what?"

"Nothing. I'm just not used to it, that's all."

"Well, let's go then. Come on. I've got a lot planned." He grabbed my bag and immediately launched into a rundown of the schedule, so involved in his own words he almost collided with two or three more people on his way to the door. Same old Bill, I thought, a little oafish, but filled with energy.

But he really wasn't the same, I noticed, as we drove out to the old neighborhood. He was quieter, almost a little shy. We talked about our friends and acquaintances—the summer had brought quite a few changes. Several couples had split up, there had been three marriages, several guys and one girl had joined the service, a fairly distant friend had been killed in a car accident, and one closer friend had been caught breaking into a house. But all our best friends had pretty much kept their lives running smoothly.

There was a pause in the conversation as we entered the streets that were so familiar to me. Here nothing much had changed, or so I thought until we passed the school ground. The basketball court had disappeared under a mountain of heavy equipment, torn earth, and concrete blocks. The swing sets and jungle gym had completely vanished. "What is that?" I yelped.

Bill glanced at me quizzically. "Oh, didn't I tell you? They're putting on an extension to the elementary school. All tied up with the busing thing. More kids from the inner city out here beginning in the fall."

"Doesn't look like it'll be ready in time."

"No. The masons' union has been on strike most of the summer. A lot of hard feelings about it too. Some of the unions are honoring the picket line, some aren't. Half the neighborhood feels one way, half the other. Nasty business."

At his house we sat down over sodas and chips. He apologized for not having any beer, but his old man was on the wagon. "On again, off again." Bill shrugged. "Hard to know from one day to the next. But he'd been hitting it pretty hard for a while and I'm glad he's trying to ease up." He sat looking at his feet for a long minute. "I guess the biggest news is I've decided not to go to college for a couple of years."

I was flabbergasted. "Why not? It's all you talked about last year."

"Ya, I know." He looked up, smiled, and shrugged. "I guess I'm just not ready to go back to the old grind. I started working for a carpet layer a month ago and I'm already making a buck over the minimum. It's nice to have some money for a change. I figure I'll enjoy it for a while before worrying about college or trade school.

I was trying to absorb this as Bill rattled on about his job. I could see he really enjoyed it, which was funny since Bill had always talked before about making a living with his head rather than his hands. The old Bill had been fond of saying how he wanted a career where he'd be driven in a limousine to work and once a week to the barbershop for a haircut and a manicure. It had just been fantasy, we both knew, but I'd expected him to get a B.S. in business or accounting and a job where he'd be able to stay away from manual labor.

But in a way I wasn't surprised either. My own attitudes about that sort of thing had changed too. I was still going to be an architect, but now I realized that I'd miss the satisfaction of working with my hands. I was completely absorbed in these thoughts when I noticed Bill had stopped talking and was watching me. Had he asked me a question? I didn't know. "I'm sorry, Bill, something you said started me thinking."

"I asked you if you wanted to go to the party alone or if we should try to get you a date." There was a touch of irritation in his voice.

"I don't know. Is it going to be mostly couples?"

"Mostly, but there'll probably be some without. I wouldn't worry about it."

I was relieved. "I'll go alone then, I guess."

"Okay. Come on, we'll put your things in my bedroom. I brought down an old mattress from the attic. Then we'll go out for hamburgers."

"Where are your folks?" I was curious because Bill's mother is a fabulous cook.

"Mom's visiting her sister in Racine. Dad's working four to twelve," he called over his shoulder, again in a hurry without reason.

The party was at Joe Allen's. I'd barely known him in school, but he and Bill had become close friends working together during the summer. It was a pretty straight party with a couple of dozen people and a pony of beer. The keg didn't get tapped right, so most of the beer came out foam and nobody could drink much. I knew quite a few people and I had some good conversations. I was glad I hadn't brought a girl since I could circulate and trade the news better this way.

I was having a relaxed talk with a couple of girls when Glen Russell, one of my closer friends from school, came in. Glen is a smiling, good-natured blond kid who has a knack of saying things that almost get him into a fight and then talking his way out. He's not mean or stupid, he just doesn't know when to shut up. When he sat down I could tell he'd already had a few. "Hiya, Rick, how's life on the farm?"

"Pretty good, Glen. How you doing?"

"Me? Just great. Just rolling along. Say, looks like you put on a little weight shoveling that manure and pulling them udders."

"A little, I guess. You don't pull udders, by the way, you pull teats."

One of the girls asked, "You don't milk by hand, do you?"

"No, we've got milking machines." I described the operation in detail. The girls were politely interested, but Glen snickered a couple of times. I ignored him and explained how eventually we hoped to install a pipeline system, so the milk would flow directly from the machines to the bulk tank.

"What a deal!" Glen cut in, laughing. "Dumb farmers don't even have to milk the cows themselves anymore. Just punch a button and wait for the money to roll in. Hardest work is loading the green into the Cadillac and hauling it to the bank."

I should have known better. Glen was a little drunk and he'd always been lippy, but I snapped back at him. "You don't know a damn thing about it, Glen. I'll put the I.Q. of any farmer I know against yours any day of the week. What are you doing? Still waiting tables? That takes a hell of a lot of talent, city boy." I said it loud and found myself standing now, glaring down at Glen, my fists clenched. The room hushed and I felt all eyes on me.

Bill pushed through the crowd around the kitchen door and

came over. "Hey, take it easy, guys," he soothed. He pulled me away gently. Glen was slouched down in his chair watching me with eyes wide in amazement. Bill pulled me outside. "What the hell is going on, Rick? Are you drunk?"

"No, I'm not drunk!" I was still furious.

"What happened?"

"Oh, he made some stupid remark about dumb farmers in their Cadillacs."

"So what? You know Glen never means that crap. He's just shooting his mouth off."

"Well, he ought to know better."

"Come on, Rick. There's no reason to get so mad. Hell, you never used to be like this."

"Ya, I know." I was starting to cool down. "It's just I've seen my folks work so damn hard this year and then to hear that silly ass call them dumb. . . . It's just too damn much."

"He didn't call your folks dumb. He was just trying to get some laughs. You shouldn't have landed on him so hard. Now take it easy."

I nodded and we went back in, but I was still too mad to apologize. As the party wound down, I finally walked over and shook Glen's hand. "I'm sorry, Glen. I shouldn't have lost my temper."

"That's okay, Rick." He was a lot more sober now and obviously embarrassed. "I shouldn't have said such a stupid thing. You know I'm good at that."

"Ya, well, take it easy."

"You too." His eyes never met mine.

In the morning I rode the bus to the campus for registration. The field house was packed with other would-be students and the procedure seemed needlessly complicated. Still, I got most of the classes I wanted and was done by early afternoon.

I ate lunch in the student union and then walked over to the bookstore, glad for the fresh air after the smoke-filled din of the cafeteria. The sidewalks were overrun and I had to walk on the

250

grass a good deal of the time. I was rounding the corner of the physical science building when a voice yelled at me, "Hey, you. Can't you read?" One of the groundskeepers stood twenty feet off, pointing angrily at a sign that read, "Freshly seeded. Keep off."

"I'm sorry, I didn't see it."

"You college boys ought to know how to read."

"I know how to read, I just didn't see it."

"If you kids would stop smoking pot, maybe your eyes would be better. Some of us have to work for a living, you know."

I felt myself flush and I guess my expression must have reflected my anger because I saw a glimmer of uncertainty cross his face. I kept my voice down. "I said I was sorry, but don't accuse me of things I don't do." I walked away. He said something about smartass kids, but I ignored him.

When I crossed the street I wasn't paying enough attention either, and a whiz of air startled me. "Watch it, jerk!" I looked down the road where a girl on a ten-speed bicycle was half turned in the saddle glaring back at me. Damn, I thought, I've got to find a quiet place for a while.

The bookstore seemed a good possibility, but I was stunned to find a line at least fifty people long waiting to get through the door. As the line moved up, I could see the crush of people inside. The sight of all the pressing, pushing, and grabbing started to make me feel a little sick to my stomach and I suddenly knew I couldn't enter that turmoil. I bolted out of the line and strode rapidly away toward the bus stop, followed, I was sure, by the startled looks of these city creatures.

I was sitting on the front step when Bill got home from work. "Hi, been back long?"

"Couple of hours."

"Must have gone fast. Get all your classes and books?"

"I got the classes, but there were too many people at the bookstore. I figure I can buy my books in the fall."

"Oh ya? Knowing you, I thought you'd have them half read by then."

"I guess that would have been nice, but we've got hay and oats to get in before then."

"Hmmm. Strikes me you like the farming more than you let on."

"It's okay . . . better than okay a lot of the time."

"Ya, well, let's get some dinner."

That night there was another party, but I spent most of it sitting by myself just watching the people. They were good people, many of them my friends, but I felt detached now, more at ease by myself than with them. It was stuffy in the apartment and after a while I went out for a walk around the neighborhood.

The rows of tract houses seemed to melt into a boring sameness. I tried to remember the feeling I'd once had about these blocks—how this had once been home for me—but it wouldn't come and I found myself feeling imprisoned and dulled by it all.

Finally, I stood in front of my old home. The windows were dark, the new owners out for the evening or already in bed. I felt no sentiment at all, no bittersweet twinge of homecoming. My home was no longer this house, this neighborhood, this city. Like it or not, I was no longer the city slicker I'd been only a few months before. Now my hands were rough and calloused from countless hours of farm work and my skin deeply tanned from the wind and the sun in the fields. I was now more comfortable in overalls and boots than anything else. I'd changed and, oddly, now that I thought about it clearly, I wasn't sorry.

Sure, I could readjust to the city. It would take a little time, but hell, I knew the ropes. The question was: Did I really want to readjust? Or at least, did I want to now? I wasn't sure. Honest to God, I wasn't sure.

A car came around the corner, its headlights illuminating

the sidewalk. I became aware that I had been standing looking at the house for a long time, a suspicious thing to be doing on a dark city street. I walked on. The car passed without slowing.

On Saturday afternoon Bill and I and three of his friends from work went out to watch the Brewers play. I enjoyed the game, the bright sunshine, and the good companionship. Still, as we left the stadium in the great stream of cheerful fans, I again felt uncomfortable. My claustrophobia grew when we joined the long line of cars waiting to get out of the parking lot and onto the highway. What with the heat, the exhaust fumes, and the constant blaring of horns, I soon felt sick to my stomach. Only a sudden break in the traffic gave us the opportunity to slip into the flow on the highway and saved me from having to vomit out of the window.

They dropped me at the bus station on their way back to the neighborhood. I'd originally planned to stay until Sunday, but I'd had enough of the city for the present. What I needed now was time to think.

Bill came into the station with me. "Well, Rick, are you sure you can't stay over tonight?"

"I'd really like to," I lied, "but I've got a lot of things to do at home in the next few days."

"Ya, well, it's been good to see you. Call when you get back. You college boys don't have to be afraid to associate with us working types."

"I'll remember that."

"Well, so long, Take care."

"You too." We shook.

I made a quick call home to say I'd be back ahead of schedule. I killed the rest of the wait for the bus trying to read a paperback novel, but I spent most of the time gazing at the scrap paper and crushed gum wads on the dirty floor.

14

ON THE WAY home on the bus I decided not to think too much about school and the city for a while. If I'd had a couple of bad moments this time, next time would be better. It was best to forget it for now. I'd talk to Lorie about it later. There would still be an hour or two of daylight left when I got home and perhaps we'd take a long walk. Maybe someone at the farm would think to call her and she'd come in to pick me up.

Instead, Judy and Connie were waiting in front of the gas station where the bus stops. I was a little disappointed, but glad to see my sisters too. They both had big grins, and it didn't take Einstein to figure out they'd both passed their driver's test. Without a doubt, they'd jumped at the chance to take the car to town to show off for big brother. "Congratulations," I called as I got off the bus.

I tried not to look nervous on the drive home. Judy drove, leaning forward in the seat with both hands gripping the wheel and her eyes squinting in the late afternoon sunlight— not exactly a picture of confidence. Connie was telling me the news as if I'd been gone for weeks instead of a couple of days. None of it was very important except what she had to say about the call from Minneapolis. ". . . And anyway, the doctors think they can make things a lot better if they operate on one of Tommy's eyes pretty soon and the other at Thanksgiving."

"That's great!" I hesitated. "But expensive too. How much is social services going to pick up?"

Connie glanced at Judy, very serious now. "Mom and Dad can't find out for sure, but probably no more than half or two-thirds."

"Ouch. That'll put a crimp in things."

"Ya, they're pretty worried about it. Dad had to go to the bank again Friday."

"Any luck?"

"A little, I think. Not as much as he wanted, though. They didn't tell us much."

Judy broke in, "You'd better give him the letter."

"Oh, ya, this is from the hot little number."

They started giggling so hard that the car swerved on to the shoulder. "Hey, keep it on the road." I tore open the envelope.

Saturday 7:00 A.M.

Dear Rick,

I wish I could tell you this in person, but I've got to catch the bus in a few minutes. Mom called last night and we had a long talk. Dad had been by to see her earlier and they decided to give it another try. She wants me to come home, because maybe that will help them stay together. In a lot of ways, I really don't want to go. I'm sick of watching them fight, and, well, I'm pretty pessimistic about things working out any better this time. I didn't have a chance to tell you much about my last visit, but it was really the pits. They're so bitter! Maybe they want to make it up, but I'm not sure they ever can. Still, I've got to do my best to help. So, I'm going to be down there for a while—I'm not sure how long.

I'm going to look around for a nursing school near Des Plaines, but I've pretty much made up my mind to come back up here in the winter to the one in Mason. You remember the nurse who was in the emergency room when we brought Pam in? Well, I went down on Friday and talked with her about the program. It sounds really good.

Anyway, Rick, I hate to end our summer so abruptly, but I guess it can't be helped. If I come back up here, maybe you can see me when you come home on weekends. Or if I stay in Des Plaines, maybe you can come down there sometime. It's not too far from Milwaukee.

Well, I don't know what else to say other than the last few weeks have been the best in my life and I hope it doesn't end here. Write to me.

Love ya, Lorie

P.S. I'm going to drop this by Bergstrom's on my way to the bus. The girls can give it to you. I'll miss them and everybody in your family. Judy especially. She's really a good kid, Rick. Try to help her along.

P.P.S. God, I'm going to miss you!

For a moment I felt like crying. I'd been depending on talking to her. But I swallowed hard and watched the passing fields now high with crops soon to be harvested.

"What did it say?" Connie asked in a small voice.

"She's going back to live with her mother for a while."

"Why didn't she tell us?"

"I don't know, I guess she doesn't like good-byes. Here." I handed the letter to Connie. Judy almost ran off the road trying to read it too. "Damn it! Watch where you're going!" I plucked the letter back. "Read it when you get home."

256

When we got to the farm, I left them reading the letter avidly by the car and went looking for Dad. Maybe I should have kept the letter to myself, but it had seemed simpler to let them read it than try to explain everything. After all, she was their friend too. I was numb with disappointment and work seemed the only immediate salvation. Later I could figure out what it all meant.

Dad was in the shed where the old combine sat. He was puffing on his pipe and shining a flashlight around underneath. He straightened when I came in. "Hi, son, have a good trip?"

"It was okay."

"How are Bill and your other friends?"

"Okay. Not too much new."

"That's good." He wasn't really listening. He relit his pipe and gazed up at the tall red machine. "Did the girls tell you what the doctors said about Tommy?"

"Ya. That's pretty great news."

"It sure is, but it means contracting for the combining is definitely out for this year, so we're going to have to get this old beast going."

"Did you find out anything new?"

"Most of the parts seem to be here. The drive train is torn up. I suspect that's what did it in last time, but I think it's fixable."

"Well, let me go change clothes and I'll crawl under."

Judy intercepted me on my way to the house. "I'm sorry she's gone, Rick."

"Ya, me too."

She was silent a second. "I saw her Friday before supper and told her I'd had a visitor."

"Oh ya? Who was that?"

"My monthly visitor, dummy."

"Oh, I see . . . well, congratulations!"

She was crimson, but smiling. "Thanks. And I want you to know how much I appreciated you coming to get me and keeping the . . . ah, you know, secret." She leaned over and gave me a quick kiss on the cheek. "You're a pretty nice guy to have for a brother." She ran off before I could reply.

Dad and I worked on the combine until nearly midnight that evening and then every spare minute the next few days. A lot more was wrong with it than we'd originally thought, but we managed to fix the problems one at a time. My discovery of the old mate to it at the junkyard in Carleyville was a blessing. Red's boss shrugged and told us to take what we needed any time. "We'll settle up when you get yours going. This heap ain't worth much to me."

Often late at night, long after Jim had gotten bored and gone inside and Dad had given up in disgust, I'd keep working on the combine. Signa was my only companion then. Her summertime bed had been under the old machine before we'd started to mess with it. She'd moved good-naturedly to a pile of rags in the corner and lay there watching our frustration with lazy good humor. When I at last dragged myself out from under the combine, she'd wag her tail and grin—*Why didn't we pay more attention to the truly important things in life?* she seemed to be asking. I'd explain to her in a half dozen carefully chosen statements, liberally laced with obscenities, that we had to get the damn combine going. And if we didn't, how she'd have to get very serious about the hunting, because we wouldn't be able to afford dog food. In reply, she'd wag her tail a little faster and I'd go in to bed.

But tired as I usually was, sleep didn't come easily these days. I'd written a long letter to Lorie about the things that were bothering me, but then thrown it away. My second lengthy attempt was no more successful. Finally, I wrote her a short letter that covered most of the news around the farm, but talked little about what I'd been trying to say. She'd been good at helping me through those times when I had trouble putting my thoughts into words. But from a distance it no longer worked and I couldn't get down what really bothered me without sounding silly. So I concentrated on news of the family.

By and large things were going okay. Jim was beginning to

gripe about the end of summer vacation and the dismal prospect of school after Labor Day, but he was still in pretty good spririts. The fall meant the fair and he was convinced Onions would be a ribbon-winner. Dad tried to keep Jim's expectations low, but Onions was indeed a fine-looking calf and I knew Dad was hopeful too.

Connie and Phil continued to see each other at every possible opportunity. He was a nice guy, though painfully shy around the family. Mom almost had to bludgeon Connie into convincing Phil to stay for dinner. I think Mom wanted to have a better look at Phil and I was rooting for him to make a good impression. (I hadn't forgotten his calm, concerned way the night Judy had disappeared.) All through the meal he sat quietly, carefully minding his table manners and smiling politely. Dad tried to draw him out and Phil answered his questions easily, but he never volunteered anything. Connie sat beside him glowing with pride. To my surprise, Judy made a particular effort to be cordial. In the end, I think Mom came away with the sense that Phil might conceivably be trusted with her daughter. I know Phil left with considerable relief.

Judy was more of a puzzle these days than ever. She didn't seem unhappy—quite the reverse actually. But she was even more quiet and businesslike. She no longer bitched if someone else was slow doing something, instead she'd quickly do it herself—anything so she could keep to her own schedule. That schedule included running several miles morning and night. Connie went with her a couple of times, but soon announced that she'd wait until school began to get in shape. She didn't seem worried at all that Judy might have an insurmountable lead in conditioning by then. Connie had come out in front in everything else, why should things change?

I summarized this and all the news in my letter to Lorie and added some awkward phrases about how much I missed her and wished she was nearby. I hesitated before putting it in the mailbox. It wasn't much of a letter—short on news and shorter on sentiment. Still, I had to mail something.

If I'd waited a couple of days I would have had more to report.

Surprisingly, Pam, the nearly model kid, finally touched off the big crisis with Mom. When I looked back on it, I could see that things had been building up for quite a awhile. Not only was Mom worried about everybody and working too hard, but she was also getting increasingly irritated with the way some, I guess all, of us were acting. A few days before she'd given me a pretty good blast for tracking up her freshly scrubbed porch with manure. A day or so later the twins got a bawling out for hurrying with the dishes and breaking a couple of plates, then hiding the pieces. Tommy could be excused for his irritability with the painful eye drops and his declining sight, but he really was being a little brat a lot of the time. And Dad was gloomy, snappish, and not overly sympathetic when Mom complained to him.

So everything was pretty well set up for a major blowup when Mom, Dad, and I got home from an auction at a nearby farm on the Thursday after I came back from Milwaukee. Dad and I had hoped to buy one of the haywagons, but they'd all gone too high. Mom had wanted to bid on some of the furniture, but hadn't really liked anything. So, we headed home early. Mom rode in the back with Tommy, who asked nonstop questions about the auction. Dad rode in the front with me. We talked about fixing the combine and didn't pay much attention to what was being said in the back seat, until, as we turned in at the farm, Mom blurted, "Oh, for Pete's sake!" I spotted what she'd seen almost immediately. In the pasture behind the barn, Pam was seated high aboard Arrow, her cast visible even from this distance. Jim was leading them proudly.

They still hadn't noticed us when I parked the car. Dad tried to calm Mom, "Now, Ellie, don't go off . . ." But she was out by then and charging for the pasture, her face red with anger. The kids saw her coming and froze. She started letting them have it when she was still twenty yards away. "Get off that horse right now, Pam! Do you hear me! Is this how you two children obey your mother? You're going to get the tanning of your lives for this!" She was up to them now. She grabbed Pam and pulled her down. Arrow whinnied and shied away, pulling the bridle out of Jim's hand, and galloping off. Mom ignored the horse. She had a hand on each of the kids and was shaking them violently, still yelling at the top of her lungs. I went after Arrow as Dad, with Tommy trailing behind, slowly walked out to intervene. That was a bad move on his part, because Mom lit into him, too, blaming him for not helping more with the kids and letting them run wild. That wasn't really fair to Dad, but I knew better than to go close and express my opinion. Instead, I advanced slowly on Arrow, who looked up from cropping a few mouthfuls of nerve-settling grass. Recovering his usual patience with the human race, he let me unsaddle him.

Finished, I turned back for the yard with the saddle and bridle. Mom, dragging the two kids, was halfway to the house. Dad, a billow of pipe smoke drifting behind him, was walking head down in the direction of the barn, his arm around Tommy, who was anxiously asking what was going on. They'd disappeared and I'd just about reached the small shed at the edge of the pasture that served as Arrow's stable when Mom let out a shriek from the porch. Oh, God, what now? I heaved the saddle through the door and ran to the house.

"Just look at what your dog's done!" Mom yelled at me.

My dog? Since when had Signa been my dog? I'd always thought she was the family's dog. I got closer and spied Signa lying in a cool hollow dug in the center of the flower bed running beside the house. The fragments of a half dozen of so marigolds lay about her and between her forepaws lay a rotting, unidentifiable hunk of dead animal. She was grinning, of course, unaware that at this moment her life was worth very little in Mom's view.

Mom glared at me. "You go bury that thing, whatever it is, then fix my flower patch. And from now on keep your dog out of it!"

I still wasn't clear how I'd suddenly become Signa's sole owner, but I wasn't going to argue about it. I nodded. Mom turned her attention back to disciplining the whimpering kids. Still giving them hell, she dragged them into the house.

I chased Signa away from her prize and went to the barn for a plastic garbage bag and a shovel. Dad and Tommy were nowhere around. When I came back out Mom was climbing into the car. She backed it around fast and, without a glance in my direction, drove away. What now? I wondered.

Mom still hadn't returned when Phil dropped off the twins after work. I saw them go into the house and followed to give them the news. Tommy came running from the barn. "Ricky, I'm supposed to . . ." He stumbled, but recovered his balance. Like everything else, running had become more difficult for him in the last few weeks. "Daddy says I'm supposed to go with you." I waited for him.

The twins were looking a bit confused when I came into the kitchen—normally Mom would be here to give them directions. I cut off their questions, sent Tommy in search of Pam and Jim, then explained to the twins what was going on. Or at least what was going on as far as I knew. Jim came to the door and listened quietly until I saw him. "Has Dad started the milking?" he asked.

"Just about to, I think." He stood there uncertainly. "Why don't you go ahead, Jim. I'll only be a couple of minutes." He left glumly. I turned back to the twins. "Judy, I think maybe you'd better skip the running tonight. And, Connie, if you're planning on going out with Phil, maybe you'd better put it off for a while. I think there's some big trouble in the wind and we'd better stick around."

"Well, where could she be?" Connie asked. "She's never done anything like this before."

"I don't know, but she's pretty pissed at all of us, I think. Dad included. So let's try to be real cool."

They nodded. The memory of the broken plates was still fresh. I had to get out to the barn, but I wanted to check on

Pam. I'd been pretty angry with her and Jim, but now I felt a little sorry for them.

She was trying to divert Tommy with a board game on the floor of their room. She'd been crying a lot and it showed. Tommy seemed to have forgotten about the incident altogether. He peered intently at the board, trying to keep track of the moves. "Hi," I said, and sat on the edge of Tommy's bed.

"Hi," Pam said.

"Ricky, I'm way ahead," Tommy crowed. "Watch. I bet I get a twelve." He tossed the dice, then picked up each one and tried to read the number of dots.

"Nine." Pam said. Tommy laboriously counted out the squares on the board, finishing with eleven. Pam didn't bother to correct him.

I watched a couple of turns, then got up and left, giving Pam a gentle pat on the head as I passed.

Mom wasn't home for dinner and everyone was getting very worried. Tommy asked about Mom, but Connie hushed him and helped him with his food. Hardly a word was spoken at the table. I think we all expected Dad to unload on us any second, but he didn't. He ate in silence, finished first, and went outside. Pam left the table and Jim followed her. I tried to think of something intelligent to say, but nothing much occurred to me. As I got up to leave, I said to the twins, "Try to keep the kids occupied. Don't give them any grief. Let's try to be cheerful."

They nodded and I went out on the porch. Maybe I should go talk to Dad. But what would I say? Jim came out the back door and by me without a word. His face had that frozen, sullen look I'd seen all too many times before. Oh, no! Not now! "Hey, Jim, wait up." He kept going and I hurried after him.

"Hey, Jim, hold on a second." I put a hand on his shoulder. He stopped and stood looking at the ground. "Jim, don't get so upset; it's not worth it."

"It was all my fault."

"No, it wasn't."

"Yes, it was. It was my idea and I got Pam in trouble and now everybody hates me."

"Jim, no one hates you. Mom's mad about a lot more than just this afternoon." It wasn't working and I felt desperate. "Look, you guys screwed up pretty good. I'm not going to tell you that you didn't, but really, you haven't been alone recently. . . ." His face was hardening. The signs were all there. Somehow I had to stop it. "Please, Jim, don't do this to yourself." I took him by the shoulders. He was as tense as a wound spring. "You know you're working up to one of your tantrums. You know how you do it: You'll start brooding, then you'll start thinking some crazy things, and pretty soon you'll lose control. But don't do it this time, Jim. You can stop it right now. Okay, you screwed up, but you don't have to punish yourself! . . ." I finished softly. "It's not worth it, Jim. You don't have to hurt yourself. . . ."

He looked up at me, his eyes filled with tears. "But it was my fault," he whispered.

"Yes, part of it was your fault, but you're sorry. That's all Mom or anybody expects. You don't have to do anything more. You really don't have to hurt yourself, Jim." He looked down and sniffed, but the terrible tenseness in him was slowly slipping away. "Come on, Jim, let's go look in on Onions." I put an arm around him and we walked down to the barn.

Mom called at 9:00 P.M. Dad was banging away on something in the machine shop and the kids were gloomily watching TV. I was sitting at the kitchen table trying to distract myself by messing with a couple of my diagrams for the perfect farm. Perhaps I should have been out helping Dad, but I wanted to stay near the phone. When it rang, I got up quickly to answer it before any of the kids.

"Hello, dear. How's everybody holding up?" Mom's voice was positively cheery.

"Fine, Mom. Well, okay, anyway. How are you?"

"Oh, I'm having a very nice time with a couple of the girls from Weight Watchers. I called them up this afternoon and we went out to eat a low-calorie meal. Now we're having a glass of wine and talking."

"Well, I'm glad you're okay. You scared the hell out of everyone. I think everybody thought maybe you'd gone to Brazil or somewhere."

She laughed. "Not yet. We're considering Mexico, right now." Then she was serious. "Everything's all right, dear. Your mother was angry and decided to make a point."

"I think you did it."

"Well, I'm going to get back to the girls. Tell your father not to worry. I'll be home in a little while. Bye now."

"Good-bye, Mom." I turned from the phone. All the kids were watching me. "It's okay. She went out to eat with some friends and she'll be home in a little while. . . . Let's be cheerful and try to be especially nice to her."

I went out to tell Dad. He was still fussing with a wheel from the combine. "She's okay, Dad." I told him what Mom had said.

He shook his head. "Well, as you said, she's made her point. We'd better tread real careful for a while."

"I think . . . Well, maybe I shouldn't say so, but I think you guys ought to go out by yourselves every once in a while. Give Mom a chance to relax."

He nodded. "Ya, maybe, but we don't have the time or money."

I was about to say more, but he'd turned back to the workbench and the wheel. "Can I help?"

"Ya, get that torch going for me."

Everybody did their best to be cheerful and cooperative in the morning, especially Pam. She fell all over herself trying to help Mom. I was checking my replanting of the marigolds when Mom came out with a basket of wash for the line. Pam rushed back and forth between the basket and the line. The cast on her arm hindered her some, but she was doing her damnedest. Tommy was trying to help too. Finally, Mom turned. "You kids are driving me absolutely nuts." Pam stood with a couple of wet sheets in her arms looking very hurt. Mom laughed, leaned down, and hugged Pam. "My little girl doesn't have to feel so bad. You're a kid. I don't expect you to be perfect." She held her out at arm's length. "I was angry with you because you disobeyed me, but more because I was afraid you'd get hurt again. Do you understand that?" Pam nodded.

"Mommy, I want a hug too." Tommy pulled at her.

Mom put an arm around him and went on talking to Pam. "You'll be able to ride Arrow soon, I promise. Be patient. Now you two go have some fun on this beautiful day." She hugged them again, laughing. "And stay out of trouble," she called after them cheerfully.

I found myself thinking of something Uncle Fritz had once said. "All the world's a wonderment, boy. But women, they're the biggest wonderment in it."

Getting the old mastodon combine going was still the major objective for Dad and me. After all the years the combine had stood idle, it didn't seem anything worked properly. But little by little we got each component working again. It was a week after we started that we hit the problem we couldn't solve. The engine and all the combining parts were fixed by now, but the power simply wouldn't transfer to the back wheels. We went through the drive train again and again for two days, but there seemed no solution. Finally, at 11:30 P.M. on the last day of August, Dad threw a hammer against the wall and stood fuming. "It's no damn good, Rick! We've put off the combining long enough. We'll get wind or hail or something if we don't start in the next couple of days."

I sat down on the floor, my head swimming with fatigue. "We're so close. If we could just find the problem."

"If we find this one, there'll just be another one. I was a damn fool to even start. Fritz was right all along."

"Maybe one more try."

"No! No more tries! I'm finished with it! I'll just go to the bank tomorrow afternoon and beg for enough money to contract out the combining. The damn milk inspector is due any day now and we've got to straighten up the barn and fix that barn cleaner." He shook his head. "Too much to do, just too damn much to mess with this piece of crap. We could have been fishing for all the good it did."

I was going to protest one more time, but he stomped out and crossed the yard, stopping to pick up a stone and send it sailing far off into the dark. I sat for a few minutes, too tired to be angry, just deadened with the fatigue and disappointment. Finally, I got up and went in to bed.

As tired as I was, the frustration wouldn't let me sleep. After a half hour of staring at the reflection of the yard light on my ceiling, I got up and sat at my desk. The combine was so old that there wasn't an exact picture in any of the manuals or books I'd collected over the summer, but there were machines not too dissimilar, and slowly, painstakingly, I started to go through the diagrams. It was another hour before I hit it. Damn, could that be it? I forced myself to stay calm and went through the diagram once again. It was, I was almost sure. A tiny bearing was missing. Why hadn't we noticed it?

I almost ran down the stairs and out to the shed. Jamming myself under the frame, I shined the light up at the place. Yes, it was the same rig, only the bearing was gone, lost somewhere over the years since the big combine had plowed its ponderous way across the oceans of oats that had once been its natural habitat. I dug around in the dirt under the machine looking for the bearing, but it was hopeless after all the years since the drive train had been torn down.

I ran to the barn and got on the phone. A sleepy voice said, "Hello."

"Red, Rick Simons here. I need a part bad."

"Christ, man, it's after one o'clock in the morning!"

"I know, Red, but I really need a part from that combine. You don't have to come in, I'll just drop by and pick up the keys. It's worth five bucks to me to get it tonight. Please, Red."

There was a pause. "Oh, what the hell, I was only sleeping anyway. I'll meet you there."

"I could pick up the keys."

"No, I'd rather catch this gig live. I've always been big into late-night craziness."

Back in the house, I opened the door to the girls' room quietly and shook Connie gently by the shoulder. "Connie, Connie, get up."

"What's the matter?" She looked up at me through sleep-fogged eyes, then tried to roll over.

"Connie, get up. It's important."

"Is something wrong?"

"No, but I need your help. Get Judy too. Be quiet. I'll tell you all about it on the way."

"Where are we going?"

"Carleyville."

Judy held the light and Connie handed me the tools. Red had stayed in the office reading a surprisingly thick and se-rious-looking paperback. In the middle of the night the junkyard was eerie with the crushed cars and jumbled piles of parts throwing weird shadows around us as we worked. The girls shivered in the mixed chill of the fear and the night air, talking in whispers and casting quick glances over their shoul-ders. Perhaps I should have waited until morning; I'd have some tall explaining to do if Mom or Dad got up and found us gone.

We were home a bit after 3:00 A.M. and I sent them to bed, swearing them to secrecy. Then I worked under the combine by the glow of a safety light until nearly dawn. I had to dis-assemble quite a bit of the drive train to get the bearing in and, putting it back together, I twisted too hard on a rusty bolt and it sheared off in my hand, the socket wrench continuing around to give me a good pop right at the hairline. Cursing, I felt for blood, but there was only a rising bump. I examined the bolt carefully with the safety light. It had broken well below the surface leaving nothing to get a vise grip on. Damn. I got the electric drill and my goggles and very carefully started to drill it out. If I could save the original threads, things would be a lot easier. I finished the drilling and ran a tap into the hole. Not bad, Rick, not bad at all.

I went to the machine shop to find another bolt, but of all the scores we had lying around, not a single one was both the right diameter and length. Damn. Well, I'd have to go back to Carleyville in the morning for one more part.

Still, as I walked back to the house nursing the throb in my forehead, I felt wonderful. The early light in the east glowed honey yellow on the horizon, promising a beautiful day, and a gentle breeze brought me the smell of rich earth and ripening crops and a faint whiff of manure, too, but now the smell seemed fragrant and good.

I didn't bother to sleep, but sat on my bed writing a letter to Lorie.

Everybody was up even earlier than usual. Jim was going to a Four-H workshop in Mason on the upcoming fair and the twins were driving him down. Mom fed everyone a big breakfast. The twins seemed to have forgotten entirely about our journey in the night. Mom had given them permission to spend the morning shopping in Mason for their fall wardrobes and they were anxious to be there when the stores opened. They'd pick Jim up at noon and drop him back at the farm before going to work at Bergstrom's in the afternoon.

Dad and I did the milking alone. I didn't mention my success with the combine. I wanted it to be a surprise, a good one for a change. He worked silent and brooding and I had trouble containing my glee.

When we were finished, Dad picked up a shovel and started to dig the impacted manure out of the barn cleaner. "If that milk inspector shows up today, we are really in for it."

"Oh, they can't be that tough."

"Oh ya? You haven't dealt with that breed long enough. He wasn't real happy last time he was out here either. Two in a row and he's going to start getting nasty. There it is." He uncovered the broken link between two paddles.

A barn cleaner is a series of paddles like a conveyer belt traveling around the barn in a concrete gutter. The gutter runs by the opening of each stall catching the manure which is then moved around and up an incline by the paddles until it drops outside into the manure spreader. It's an ingenious rig, but prone to breakdowns. Since a barn has to be very clean for health reasons, a breakdown of the barn cleaner means a lot of shoveling and real problems if the milk inspector suspects you've been slow in fixing it. And with trying to repair the combine, we had been.

Together we worked the broken link back into position, our hands slimy with the manure. Dad twisted several turns of heavy wire around it and with a final tug on the pliers, sat back on his haunches. "That'll have to do for now. We've got to get this place cleaned. He was down the road on Friday, he's sure to hit us today."

I was aching to be off for Carleyville to get the last part for the combine, but I knew this had to come first. Dad looked carefully at my face. "You look tired, son, and you've got a bump on your forehead."

"Ya, nicked myself with a wrench trying one more time on that stupid combine." I smiled inwardly.

"Not worth it, that damned thing is hexed." He got up. "Your mother wants you to go up to Carleyville for some things from the drugstore. She's not feeling too perky and she's got to look after the kids, so you'd better go. I'll get started here."

I almost jumped for joy. I left the barn at a dogtrot, almost forgetting to stop by the house to wash my hands and get the list from Mom. She explained it all slowly and carefully as I waited impatiently. Then I was out the door almost running. As I swung the pickup out the drive and down the road to the highway, I thought, This is going to be a big boost for them. Something good for a change.

I recognized the milk inspector from the back as I came into the office at the junkyard to tell Red's boss I'd gotten the last part I needed and he could figure up the bill. The milk inspector and the boss were looking at a diagram in a parts book. "So you don't have one?"

"Nope, afraid not. Kind of a rare bird."

"I guess so. The auto parts store didn't have one either. Well, I guess I'll limp back to Hawthorne and see if I can find one there."

"Ya, it should hold that long."

The milk inspector turned from the desk. "Hi, Mr. Farrell," I said.

"Oh, hi. Young Simons, isn't it?"

"That's right."

"I was going to swing out by your place today, but the old buggy is complaining a bit."

"That's too bad."

"Ya, well, I'll probably be back up around here the end of the week."

"We'll be waiting."

"Good enough. Well, thanks, Ed. See you later, Simons."

I settled with the junkman for less than I'd dared hope, stopped at the drugstore, and started home, humming with all the good news I had. I went first to the house and gave Mom her things and then walked out to the barn to tell Dad about the milk inspector. It was very rare for one of them to tell when he was coming.

Dad sat on the edge of the gutter with the barn cleaner torn apart in front of him. The wire we'd used to jury-rig the link had parted and ripped loose two or three more sections. His hands and clothes were wet with the manure and he sat hanging his head, slow tears of frustration cutting tiny eddies in the dirt and manure on his face.

I slipped back out and crossed the yard to the shed with a sick feeling down deep in the pit of my stomach. I crawled under the combine, trying not to think of how small and

lonely my father had looked sitting there. By the time I finished getting the bolt in, I'd made a decision.

Sitting high on top with the door wide in front of me, I
prayed, "Dear God, let it work." I turned the key and the
engine roared to life. Slowly I let out the clutch and with a jerk
and a grunt we rolled out into the sunlight. If it had had a horn
I'd have blown it all the way to the barn, but it wasn't necessary. In seconds Mom, Pam, and Tommy were at the door to
the house and Dad came running out of the barn. He stopped
and stood frozen, then he started to laugh. I drove the big
machine triumphantly around the loop of the drive until we
stood in front of Dad. He was still laughing, but mopping his
eyes at the same time. Mom and the kids came clustering
around as I turned off the motor and climbed down.

"How in hell?" Dad began.

As I told him, he just walked around the machine with a
wide grin on his face. Finally, he stopped and stood. "Boy, is
this going to take the heat off!" He slapped me about eight
times on the back, laughing again. Then he sobered. "But the
barn cleaner is broken again. I guess we'd better fix that and
congratulate ourselves later. We're not out of the woods yet."

Amid everything I'd forgotten to tell him what the milk
inspector had said. Relief drained into Dad's face then and we
went to sit in the shade while Mom brought coffee. I was so
happy I could hardly sit still. "Dad, let's go fishing." He
laughed and sucked on his pipe, his eyes caressing the combine. "Really, let's go fishing."

"We've got a lot of work to do."

"Not so much we can't go fishing for a couple of hours.
You've talked about it all summer."

"Won't catch much this time of day."

"I don't care, let's go anyway."

He looked at me, for the first time realizing I was serious.
"Well, I guess we could at that."

In ten minutes I had the poles and gear in the truck. Mom
scurried over to hand a bag of sandwiches and a thermos of

lemonade through the window. Her face was radiant as she hustled Dad into the truck. "Where will you be? Jim will want to join you when he gets back from Mason."

"Tell him the old railroad bridge. It's only a couple of miles, he can ride his bike down," I called. Dad closed the door, still looking a bit bemused, and we bumped off.

The smell of the tarred timbers baking in the noon sun rose around us as we walked from the old roadbed on to the trestle. The river slipped wide and shallow under the overhanging brush into a deep pool below the bridge. We baited our hooks and fished with only casual attention, drinking the lemonade and letting the sun and the quiet settle us.

Finally, I took a deep breath. Here goes, I thought. I looked over to where Dad leaned against the rail gazing meditatively down to where his line dimpled the barely moving water of the pool. "Dad, I've decided to stick around for another few months."

"Oh?" He gave me a startled look. "What happened to your college plans?"

"Well, I don't know for sure. I still want to go, but I guess not right now."

He looked back into the water, his face troubled. "I don't want you to give up your dreams just for us, Rick. You've already given more than I could reasonably expect."

"The family really isn't it, Dad. I like it here and right now I feel like farming. Not forever, but now it's what I want to do."

His voice was thick and I thought for a second he was going to cry again. "That's great, son. Whatever the reason, I'm glad you'll stay for a while. . . ."

He was going to say more, but a bite on his line almost jerked the pole out of his hands and, yelling and laughing, we forgot everything else as he fought the big rainbow trout dancing silver in the stream.

Epilogue

A LIGHT SNOW blew across the drifted fields as we walked down to the barn for the milking in the fading light. Behind us the lights of the Christmas tree shone through the frost on the living room windows and reflected on the blanket of white around the house.

The twins hauled open the door and let Pam and Tommy through into the warm interior of the barn with their buckets of overripe carrots and apples—Christmas gifts for the cows.

Jim walked beside me, huddled close in his coat. "Do you think the kids really believe in Santa Claus anymore?" he asked.

"Oh, Pam is probably just playing along for Tommy's sake. No harm in it. He'll find out soon enough."

"I guess." He turned and looked back at the house. Inside, Mom and Dad were hustling about, getting the presents under the tree before hurrying down to the barn where we'd all wait to hear sleighbells and reindeer hooves. It seemed pretty transparent, but who cared? It was the fun of believing that counted.

It's hard to remember Uncle Fritz is gone, but we have a lot

274

to be thankful for this Christmas. Money is still short with the bills from Tommy's operations coming in. But although the presents may be a little scant, we already have the important things. Tommy still wears a patch over one eye and the doctors won't be sure how successful they were for weeks yet, but the other eye is stronger and healthier than it has ever been before. His vision will never be good, but now there is at least the promise of lifelong sight.

The other kids are back in school and doing well, even Jim, who has discovered biology and now bubbles with arcane facts and names. He's joined Four-H too and pours his love of farming into the activities. Onions got an honorable mention at the fair and the plaque is Jim's proudest possession—next to Onions, of course.

Pam's arm healed perfectly, and somehow the whole experience seemed to give her confidence. She stands up to Jim and the twins more often now, and even if the attention is negative sometimes, it's attention. She still complains now and then about being the littlest in her class, but she's popular, spunky, and happy. And still my favorite.

Connie had a bit part in the school musical in the fall. (Fortunately, she didn't have to sing much.) She hopes for a bigger part in the spring play and talks about it endlessly. She and Phil still go out quite a bit and, although that relationship may be cooling a bit, Connie seems to be having the time of her life.

Still, Judy, or Boots as she likes to be called around school, has had the happiest fall of all. The twins went out for cross-country in September, but Connie found an excuse to quit after a week. Judy, on the other hand, not only made the team, but pushed the top couple of girls pretty hard. I don't think she's naturally very talented, she just works harder than the others. All fall she wore boots at practice, figuring they would strengthen her legs. Now most people think that's how she got the nickname. When the coach was quoted in the school newspaper saying that, "Judy 'Boots' Simons is one of the best young runners I've ever coached," the conversion of the nickname was complete.

But all that didn't make Judy nearly as happy as getting Brad. I think it's fair to say she chased him. She ran with him in practice, asked his advice, called him on the phone to discuss meets, suggested practicing together before school, and eventually Brad noticed that she wasn't only a fellow running addict, but also a girl. They've been going out for a couple of months now and he's a real nice guy from what I've seen. Connie says they're a bore to be around, because all they talk about is track season in the spring.

I thought about all that had happened, good and bad, since last Christmas as Jim, the twins, and I got the milking started. Pam and Tommy doled out the carrots and apples to the cows, who sniffed loudly at the strange objects before taking them in their mouths. The kids crowed with laughter and we stopped to watch and laugh too. Ya, I thought, maybe nothing we're doing is very momentous or any of the progress we've made very earthshaking, but it's still progress, a step at a time. Going forward.

The door swung open and Mom and Dad came in, brushing the snow from their coats and stamping their feet. "Picking up out there," Dad called. "Going to be a real storm. Bad night to be driving a sleigh, I don't know if he'll get through or not."

"Oh, Paul, don't tell them that."

"Just telling the truth." He winked at me.

Mom took off her outer coat and came over to help. She's lost maybe twenty pounds, although you have to look hard to tell the difference. Dad is proud of her. The other day he announced at the kitchen table, "Why pretty soon she'll be able to sit on a dime and still read 'In God We Trust' around the rim." We all laughed and she blushed, but she's proud of herself too.

Mom still doesn't get out as often as I think she should, but every once in a while she does take an afternoon or evening for herself and that seems to help.

Dad is back in a better mood, too. The oats in August and the corn crop in the fall were better than we'd hoped for, and with the price pretty good because of the drought in the lower Midwest, we made a nice profit from the extra we didn't need for the cows. That's not to say things aren't still tight, but at least we made it through the first year in the black. Next year, things will be smoother, I'm sure.

Me? I'm getting along. I'm not sure what the future holds, but the present is fine for now. Lorie writes from Des Plaines. She's working as an aide in a nursing home and plans to come up for school in Mason in January. I haven't seen her since I took a weekend off in October and I'm looking forward to next month.

I've been rethinking my own plans for school. I've really become interested in agricultural design. A tremendous number of farms could use redesigning and I've got a lot of ideas about building from scratch too. I've sent out a few letters inquiring about programs at colleges around the Midwest. I'm not sure when I'll make the break, but it can wait awhile. I'm not worried about it. Right now, I'm just waiting to see if I'll really hear the sleighbells this time.